C000039564

Helen Buckley

STAR IN THE SHADOWS

Limited Special Edition. No. 8 of 25 Paperbacks

Helen has spent over thirteen years working and volunteering for charities in the UK and abroad, including four years in Honduras. She currently works as a charity communications manager and lives in Bedfordshire with her husband and son.

For Donovan – my little star

Helen Buckley

STAR IN THE SHADOWS

Dear Martin & Margot,

Thankyou so much for all your support and encouragement!!

Love, Helen
xx

AUSTIN MACAULEY PUBLISHERS™

LONDON • CAMBRIDGE • NEW YORK • SHARJAH

A CIP catalogue record for this title is available from the British Library.

ISBN 9781528932004 (Paperback)
ISBN 9781528966887 (ePub e-book)

www.austinmacauley.com

First Published (2019)
Austin Macauley Publishers Ltd
25 Canada Square
Canary Wharf
London
E14 5LQ

I want to say a big thank you to Helen Bowen and Mum – for all your unswerving support and for taking the time to read pages and pages of drafts. I'm so grateful to my friends in the States – Amanda Knauss, Jennifer Jenkins-Butts, Beverly Chesser, and Jana Richardson – who helped me with checking the American vocabulary. And thank you to my husband, David, who listened patiently and encouraged constantly.

Part One
Surviving

An order

Marco breezed into the apartment and sat down, his dark hair gelled back with a greasy shine. He always moved with a cat-like arrogance, an air of entitlement and ownership, regardless of whether he was in her hotel room or her apartment. It was one of the qualities Kiara envied about him – his ability to seem so at home and in control no matter where he was. She slid onto the red leather couch next to him, extending her legs onto the coffee table, ankles crossed, her pale skin a contrast to his deep tan.

"Well, good news," he began. "You've been asked to do an exclusive TV interview with Beth Winters."

Kiara's mouth opened in surprise. "What?"

Marco grinned, flashing his white teeth at her. "Isn't it great? Her ratings are amazing."

"But why would she want to do an interview with me?" she stammered.

"Why not? You're gorgeous, you're number one all over the world, and you've got a great story to tell," Marco put his arm around her and gave her a squeeze.

Kiara shook her head. "Marco, I can't talk to her. She likes to go in deep, uncover private stuff. She'll want to know real things about me, about my past…" she trailed off.

Marco's smile faded, and his mouth pressed into a thin line.

"Time's up Kiara," he said, his gaze hardening. "Beth's team already knows plenty about you as do lots of other people sniffing around."

She sat there silently, palms moist and stomach churning.

"You need to tell the story in your own words, make it your own exclusive. Get ahead of this now and we'll help you make sure it comes out the way you want it to," he continued.

"Do I have to tell them everything Marco?" she asked, her heart starting to flutter with anxiety.

"Not everything," said Marco thoughtfully, rubbing his chin with his finger. "But you'll need to talk about your dad, about running away when you were seventeen…"

"About why I ran away?" she interrupted, her voice tight and lips numb.

"Yes," he said, and her stomach somersaulted.

Kiara put her head in her hands, the ground starting to lurch beneath her feet. "Marco please, I don't want to do this on camera, it's too hard."

"I don't care," he said bluntly.

She looked up at him, shocked. "Excuse me?"

"You will listen to me and you will do what I say Kiara. This is not optional. We have protected you so far and we will continue to do so but only if you take our advice." Marco jabbed a finger at her and she sat in anxious silence, trembling at his change of tone. "You have a lot of dirt to cover up and I'll help you do it but don't question me. I don't want any tears or panic attacks or begging. You'll do it and you will be fine."

She nodded, eyes downcast, unable to meet the intensity of his dark gaze. His voice softened, and he stroked her hair. "This is best for you and it's best for the group. You trust me, don't you?"

She nodded.

The interview

Kiara settled herself on the oversize velvet chair. People with clipboards and headsets were flitting around her, checking light and sound levels, preparing to start recording. She fiddled with the lead of the mic running up inside her sweater. The lights were so hot that a slight sheen of sweat dampened her chest and stomach, and she could feel her face glowing underneath the thick film of studio makeup.

Beth Winters strode over and sat on the chair opposite hers. Tanned, tall and wiry, Beth Winters was famous for her exclusive television interviews. One steely glance of her grey eyes would have celebrities spilling their deepest secrets, all captured on camera and ready for the audience to devour.

"You ready Kiara?" she said in her trademark southern drawl, waving away an assistant with her perfectly manicured hand, her bright coral nail polish shining sharply under the lights.

"Sure, let's do it." Kiara flashed a huge smile, sticky with lip gloss. Feeling the sweat bead down her back, she sat up a little straighter and focused on Beth, thankful the interview wasn't going to be filmed live or in front of an audience.

The cameras switched on, the red lights trained impassive and unblinking on her and Beth.

Beth turned towards the cameras. "Tonight, I'm delighted to welcome Kiara Anderson, lead singer of the chart-topping group Femme Fatale. She'll be telling us about her journey to the top as a member of one of the sexiest and most successful groups in the charts."

Beth paused and turned to Kiara, running a bright fingernail up and down the papers she held in her hand. "Kiara, we're just delighted to have you on the show tonight. I'm actually a huge fan of Femme Fatale," she said.

"Thanks Beth. It's great to be here," Kiara replied, widening her smile. She began to sweat through her jeans onto the plush velvet beneath her.

"I must say, I'm just dying to get to know you better, as I'm sure our viewers at home are too." Beth smiled at the camera and then leaned in towards her.

"Tell me, how does it feel to be one of the most desired women on the planet?" she asked Kiara.

Kiara smiled coyly, arching an eyebrow. "Oh, I don't know about that…" she giggled, tossing her red curls over her shoulder, tumbling down her back over the cropped white jumper that revealed her slender waist and hung off one pale shoulder. It was Marco's choice – he was better at picking out her clothes than she was.

"You were recently voted number nine on the list of the world's sexiest women, and your latest single is currently topping the charts all over the world. You've made a big impact since Femme Fatale came onto the scene just under two years ago."

Kiara nodded and smiled. "It's been a crazy journey. Sometimes I don't know where I am and what day it is!" She had never expected this level of fame and attention so quickly and her and the girls were still adjusting to the frenetic pace – days of seemingly endless travel, sleeping on tour buses, constant movement, endless noise, and the shouting of crowds calling out their names.

Beth nodded. "It's been described as a 'meteoric rise to the top' – how you went from working in a hotel bar to being a worldwide superstar. But what I'm interested in is where you come from and where this journey started for you."

Beth leaned back into her velvet chair. They had agreed to give Kiara space to say things in her own words, exclusively and for the first time, but now that it was time to talk, Kiara's heart was thrumming and her head was a jumble of words and memories that wouldn't come out. Until now, Marco was the only person who knew the story completely, but he had coaxed it out of her while drunk and panicky one evening.

Seeing her uncertainty, Beth prompted her along. "Well, why don't we start at the beginning – tell us about your family." Beth gave her a nod and tapped her fingertips together, gently demanding. Kiara took a breath – time to start talking.

Twenty years ago

"Mrs Jacobs?" Ted leaned round the door to the kitchen. His face, like his hands, were weathered, like soft leather, tanned and lined from the sun. "There's a lil' girl in your garden."

Janet turned from the coffee she had been pouring. Despite being a mom of two, she was still slight, lithe like a ballet dancer and just as graceful. "A girl, Ted?"

"Yup. I'll show you." Ted walked away from the doors leading to the back garden, and Janet followed.

Janet loved this house. It was more than she could ever have imagined owning, with large airy rooms and huge windows to let the Connecticut sun stream in. The double doors at the back of the kitchen led to the side of the garden, lush and green with roses everywhere they would grow. Following the path led to a large white stone patio where her and Victor had entertained hundreds of guests over the years – with intimate cocktails, raucous barbecues, and extravagant parties. The catering from last night's party was still there, arranged elegantly on tables, discarded glasses with lipstick stains scattered in between the plants. The pool glimmered silently to the side of the patio.

As she walked onto the patio she could see the girl Ted was talking about – a shock of red curls and faded denim, tucked up on one of their sun loungers, eating one of yesterday's sandwiches. Janet nodded to Ted to indicate he could go and he ambled off down the path to carry on pruning the roses.

Janet walked up to the girl on the sun lounger and saw that she couldn't have been more than five years old. The girl looked up as Janet approached, finishing the sandwich in her hand and swallowing quickly, furtively.

"Hello," the girl said, smiling. Her eyes were powder blue, like the sky that day, and narrowed against the glare from the clean white patio.

Janet sat down on the lounger next to her. "Where did you come from sweetheart? Where's your mommy and daddy?"

The little girl shrugged. "Daddy is sleeping so I went for a walk. Your house is really pretty." She grinned up at Janet.

"Thanks. So how did you get here?" Janet asked. She cast her eye over the girl and could see her pants were worn and too small, her sneakers worse for wear. She wore a faded black t-shirt that was clearly meant for a boy about twice her age, with a peeled and faded Batman logo.

"I walked here through the fence. Can I have another sandwich please?" She smiled at Janet hopefully.

"I'll give you something to eat," said Janet, "but then you'll show me how you got here, okay?" The little girl looked at her eagerly at the promise of more food and nodded.

They walked to the kitchen. "What's your name?" Janet asked the little girl.

"Kiara," she replied.

***

Victor purred down the drive, looking forward to getting home after a busy day of work. It was past 6pm and the sky had turned deep blue with bands of red and orange blushing over the horizon.

He let himself into the house and headed for the kitchen. Warm air drifted in lazily from the patio doors and the sound of gentle chirruping from the birds filtered through the dusky twilight.

"Dad!" Shane and Sarah yelled excitedly when he rounded the corner.

Janet handed him a bottle of beer with a kiss on the cheek. "Hi darling," she said. Victor kissed her back. She had barely aged in the years they had been married, her waist still trim, with only one or two gleaming strands of grey shining amongst the highlights in her hair. Some of his friends were busy managing multiple affairs with younger women while their wives raised their children, but he had never felt the need to turn somewhere else for attention, never wanted a taste of something new.

"Who's Sarah's friend?" he asked, pointing his beer at the little red-haired visitor peeking over the table at him.

Janet motioned for Victor to follow her behind the counter. Looking over at their visitor, she lowered her voice – "I found her in the garden today. She came in through a hole in the fence towards the back and started eating the leftovers from last night."

Victor widened his eyes, pale blue with a hint of grey round the pupils. "And now she's here for dinner? Where are her parents?"

Janet looked embarrassed, lowering her eyes to the floor. She had meant to take the girl home, but once she had prepared her some lunch and the girl had shown her the hole in the fence, Shane and Sarah came home from school and then it was dinner and the little girl had seemed so hungry…

Victor sighed and patted her on the shoulder. He knew his wife was a soft-hearted woman, and would happily take in any waif and stray, animal or human, without thinking of the consequences.

"Daddy!" Sarah interrupted them, running over and throwing her arms around Victor's waist.

"Hi sweetheart," he said, grinning. She was only eight and he already thought she was growing up to be beautiful, with honey-blonde hair half-way down her back to her waist, and blue eyes like his but a warmer hue, like a summer sky in the early morning light.

Shane came over and reached into his pockets for the treats Victor usually kept there. "Thanks dad!" he yelled when he found the candy, and ran off, sneakers screeching on the shiny floors. He was ten and tall for his age, constantly distracted and always on the move. He had the same tender heart as his mother, Victor had seen it in the way they had both cared for a small bird with a broken wing they found one winter, their two heads bent over it, worry creasing their foreheads, hoping to save it.

"I'm going to play with my new friend Kiara," Sarah grabbed the little girl's hand and started dragging her from the table, but Victor stopped her. "Kiara needs to go home now."

He looked down at the little girl, who turned her eyes up to meet his, cautious and uncertain. She was shabby and scrawny, just like him when he was a kid. He shuddered at the memory of the hand-me-down clothes and tight shoes and told Kiara – "It's time to go home." He tried to ignore the look of disappointment etched on her face.

Kiara's father wasn't home when Victor took Kiara back, walking with her as she showed him the gap in the fence leading to the land beyond their garden, and then following her back along the dirt path to the trailer where she lived. She walked up the steps and opened the front door to let herself in, barely tall enough to reach the handle.

"Maybe I should stay here till your dad gets back," Victor said, hesitantly.

Kiara shook her head, paused in the doorway of the trailer. "It's okay. Daddy will be back soon."

"And what about your mom?" Victor asked.

Kiara shook her head, her red curls dancing. "I don't have a mom."

The interview

Kiara cleared her throat. Her mouth was dry, and the gloss was starting to shrink into the lines in her upper lip.

"I never knew my mom. My daddy raised me," she said.

Kiara never really knew her mother. Her departure when Kiara was still in diapers was a constant font of bitterness for her father. When she was little Kiara used to dream that her mother would come back for her and be kind and loving and gentle, like Janet was, but when Kiara was eight years old her father told her that her mother had died. She remembered what he said as she started to cry, her childish hopes shattered: *That's what happens to girls who act like whores, sweetheart. All that waits for them is death."*

Kiara hadn't really understood what he meant, but she knew that something significant was missing from her life, and that now there was no chance to get it back. She used to look in the mirror and wonder what her mother had looked like, imagining someone with the same hair and the same eyes, because her father used to say that she looked like her mother. Maybe that's why he eventually hated her so much.

Beth was tapping the point of her black patent shoes, urging her to carry on with a nod. Kiara continued. "We lived in a trailer, just outside the main town. It was hidden off the street, up a dirt road and surrounded by trees."

"What was your daddy like?" Beth asked.

Kiara paused. There were a lot of words she could use to describe him, none suitable for this interview. "He was a drunk."

Twenty years ago

"Bill Anderson is a drunk bum Janet. He may even be dangerous – if I were you I would keep away."

Janet sat with her usual crowd of friends, at their usual table at Crawford's – their favourite lunch spot in the town. It was the place where the rich moms went for leisurely lunches, where business deals were conducted, and engagements celebrated.

Janet always enjoyed these lunches with the other mothers. Janet presided at the head of the table, organising the parties, as wealthy as, maybe wealthier, than the rest of them, yet inwardly she was still the girl from the farm in Ohio who had cried over the hens when they died.

Ronnie, a pale woman with a frizzy mass of dark hair and crimson lips, wrinkled her nose as she pressed her fork onto a moist slab of chicken. "I agree with Alma, Janet. Bill is one of those people who should be removed from the town and sent somewhere…more fitting."

Alma pursed her lips and nodded, pleased that the other women were on her side. "So, the Anderson girl just strolled right into your garden, Janet? And you invited her inside? With your children?"

Janet nodded. The women at the table looked concerned and shook their heads.

Alma tapped her long nails on the wine glass in front of her, beads of moisture moving slowly from the glass down to her cuticles. "Listen Janet. Bill is not the type of person you want to have in your life, and that includes his little girl. She may look like a cutie-pie, but she's trash – they both are. I warn you it'll only end in tears."

Janet felt her throat tighten. She knew that what they were saying made sense, at least about the father, but the girl had seemed so sweet. Twisting her thick linen napkin in her hand, she looked around the table. "I think she needs someone to look out for her, just to make sure she's alright. After all, Victor told me her mother isn't around."

Ronnie arched an eyebrow. "Yes, well we all know why that is."

Janet shook her head. "I never really listened to that gossip."

Clarissa, a thin woman with straw-coloured hair, smiled coolly and proceeded to fill Janet in.

***

Bill Anderson met Suzanne when they were both eighteen. The baby hadn't been planned and Bill promised he would take care of it all, but Suzanne had shook her head at him and twisted her mouth in displeasure at her changing body, glaring at her growing stomach, resentfully tracing the stretch marks spreading across her skin. Bill hoped that when she had the baby she would feel differently, but she didn't.

She felt her body had been taken over by the baby, born puce-faced and spongy, with a wisp of red hair, greedy for her from the outset. She resented its neediness and expectation, its constant mewling cutting through her thoughts and her sleep. Everything felt soiled all the time – her clothes were sodden with its tears, vomit, and her own milk seeping through underneath, her swollen breasts aching and repulsive to her.

She had picked the name carelessly, a name in a cheap paperback she once read that sprung to mind. Bill wasn't with the baby much, he was too busy working or too tired from working and he thought it would be easy for her now she was a mom.

The baby was six months old when Suzanne started her affair with Carl Murphy, and eleven months old when she left in the middle of the day. She swiftly and quietly gathered her clothes and met Carl, climbing into his car, driving fast and far, her brief fling with motherhood discarded like the soiled diapers she could barely bring herself to touch.

Bill's anger and humiliation burned inside him, mixed with the bourbon he tipped down his throat, trying to forget. He had burned her remaining possessions in a fury, leaving them in a charred heap outside the trailer, the black embers floating on the breeze for weeks afterwards. Every time thoughts of her betrayal washed into his mind, like a wave carrying garbage from the ocean, he took a swig of whatever was closest.

There was no one to take the baby. Suzanne's father had died and the mother wasn't well in the head. She spent days wrapped in a white robe, wandering round her home muttering, and talking to the cats in the yard. Bill had only the remnants of a family, his half-sister dead, and a distant nephew in New York.

He moved the trailer they had shared to a bit of land no one seemed to know or care about enough to charge rent for, in the woods nestled at the back of someone else's property, the trailer not far from the edge of their land, where their perfectly manicured garden ended with a wooden fence.

He would sit at home, the drapes drawn, clutching a bottle of bourbon to his chest every night till he fell asleep on the couch and could ignore the baby crying as he dozed in an alcohol-soaked daze. Somehow, the baby stayed alive, and grew to look more and more like her mother every day.

***

Janet sighed, unable to understand how a mother could leave her child behind. She thought of Kiara's bright eyes and how she

19

had smiled with pleasure at playing with Sarah's toys, and felt desperately sad that she was missing out on a mother's love.

"I think Kiara could use someone to look out for her, especially if her father isn't taking good care of her," Janet said firmly to the women at the table. "She's only five years old," she added, surprised at their cynicism.

Clarissa sighed. "You're such a good person, Janet. You always want to help people."

Alma sniffed. "Some people can't be helped. You mark my words – you'll regret the day you invited that girl into your home."

The interview

Beth widened her eyes. "That must have been terribly difficult for you to grow up without your mother," she said, gently.

Kiara nodded. "I knew I was missing out on what other children had. It did make me sad," she said, thoughtfully.

"I understand that there was another family that helped you and took care of you, is that right?" Beth asked.

Kiara placed the fingertips of her hands together, hoping no one could see them trembling. "They were my neighbours. Our trailer was right up against the border of their land, and they told me I could always come, always visit, anytime I wanted to," she paused. "For many years, they were my real family, much more so than my father."

Beth nodded. "They sound like really kind people, Kiara. What do they think about your singing career now? I'll bet they're very proud."

Kiara lowered her eyes. It was so much more painful to talk about them than she had expected it to be. She exhaled slowly. "I haven't seen them for a long time."

Twenty years ago

Victor could hear the shouts of the children in the pool. It was another bright summer day, sunshine filtering into his home office and warming the back of his neck, a light breeze carrying the smell of the BBQ right to him at his desk, the scent of meat and paprika in the air. The study was full of framed photos of famous sports men he had represented over the years, lit up with stripes of sunshine through the slats of the blinds, with alternate lines of light and shade patterned over the walls.

Janet peeped round the door.

"Anyone for lemonade?"

He smiled at her. "Perfect – you read my mind."

She handed him a glass of lemonade, clinking with ice, and lingered by his desk to rub his shoulders. "Do you have to work on a Sunday?"

Victor nodded. Setting up his own sports agency meant the work was constant, but he thrived on it, and most importantly it was his own company that he would be able to pass on to Shane and Sarah one day. He wanted a legacy for his own kids that consisted of more than his own father had given him, who had just left him with bruises and bad memories.

"Kiara out there too?" he asked, not looking up from the stack of papers he was sorting through.

"Yep." Janet drifted to the window and picked up an old coffee mug to take back to the kitchen.

She had told Victor what she knew about the girl after lunch with her friends, but he already knew about Bill Anderson. Bill had been involved in an altercation in town not long ago, and Victor was friends with the police chief who had been called to 'diffuse' the situation.

"Remember Janet – anything she needs, anytime she wants to be here…" Victor trailed off. Janet smiled and kissed him on the cheek before leaving him to his work.

Janet walked back to the kitchen, towards the gleam of the white patio and the splashes of the pool. He wasn't usually so supportive of what he called her charity projects, the people she took an interest in and wanted to nurture. He was always concerned that she would get taken advantage of.

But Janet could see that Kiara had struck a chord with him and that he had grown deeply fond of her. Not in the same way as he doted on Sarah of course, his only daughter. But Kiara had untapped something in him, and Janet was glad of it. She often didn't know what he was thinking but she knew he had memories he kept locked away and stories he never shared of a childhood that was more painful than pleasant. If helping Kiara would somehow make him more open, Janet would consider it as a just reward for helping the girl. She headed out towards the patio, the BBQ nearly ready.

The interview

"Now Kiara, I've heard rumours that the family who helped you was in fact the Jacobs family, owners of the famous Jacobs Sports

Management agency. Was it Victor and Janet Jacobs who supported you through your childhood?"

Beth leaned back in her chair, her long limbs extended and expectant. She always did that when she dropped a big question, as if she were throwing an emotional grenade and settling back to watch the blast.

Kiara winced inwardly. She knew the question would be coming – Marco had told her it would be. Of course, he knew her whole backstory and had been determined from the outset to use it to best advantage.

She shook her head. "I'm not going to name the family. I don't want to violate their privacy."

Beth looked discomforted, the big reveal not forthcoming, though Kiara knew she would get one later anyway.

"I appreciate that you want to keep their names out of it. You said they have two children of their own, a boy and a girl, both older than you. How did you get on with them?"

Kiara smiled at the thought of Shane and Sarah. She carried many bad memories with her, always threatening to crowd into her mind, like a group of wild animals she had to keep tamed and tucked away, but the happy memories she did have always featured Shane or Sarah or both of them together.

"They were like my older brother and big sister, and my only friends. I loved them. I still do."

Seventeen years ago

Sarah curled up in her sleeping bag, a bowl of popcorn balancing precariously on her knees. The floor was covered with sleeping bags, one for each of the six girls staying at Barb's house for her tenth birthday. Sarah was always invited to parties – she was beautiful, confident, and wealthy – and even girls at age ten understand that these things open doors to parties, friends and popularity.

Janey was telling them about her older brother, Sam, and how unbelievably gross he was. "It's cootie-central at my house," she said, to the squeals and laughter of the other girls.

Amber turned to Sarah and poked her with a tanned foot with glittery pink nail polish smeared inexpertly on each toenail. "Your brother is the cutest Sarah," she said, sighing dramatically.

"Ew! No! Don't be gross!" Sarah shrieked. All of Sarah's friends loved Shane. At thirteen, he was old enough to be an object of complete fascination, yet appropriately unobtainable enough to spark ardent yearning crushes in Sarah's friends. Her house always had troops of blushing giggling girls whispering behind their hands when they came to visit, and Shane found it infuriating.

"How's your little sister, Sarah?" Rachel said, teasingly.

"I don't have a sister," Sarah muttered. The popcorn had spilled into her lap. She picked up the kernels one by one, deliberately focusing on putting each one back into the bowl and hoped the conversation would move on.

"Are your mom and dad going to adopt her for real?" Barbara said, trying to talk with her mouth full of candy.

Janey, sitting cross-legged and leaning on Amber, made a face. "Doesn't she, like, smell bad or something? My mom says she's trash." The other girls snickered.

"Shut up! *Please*," Sarah wailed.

The girls' attention soon turned to other things, but Sarah's cheeks still burned. She wasn't used to being made fun of, and increasingly Kiara was becoming an unwanted source of jokes at her expense. It annoyed her when Kiara got to wear Sarah's old clothes and the other girls saw her in Sarah's cast offs. She didn't like seeing the younger girl being lifted in the air by *her* dad in that special way when he whirled you so fast you were both scared and thrilled at the same time and didn't know whether to laugh or cry, and your heart felt like it would just fly away. Sarah didn't want to share that experience with anyone else, especially not the scrawny interloper that her mom told her to be nice to.

Sarah sulked for a while and only cheered up when Barb's mom bought the pizza and ice cream and let them eat it in Barb's bedroom, even though they really weren't supposed to.

***

Shane dumped his backpack in the hallway and headed straight to the kitchen to grab a soda from the fridge, then he went to the living room and jumped onto the couch, switching on the TV and flicking rapidly between the channels. He could hear his mom outside with Ted, obsessing over her roses.

On hearing the TV, Mary walked in. "Hi Shane. How's school?" she asked. Sarah and Shane loved Mary – a tiny woman who never seemed quite upright, always a little bit crooked or leaning to one side. It gave her a furtive, fragile air, like a bird recovering from a bad flight. She had been housekeeping for them since Shane was two, and despite her appearance she was still energetic enough to join in with the kids when they were horsing around.

"Good." Shane replied, distracted by a basketball match. One of the top NBA players was represented by his dad's agency and Shane had met him a few times and got a signed jersey and a photo together. The other kids at school were practically feral with jealousy when he told them.

Mary leaned over to tousle his thick dark hair. He grinned at her and playfully swatted her hand away. "Use a coaster!" she shouted to him as she walked back to the kitchen.

He settled in to watch the match. He tried to watch as much sport as possible so he could follow his dad's players, know the results, and talk to his dad about them when he got back from his office in the late evenings. His dad always told him it would be his business one day.

He was so fixated on the TV he didn't notice Kiara had crept in beside him. She was still small for her age and seemed almost absorbed by the pillowy couch. "Hi Shane," she half-whispered, poking his arm with the tip of her pinky.

"Hey! I didn't see you there," he said, smiling at her. "Want some soda?"

"Sure." He handed her the cola which she took and held in both hands, raising it to her mouth with great ceremony. "Thanks Shane," she said, solemnly.

"Where's Sarah? Why aren't you playing with her?" he asked, tugging gently on one of her red curls.

Kiara looked down at the floor and sniffed, her mouth turning downward. "She told me to go away," she said, mournfully.

Shane looked at her with pity. He had heard his parents talking about Kiara and about her dad. One evening he had walked her back to the trailer from the garden and he had seen it for himself, although Kiara told him very firmly and seriously that he was not to come any closer. Even though she was only eight, she was very adept at keeping that part of her life separate.

Shane felt sad for her, and never really minded her being around the house, she was easy to boss around so she would always do what either Sarah or Shane wanted.

"Sarah's just being grumpy. You can sit and watch sports with me if you want?" he offered. "You'll have to be quiet though."

He turned the volume back up and Kiara sat very still and silent so Shane would let her stay and she wouldn't be told to go away again.

Kiara had gotten very good at practicing being silent. Holding each muscle still until she ached, breathing gently, her mouth slightly open, taking quick shallow breaths. Her daddy liked peace and quiet and she didn't like to make him angry.

There was a rainstorm pushing heavy on the skies when Shane walked her back that evening. They had taken a panel out of the fence and replaced it with a gate, as she had gotten too big for the gap she had originally squirmed through and kept snagging clothes on it. Janet had always mended the holes before her dad could notice. Sometimes Janet washed her clothes too and she got to wear something from Sarah's closet while they dried. She would close her eyes and wish clothes had the power to change her into a different person with another life.

It wasn't long before the skies dropped their burden, tipping the water down heavily as though the clouds were eager to be rid of it. The droplets bounced hard off the trailer and plopped softly onto the dirt. Kiara liked to watch the rain running down the small window in her room. If she watched it for long enough she felt like she could be part of it, running away down the walls outside and into the ground.

She gently pulled the blanket up over her knees. It had gotten wet the other day and still smelled damp and mouldy. The blankets in Sarah and Shane's house smelled like a meadow in summer, she could lay face down on the beds there and just lie breathing it in for hours. There were never any summer meadows in the trailer, only autumn moulds and winter mulch.

The trailer had two bedrooms. The door to her room was a brown folding plastic door that was supposed to shut with a magnetic clasp but it never quite stuck. She had a narrow bed with a few blankets and cushions underneath the window. A few shelves lined the sides of the room, with clothes piled on them, in no particular order. She didn't have a lot of things to put in her room. Just herself and her silence, and a few clothes with mended holes.

"Kiara!" her dad called out for her. She pushed the blanket back and stretched her legs. They had grown stiff from where she had sat for hours watching the rain course down the window.

"Yes daddy?" She said, walking into the other end of the trailer, where there was a small couch, on which her dad was lying. The couch used to have a pattern, but it had all merged into one murky brown stain that had slowly enveloped the entire fabric. Opposite the couch there was a TV and if she moved the aerial the right way she could sometimes find cartoons, but it was usually buzzing with static and she could never hear it properly.

The trailer had a small kitchen area – a few cupboards, some with doors, and a fridge. She sometimes made food for her and her dad if there was any around. Once she even fried an egg on the two-burner stove but it didn't look how it was supposed to, with the white and yellow round and glossy and smooth. The colours all got caught together somehow and she couldn't pull them apart again even though she tried with the spatula and then her hands. She had burns on her fingers when she went to school the next day. She since stuck to making sandwiches, when there was bread around.

Her dad narrowed his eyes at her. "You hungry?"

"Yes daddy."

He pointed a rough finger towards the fridge. "Get me a beer from there. There's some ham if you want it."

Kiara went to the fridge, where there were a few greasy slices of ham separated by thin strips of plastic. She took her dad the beer and he accepted it with a curt nod.

Bill was much younger than Victor, but he looked far older. His skin was coarse and dry, his thinning sandy hair tucked under a cap. He wore plaid shirts with grease stains from when he was able to get work fixing cars, although Kiara didn't know how he was able to fix anything the way his hands trembled all the time. Mostly he was a taciturn, slovenly drunk, with an undertone of anger in every word and every gesture, regardless of who he was speaking to.

Victor had come to the trailer one afternoon, when Kiara had started visiting them. Bill had sent Kiara to her room, but she had pressed against the plastic door to listen to Victor and her father talking. Victor had asked Bill if he was okay for Kiara to pop over every now and then, to play with his daughter Sarah. Bill had nodded silently, then narrowed his eyes and asked Victor, "*What are you hoping to get out of this?*" Victor had been taken aback at the question, and held his hands up, as if Bill had said something threatening. Only a playmate for Sarah, he had said, shaking his head. Bill had agreed, on the condition that Victor didn't come and disturb him again. Bill didn't really notice when Kiara was there or when she was gone, and if the Jacobs fed her that was a bonus, as it saved him some money.

Kiara got a plate and took one of the slices of ham. It glistened wetly. Kiara took it to her room and imagined watching sports with Shane and lying on a bed that smelled like a meadow.

The interview

Beth unfolded her long legs and stood up as the cameras stopped blinking. "We'll just have a five-minute break, then we'll get right back to it."

It had been fifteen minutes since they started and Kiara could tell Beth was a little frustrated at the slow pace. She waved over Marco, who was trying to flirt with an assistant to one side of the set. He bounded over. "Hey, you're doing great!" he said, flashing her a smile that was too white to be natural.

"It is going okay? Is she getting bored? What shall I talk about?" Kiara hissed at him, anxiously.

She felt tense and sticky with sweat. She had done lots of interviews before but this was the first time she had done an interview talking about herself rather than the group or their music. Although it wasn't that that bothered her most. She knew that somewhere out there beyond the red eyes of the cameras, the Jacobs might watch this when it aired, hearing her talk about their shared past, dusting off old memories and displaying them to the world. She thought it was likely they had seen her on TV or in magazines, but maybe too much time had passed for them to care, and perhaps they wouldn't even watch it. Maybe she was just a shadow of a memory, an extra person in a photo here and there, a fragment of an anecdote.

Her mouth dry, she tried to swallow. "Look Kiara, angel, you're doing fine. You need to relax and refresh your lip gloss. Stop looking so intense – it's not attractive," Marco said to her, although his head was turned away towards the cute assistant.

"You're not giving her much detail either," he said, finally turning back to her, the assistant called away. "So far you've talked about your dad being a drunk and how you got to know the family. Give her a bit more to work with, okay?"

Kiara nodded. The makeup artist popped over and reapplied Kiara's lip gloss, gently tracing the outline of each lip and loading each one with a fresh layer, then spritzing her face and patting down a few stray curls.

Beth marched back to her chair. "Ready?"

"Sure, okay."

The cameras flickered on again, and Beth recorded a brief introduction to use after a commercial break when the interview would air in a few days' time.

"Welcome back folks. In case you're just tuning in, I'm talking to Kiara Anderson of Femme Fatale and she's sharing with us the amazing story of her rise from poverty to international pop star."

Kiara tried not to wince at the word "poverty". She associated that word with photos of children with concave stomachs and pleading eyes, sitting outside wooden shacks in a dusty land. The trailer had been shitty, but it wasn't on quite the same level as that.

"Kiara, you've shared with us about your dad and how your neighbours looked out for you. Did anyone at school notice what you were going through? Were you a good student?"

Kiara nibbled on her lower lip. "School was difficult."

Fifteen years ago

Kiara sat at the back of the class, as always. She found that if she kept quiet long enough a whole day could go by and no one would notice her.

Now she was in fifth grade, things were definitely worse. The other kids noticed stuff, and they knew she wasn't quite like them, that she didn't have the right things. Last week her pencils had gone missing when she came back from the bathroom. That was new, normally the other kids threw things at her or laughed at her, but they'd now graduated to taking her things too. Not that she had much to take, but she guessed that's why they did it, they knew it would hurt her more because she couldn't replace things like they could.

Kiara had a strategy, just as she did with her dad, three simple things she repeated to herself like a mantra: Stay quiet, don't cry, and be small. She tried to imagine every fibre, every piece of her flesh, pulling inwards and shrinking down so eventually she would be able to slip inside her own backpack and hide. But even as she said it to herself as she searched for her missing pencils, her cheeks burned and her eyes filled with tears, and the other kids knew they had got to her.

Gym class was always the worst time of the week. All the girls clustered into groups, chatting, laughing, comparing. Kiara was always jealous of their sneakers – most of the other girls had new sneakers every year, while Kiara had a pair from goodwill, stained boy's shoes with the sole flapping sadly at the bottom like a saggy lower lip, and furled Velcro straps that no longer stuck. Kiara hated how the other girls pointed and laughed at her during gym class as she ran and her soles flapped on the floor. They never stopped finding it funny.

"Kiara?" She looked up. The class was staring, while Mrs Willis looked at her enquiringly. "What planet are we on today?" There was a murmur of laughter in the class.

"Sorry miss," she muttered. Mrs Willis turned back to the board, not bothering to press her for an answer to the question she never heard in the first place.

As a student with no discernible academic gifts the teachers were coolly disinterested in her, content to leave her silent and scraping through. She knew her grades were terrible but her dad always signed her report card and never turned up to school meetings so she figured it didn't really matter.

The only class she did well in was music with Miss Hitchen, who always praised her in front of the other kids. They didn't like it and it always surprised her, but she guessed Miss Hitchen was just trying to be nice. That day in music class, Kiara had been the only one who could improvise a melody and get the right key. Miss Hitchen had been impressed and one of the other girls had even said she liked Kiara's tune. As far as her academic career went, that was probably the highlight so far.

When the school day was over Kiara always felt a huge sense of relief – she could breathe easier, stand taller. She knew she could go to the Jacob's house any day after school was over, and just being there made her feel happy, even when everyone was out and it was just her and Ted, helping him to prune the roses in the garden and talking about the best ways to make them grow. She was safe at the Jacob's house, she didn't have to look out the corner of her eyes or hear laughter behind her back and know it was aimed at her. The sense of awkwardness and apprehension left her when she walked outside the school doors, free again till the next day.

When the bell rang, Kiara grabbed her backpack and headed outside, the warm yellow of the sunshine turning a deeper golden as the afternoon marched on. She breathed in, wanting as much to breathe in the air as the sunlight itself, if such a thing were possible. She started to walk towards the Jacob's house, enjoying the warmth of the sun, wishing the moments from now until she had to go back to the trailer would slow down and extend.

She hadn't been paying attention to the journey, daydreaming while her feet traced her regular route, when she was jerked backwards and pulled onto the ground. She landed hard on her tailbone, a dull pain spreading across her back, small sharp stones digging into her hands.

A group of three girls stood over her. Kiara leaned back and looked up at them silently, hearing her heartbeat coursing in her ears and jumping at her throat. *Stay quiet, don't cry, and be small,* she repeated in time with her pulse, praying that they would leave her alone.

"Hey Kiara," sang one of the girls. Jade was always the meanest and always started the jokes. Tall and slender, she had dark hair with green eyes that flashed bright and cat-like in the sun, a smile unfolding over her pale face as she looked down at Kiara.

Diana, hanging onto Jade's arm, pinched her nose, twisting her mouth into a dramatic expression of disgust. "What's that smell?" she said, and the girls all laughed together.

Kiara's throat tightened with a sob, but she clamped her mouth shut and blinked furiously to keep the tears from her eyes. Other kids often made fun of her for smelling bad. She wasn't sure if she did or if they were just saying it to be mean, but she hoped she didn't smell like the blankets in the trailer, damp and sour. Kiara looked around, hoping someone might pass and interrupt the girls in their cruel game, but the smattering of people nearby were other students and they averted their eyes and crossed the street. No one liked to get involved in someone else's issues, there were unspoken rules to keep.

She looked down at the ground, while Jade pulled her backpack up off her, a sad sagging drawstring bag with fraying cords and a black logo that peeled and left little flakes settling around it, like black dandruff. Jade casually tossed it over her shoulder, landing with a soft thump on the grass a few feet away, a sneer over her rosy mouth.

"Why don't you write a song about it Kiara?" she said sarcastically, and walked off with the other girls, arm in arm.

Kiara exhaled shakily, thankful they were gone. She pushed herself up and inspected the damage – a few scrapes to her arms and hands where she had landed, no blood. She trotted down the street after her backpack and carried on her way to her refuge.

Sarah stood frozen a little way down the street, watching Kiara bound away, her curls bobbing up and down. Sarah's friend Amber was collecting her younger sister from elementary school, and they were on their way to Amber's house to watch TV.

"Hey, what are you staring at over there?" Amber asked her, giving her a wide-eyed look and tilting her head to one side. She hadn't seen Kiara and the other girls, she had been busy talking to her little sister.

"Nothing," Sarah said. All of a sudden, she felt a guilty chill creep into her belly. She was far enough not to be noticed but she could have run up the street, told the girls to stop or helped Kiara up, given her a hug or some comforting words. She turned and followed Amber with her little sister. Maybe she'd say something to Kiara later.

***

Janet frowned at the cake mix selection. She knew Shane would prefer Devil's food cake but Sarah and Victor were going through a red velvet phase. She decided on a chocolate brownie mix instead.

She popped the mix into her bright plastic cart and walked slowly down the aisles. She enjoyed grocery shopping – it reminded her of shopping with her mother when she was little.

It was cool and quiet in the store that early on a Saturday. She rolled the cart down the stationary aisle and picked up a packet of pencils. Kiara had lost some recently, and Janet didn't mind getting her a few more, knowing her dad wouldn't be buying her any. Janet looked at the cart of groceries. Her children always had food in the house, nice clothes to wear and things to look forward to. She just couldn't understand how Kiara's father could stand to sit by and watch his daughter be in need.

"Mrs Jacobs?" Janet looked around, startled from her reverie. Her daughter's former music teacher, Harriet Hitchen, was next to her, smiling.

"Stocking up on some supplies for my class," she said, holding up a packet of coloured paper. "I figure if I put things on bright colours they might pay more attention," she laughed.

Harriet was a young woman, but signs of tiredness were starting to creep in around her eyes and mouth. She often found that the kids were more unruly than she could handle, although Sarah had been polite and good-natured and Harriet had always enjoyed speaking to Janet about her daughter's progress.

Janet smiled back at her. "How are things Harriet?"

Harriet nodded at her "Good thanks. How is Sarah getting on in middle school?"

"She's doing well, she has lots of friends, and good grades. She's stopped playing the piano though," Janet shook her head as she said it. Sarah was a clever girl and didn't need to study hard to maintain her grades, but her piano practice was inconsistent and she had given it up a year ago.

"Oh, such a shame. What about Shane, isn't he in high school now?" Harriet asked.

Janet nodded. "He's a sophomore now, and growing up fast," she sighed. In a very short space of time Shane had started to look like a young man and behave like one too. He was still her boy, but sometimes they felt more like friendly strangers than mother and son. He was losing his soft edges, growing taller than her, becoming more distant.

Harriet hesitated. "There was something I wanted to ask you Janet, about Kiara Anderson. I understand you know her quite well?" Harriet had sent notes home with Kiara a number of times and never received a reply. Her father had been one of the hardest parents to engage with his child's progress, or distinct lack of it, and Harriet was concerned about the girl. It wasn't that she was disruptive, entirely the opposite in fact. Her silence and obvious disengagement from her classes was a cause of growing concern amongst the teachers.

"I know Kiara very well Harriet. Is she doing okay?" Janet squeezed her hands together anxiously. She and Victor were worried about Kiara too. They both had a sense of apprehension about the years to come as Kiara got older and her father increasingly checked out of his parental duties, and they weren't sure what to do next to help her.

"Kiara is a lovely girl and she is showing some real talent for music. She's just clearly…" Harriet paused, "…a little switched off. Her grades aren't good and she's not participating much in her other classes. I think that maybe she lacks a bit of confidence and I was thinking that nurturing her musical abilities would help?"

Janet nodded, agreeing that if they could help Kiara find something she was good at, it could help her self-esteem.

"How can I help?" Janet asked.

"I was going to suggest some piano lessons but I know there's no way that girl has a piano to practice on. But I hear she's at your house a lot and maybe you still have the piano Sarah was using?"

Janet nodded, thoughtfully. "Yes, that's right."

Harriet carried on quickly. "If she can practice at your house, I can make sure she gets a music tutor once a week."

Janet had no problem with having Kiara practice at the house. In fact, she was glad the piano would get used. She had inherited it from her parents – her sister Moira hadn't wanted it. She could still picture her mother stroking the keys lovingly, her foot gently tapping the brass pedals, and could remember the smell of the wood

32

as Janet stood leaning against the piano to listen, head resting on the side. Her mother had played Christmas songs every year, Janet, Moira and their father sitting nearby with steaming mugs of cocoa warming their hands and faces. The tradition had continued for a while when Sarah and Shane were little, when her mom would come to stay over Christmas before she passed away and the piano now stayed largely unused.

"Alright Harriet. If you talk to her about the lessons I'll let her know she can use our piano anytime to practice," Janet paused and added, "maybe best not to tell her we came up with this together."

Harriet nodded, "Agreed." She smiled as she turned back to continue her shopping.

Thirteen years ago

It was the type of rainy Saturday that was made for staying in bed watching movies all day. The skies were leaden and sluggish, like a shroud hovering over the town. The rain was relentless, the ground overflowing. Huge puddles squatted in every crevice and sent up waves of greyish water with each passing car.

Shane had been lying in bed most of the morning. He and his friends had planned to go out but on days like this everyone would stay indoors.

Rolling over lazily, he stood up and stretched. His mom had made soup and the smell of simmering lentils and salty smoked bacon had wafted up to his room, so he pulled on a t-shirt and headed downstairs to grab some food. The rain thrashed against the windows as he walked down the stairs. He could hear Sarah in the living room watching a movie with a friend, girlish giggles drifting up from where they sat. Shane couldn't stand Sarah's friends – they followed him round the house, laughing and whispering.

He could hear his mom organising plates in the kitchen with Mary, their voices a cheery murmur against the violence of the wind outside.

Piano notes rung out over the top of the voices and giggles, with a voice repeating back the scales, clear and bright at the top notes and soft and tremulous at the lower register.

Shane walked over past the living room entrance, quickly and softly, hoping he wouldn't be seen by Sarah's friends, then around to the back where the dining area was. They didn't use this room all the time, only for big family dinners or special occasions. It had two large glass doors that could be opened out to join the room with the rest of the house, so people could swish in and out.

He grabbed one of the handles and pulled the door open, sliding into the room and shutting the door with a soft click. The room was dominated by a large dark wooden table and chairs. It looked empty and fruitless now, but usually was laden with tastefully chosen china, gleaming silver, trays overflowing with food, candles holding up a steady bright flame to light the faces of guests. Towards the back of the room was the piano where Kiara sat, her head bowed in concentration, forehead furrowed, her hair pulled back off her face.

Shane remembered his grandma playing the piano when he was little. She'd play Christmas tunes for them and mom would try to get them to sing in tune with her, but it seemed that no one had inherited his grandma's musical talent. Sarah had gotten bored of the piano pretty quickly, it required too much effort and she wasn't someone to anchor herself down to anything for too long. Aunt Moira, his mom's sister, had tried but she had no love for playing music, only for listening to it on scratchy old records.

Shane walked up to Kiara and leaned against the side of the piano, resting his head against the wood the way his mom always used to when grandma played. Kiara looked up, her forehead unfurrowing, tense mouth relaxing into a grin.

"Hey. How long have you been in here?" she said, looking round to see if anyone else had joined them.

"A few minutes – it sounds good. What are you working on?" He slid onto the bench next to her. It wasn't really big enough for two, and Shane at seventeen was tall with broad shoulders, but Kiara was still as slight as a willow branch. She made room for him.

"Thanks Shane. I've got a few pieces by Chopin to study." She pointed at the printed sheet music in front of her, covered in scrawled pencil notes from her tutor. She had been playing the piano for two years since Miss Hitchen arranged for her to have a tutor. Even though she was now twelve and had moved up to middle school, the lessons with Peter had continued. He was teaching her to sing too. As soon as she started to play, it was like the rest of her life dimmed all around her and there was no one else besides her and the piano. Hours would pass like minutes, as if the clock was set to fast forward.

"You're getting so good, much better than Sarah ever was." He nudged her with his shoulder and she laughed. "You hanging out here with us today?"

"Yup. It's poker night, so you guys get me for the whole night." She gave a wry smile. Her dad had started regular poker nights with a group of guys, although she wasn't sure if they were actually his friends or just men who were out to make money. Either way, he didn't want her around on poker nights and would tell her gruffly to go and stay with her friends. Poker nights were her chance to be away from the trailer and spend a little more time at the Jacobs' house.

"Awesome. You know it's movie night tonight?" Shane asked. Kiara nodded happily. The Jacobs had a movie night once a month when the whole family ordered pizzas and watched movies. They even had a rota for who got to choose, and it was Shane's turn tonight. Kiara rarely got to stay for movie nights but sometimes poker nights at the trailer coincided with movie nights, a welcome rarity.

"What are we going to watch?"

Shane grinned. "Not sure yet but I'll think of something. Ideally something that'll piss Sarah off."

Kiara laughed. Sarah and Shane never agreed on their movie choices, but the rule was the rule – the person whose turn it was got to choose and no one could complain.

"You're not hanging out with Sarah and her friend, which one is it today, Janey?"

"It's Barb. And no," Kiara shook her head.

"How come?" Shane had noticed Sarah and Kiara didn't really spend that much time together anymore. He'd asked Sarah about it once, and she had started complaining about the younger girl "intruding" on their space and that her friends didn't like her. He had told her not to be such a brat but clearly, she hadn't taken his advice.

"C'mon Shane, Sarah has her own group of friends her age. They're all in the same class, they want to hang out together. I don't mind." Kiara didn't expect Sarah to make a space for her in her social circle. Sarah was two years older, and friends with the prettiest and the most popular girls. Kiara wasn't one of them and she would rather be on her own with the piano.

She reached out to shuffle the sheet music around. As she stretched out Shane could see a smattering of bruises on her arm just below the elbow. They were faded yellow marks, three circles dancing over the pale skin. He reached out to grab her wrist and turn her arm towards him.

"Hey!" She leaned back and nearly fell off the narrow bench.

He stared at her with insistent brown eyes. "Where did these come from?"

She turned, thin lipped, back to the music, and pulled her arm out of his warm hands.

"I asked you a question," he said, tapping her knee with his middle finger, still staring at her pointedly.

"It's nothing Shane, honestly. Just some bruises, no big deal." She turned her eyes sideways to look at him, then back to the piano.

Shane swallowed hard. The bruises looked like fingerprints to him, and he didn't want to ask but he knew he had to.

"Was it your dad?" he said finally, this time not looking at her.

Kiara gave a snort. "Shane, he barely knows I exist. Trust me he doesn't have the time or the energy to pay me any kind of attention, good or bad."

He looked back at her again. "So, where did they come from?"

"It was just some stuff at school, okay? It's nothing, really." Shane knew that some kids had been cruel to Kiara before. She had told him tearfully one day about the name-calling, and he knew she didn't really have any friends. He reached out his arm and put it round her, pulling her to him. He'd known her since she was five, when she was just a little kid looking for something to eat. Seven years later she was so much part of the family she was like another younger sister to him, and one he didn't find half as annoying as the other one.

"You need some help with it?" he said softly, into the top of her head. Shane was almost a senior, a handsome sports star with good grades and the son of the owner of one of America's premier sports agencies. He spent his weekends meeting the stars represented by his dad, had a great car and went to the best parties. Kiara knew that he would come to the school with her and try to let some of his star dust rub off on her, but she also knew that jealousy was as big a motivator for cruelty than any, and being seen with him could spark off a fury in the girls who seemed to dislike her so much already. It would just make things worse.

"Nope. I can handle it," she told him, firmly.

He nodded. "Okay. But you tell me if you need me, alright?"

"Sure."

He gave her a squeeze and then stood up to leave to let her continue practicing. He wasn't happy with the conversation, but he knew her well enough to know when she had said all she would say.

The interview

Kiara dabbed at her eyes with a tissue, careful not to smudge the thick makeup. She knew Beth would love it that she cried during the interview. She was once said to have remarked that *"every tear gets me another thousand viewers, at least."*

It was painful to have to talk about things she had buried and left behind, a previous life she had hoped would stay hidden. She was Kiara Anderson of Femme Fatale, not Kiara from the trailer anymore. Marco kept telling her to *"embrace her past,"* that the public love a rags-to-riches story, but she would rather take those rags and set them on fire than wave them around for all to see.

"It must have been so hard for you, Kiara. Kids can be so cruel, can't they?" Beth said, tilting her head to show her sympathy and her best side to the camera.

Kiara nodded and pressed her lips together. "I'm not the only one to have ever been bullied. But yes, it still hurts remembering what that was like."

"Of course, it does. Sometimes we carry these wounds with us all our lives." Beth leaned in.

"Did you ever have anyone sticking up for you? A boyfriend, maybe?" she asked.

Kiara resisted the urge to roll her eyes. Beth loved to pry about her guests' love lives and given that Kiara had never dated anyone while in the public eye, though there were always rumours linking her with this man or that, the question was inevitable.

"No boyfriend. In fact, I've never really been in love at all."

***

"Did you ever have anyone sticking up for you? A boyfriend maybe?"

Shane tensed as Beth asked Kiara her next question. He wondered whether or not she would mention him at all, but she didn't.

Victor, Janet, Sarah and Shane had gathered at Sarah's New York home to watch the interview. It was a shock to see Kiara be herself after seeing her as part of Femme Fatale, where it was like she inhabited someone else's skin entirely. The Kiara of Femme Fatale wasn't someone they felt they knew at all, though the red curls and the china blue eyes were the same.

It had been ten months since Sarah had rung them all breathlessly, promising HUGE news, and demanding that they all meet immediately. Shane had been the last one to arrive at the family house in Connecticut, his mom, dad and Sarah already there, Sarah flushed pink and practically dancing with excitement, but her husband Tim was nowhere to be seen.

Sarah gathered them on the couch in the living room, flipped open her laptop to YouTube and pressed play on a music video to a song they had all heard, riding high in the charts.

Victor huffed impatiently. "What the hell Sarah? Why are we here watching some girls writhe around to a song I have no desire to listen to?"

"Wait, you'll see, I promise!" Sarah flapped a hand at him, a manic smile on her face.

The music video scenes flicked from one group member to the next, low lit in a beautiful hotel suite, wearing only underwear, the shots lingering on seductive gazes and pouting lips. The camera focused on the main singer, mouthing the words to the song with a sideways glance at the camera over a bare shoulder, head tilted so her long red curls cascaded down over her back, with heavy dark makeup framing her blue eyes.

It was Shane who realised first. He put a hand to his mouth and turned to Sarah. She grinned and nodded her head. Janet wasn't far behind Shane. She gasped when she realised, tears coming to her eyes, and grabbed Sarah's hand. "It's her, isn't it?"

"Who?" said Victor, looking around, "What am I missing?"

They all started laughing then, Sarah and Janet's laughter blurred with tears, Shane shaking his head in shock. "It's her daddy, it's Kiara," Sarah told him, pointing to the video, and paused it when Kiara came into shot again.

Victor looked at Kiara, the same features but yet an entirely different person, a woman exuding power and confidence where there was once uncertainty and shyness. He kept shaking his head back and forth, exhaling loudly, looking from Sarah to Janet to Shane to the screen, unable to speak, as it finally sunk in that she was okay, after the years of not knowing where she was.

As they now sat watching Beth interview Kiara, Shane remembered that moment of discovery just ten months ago, the realisation that Kiara was actually alive and that there was a chance to see her again, to see her eyes dancing in the sunshine, to laugh with her, to sit and listen to her play the piano, to know absolutely for sure that she was safe and well.

In the past ten months, Sarah sent round emails when she found clips online or news articles, but they hadn't contacted Kiara, and nor had she contacted them. They had wanted to that first day they saw her on YouTube but Victor said not to. He had said they should wait until she decided to contact them herself, that it had to be her decision. After all, she was the one who had run away when she was seventeen, without saying why. Janet had grimly accepted Victor's advice but both she and Shane weren't happy about it.

There was another commercial break during the interview. Sarah, Shane, Victor and Janet had watched largely in silence so far. Nothing had surprised or shocked them, it was a pretty faithful report of all that they knew about Kiara, though none of them had quite realised how bad things had been at school.

"I should have known," Janet said. "She never had any friends, never spoke about any other kids she hung out with."

Sarah looked down at the floor uneasily. She felt that same guilty chill poke her in the belly, like a cold finger pointing at her, accusingly. She had seen what the other kids were like with Kiara, she knew she was going through a hard time. Why hadn't she ever stepped in to help, or spoken words of comfort? Maybe Kiara knew all along that Sarah had seen the bullying and never once tried to help her. Maybe Kiara had overheard Sarah that night she left, heard those hurtful murmurs, and perhaps that's why she ran away. Sarah felt sick. If that was the reason why she left she might say so to Beth Winters and her family would know and blame her forever. She stood up abruptly to go to the kitchen and grab a drink. "Anyone want anything?"

"Grab me a soda sweetheart," Victor said.

Sarah nodded and walked to the kitchen.

Shane was silent, thinking of the bruises Kiara often had, the bruises she begged him not to tell his parents about, and he never did. He had offered to help her and she had always said no. He never knew how bad it really was though and he had never enquired too deeply. Hearing it from her lips on TV was a shock to him, though not quite as much as to his mom, dad and sister, who seemed to have had no idea what Kiara was going through. He pressed his hands together nervously, one foot tapping the floor. He had a good idea of why Kiara had run away. He wondered if she would reveal that it was his fault.

Janet was still shaking her head, and Victor had his arm round her. "She didn't say anything, how were you supposed to know?" He was trying to comfort her. "Maybe if we had done something, told the school, helped her, maybe she would have stayed…" Janet wiped tears from the corner of her eye with a tissue.

Shane was about to say something to his mom but the interview had started again. Sarah came dashing in with the soda and settled back on the couch. Shane leaned across and squeezed his mom's hand, sure that she would find out it wasn't her fault soon enough anyway.

Twelve years ago

"Shane has a girlfriend," Sarah announced to the table. At fifteen she had assumed her place as the family town crier, the house gossip. If Sarah knew something about anyone she would happily share it, a terrible secret-keeper but quite happy to take a bribe to keep quiet. On this occasion, Shane had refused to bribe her when she said she would tell his secret, so this was her revenge. She had seen Shane and Melanie kissing, and one of Sarah's friends said *everyone* knew that Shane and Melanie were going steady. The secret was out.

Janet looked up from her plate, while Kiara stared wide-eyed at Shane, and Victor laughed.

"Is that so?" he said, looking across at his son.

Shane rolled his eyes. "Yes. No big deal."

"Are you in love, Shane?" Kiara half-whispered across the table to him.

He laughed, a slight flush creeping over his t-shirt collar, and didn't answer.

"Who is it Shane?" Janet asked. She wasn't surprised – it was fairly obvious to her that Shane had a girlfriend. He was out much more than usual, heavy-handed on the cologne, and making secretive late-night phone calls in his room.

Shane answered quickly, before Sarah could open her mouth. "Melanie."

"Oh, Alma's daughter, beautiful girl, very polite. Victor, you know Alma and Kent, right? Melanie's their eldest." Janet nudged Victor.

"Hmm yes, I think I remember Melanie. Nice girl – good for you Shane." He nodded at Shane, his approval granted.

"You'll have to ask her over to dinner." Janet looked over at Shane, her eyebrows half-raised.

"Sure."

Sarah looked disappointed at the lack of scandal, and huffed dramatically, prodding her meatloaf.

"And you, young lady, what have I told you about gossip?" Victor said to Sarah. He was trying to be stern, but his eyes were softened by a smile at the corner of his mouth.

"Sorry daddy," she smiled back at him.

"Good. That's settled then, Shane you'll invite Melanie over for dinner. Janet you may as well ask Alma and Kent to come along too." Victor leaned back and sipped his beer. "And you Kiara, you'll come too. You can tell Shane if you approve of his choice," he said to Kiara. She grinned and nodded.

Shane was pleased – Sarah had saved him trying to find a way to tell his parents about Melanie, the embarrassment of trying to find the right words, hoping his mom wouldn't make a big deal out of it. Sarah had done it like ripping off a Band-Aid, quick and largely painless.

He had been dating Melanie for about six months, but they had been an item on and off for much longer, since sophomore year. It was only now they were in senior year they had decided to go steady. She was the ideal girl for him – smart, pretty, and popular. She had pale skin dusted with light freckles, bright green eyes, and dark shiny hair that smelled of coconut. She teased him endlessly, laughing at him with a throaty chuckle that both drove him crazy and turned him on.

Before they had agreed to be exclusive, she had dated other guys, fooling around with them at parties they both went to, giggling with them in dark corners and chugging back beer. He couldn't stand it and had always left early, in a mild fury, fists clenched, and gone home to do endless push-ups in his bedroom till his muscles burned and the sweat stung his eyes. But now she was all his and it was official.

The dinner was set for that weekend. Kiara came over in the late afternoon to practice on the piano. Shane could hear her singing downstairs as he showered and pulled on some fresh clothes. The steam from the shower filled his room with a sweet mist, and he smiled as he listened to their visiting songbird. The sun had already set and the sky was turning a velvet blue, the first stars already peeping through the darkest swathe at the top of the sky.

The doorbell rang and Shane ran down the stairs swiftly, sliding his hand along the smooth polished stair rail of dark walnut wood. He was first to the door, although Janet was just emerging from the kitchen to greet their guests as he opened it.

"Hey Shane," Alma greeted him with a kiss on the cheek and breezed past him, in a waft of expensive perfume and hairspray. Alma knew he and Melanie were dating – Melanie had told her as soon as it became exclusive – but she was a particularly non-interfering mom and wasn't massively involved in their relationship. Shane was grateful for her cool apathy. Alma headed

41

towards Janet, greeting each other with kisses on each cheek, Janet thanking her for the wine she brought with her.

Kent followed her, giving Shane a quick shake of the hand and a nod of the head. He was a thickset man with a full head of sandy white hair and a tan with a hint of redness underneath, like he was constantly mildly embarrassed. He was a man of few words, as if he had long ago nominated his wife to do the talking for both of them and was out of practice.

Melanie followed, grabbing Shane and squeezing him close, unembarrassed by Sarah staring at them from the living room door and the group of parents behind in the hall. He wrapped his arms around her and looked into her eyes. "Ready for this?" he murmured.

"Sure," she whispered back, "how awkward can it be?" followed by her low laugh, with its peculiar smoky quality, though she never actually smoked *("I don't want yellow teeth,"* she would always say, tossing her shiny head, when offered a cigarette.)

Jade pushed in the door behind Melanie. "Get a room you two!" she said, making a face. Jade had always felt envious of her older sister, getting to do everything before her – kissing, driving, parties, sex. Life was moving far too slowly and she felt irritated and frustrated with being the one left behind.

The two sisters looked very similar, with the same complexions, the bright green eyes, and the tall leanness both of them had from their mother, moving with an easy grace across rooms, hallways or dance floors.

Kiara was standing at the doors to the dining room as the Harris family came in, and her cheeks flushed to see Shane and Melanie kissing in the doorway. When Jade came in behind them, her heart lost its rhythm, pulsing erratically, fluttering in her chest. Her fingers began to sweat, slippery on the door handle. If she had known Jade was Melanie's sister she would never have agreed to come to this dinner.

Janet turned to Kiara, away from her conversation with Alma and Kent. "Kiara, I think Melanie's sister Jade is in your class at school." She motioned for Kiara to come over. She walked over reluctantly, feet heavy with every step, her heart a sick pounding in her stomach and throat.

"Hi Mr and Mrs Harris," she said politely, "yes, Jade is in my class."

Jade smirked by her father's side. "Kiara, I didn't know *you* would be here, at the Jacobs' house." Her green eyes looked Kiara up and down slowly, a smile lingering at the corners of her mouth. Kiara looked at the floor and studied her shoes.

Jade wasn't at all surprised to see Kiara there. Shane had told Melanie a long time ago that his parents were helping the poor girl next door. Melanie and Jade weren't close, but they had enough late-night conversations about boys to pore over this perceived oddity of Melanie's potential in-laws, and Jade's mother had often commented on Janet's naivety in helping the girl with the drunken father. Jade thought it was quite possibly one of the most pathetic things she had ever heard.

Victor gestured towards the dining room with his arm. "Let's all go through, shall we?"

Alma, Kent and Janet entered the dining room, Jade following with a thinly disguised sneer at Kiara as she passed by her. Sarah saw Kiara's face flush and felt a wave of sympathy. She had seen the way Jade and the other girls treated Kiara, especially the year when they had both been at middle school at the same time.

"C'mon," she said to Kiara, giving her a small nudge in the back towards the dining room.

Shane and Melanie followed, lost in conversation, inside their own lovers' world.

Kiara walked rubber kneed into the dining room and sat as far from Jade as she could get, wanting to put as much distance between her and those flashing green eyes as she could. Alma turned to Kent and raised her eyebrows as Kiara sat down. She thought it almost cruel of Janet to take a girl from her natural environment and make her mix with people who were far socially superior, where she would surely feel uncomfortable.

The dinner wasn't as awkward as anyone had feared. Mary had helped with cooking the roast and the food was plentiful. The candles lit the room with a warm glow, flames swaying gently. The adults had glasses of wine and plenty of conversation, Shane and Melanie were fixed on each other, while Sarah and Jade discussed the latest boyband, arguing over who was cutest. Kiara felt relieved to linger quietly on the edges of the conversation.

After dinner the adults carried on drinking and talking. Shane and Melanie went to sit on the patio, arms wrapped around each other, their two dark heads pressed together. Sarah and Jade went to the living room, chattering and laughing. Kiara went to the kitchen to help Mary clean up. Kiara loved spending time with Mary, listening to her tales of growing up in Little Rock, Arkansas, while they both swiftly cleaned plates and wiped glasses.

"How's your daddy?" Mary asked Kiara as they arranged the warm clean cutlery in the drawers. Kiara shrugged, "Fine." She didn't like to talk about her dad with anyone. It was like another world when she was in the Jacobs' house, with music and singing, clean dishes, hugs, and laughter. The trailer and her dad were part of a different life and a different her she would avoid if she could. Talking about that life here would invite the two worlds to collide and Kiara didn't want that to happen if she could help it.

Janet walked into the kitchen to fetch another bottle of wine. "Kiara, you don't have to do the cleaning up dear. Why don't you go and talk to Sarah and Jade in the living room?"

"No, it's okay, I have to go home now anyway," Kiara said, looking anxiously at the clock. It was already 8.15pm and it was later than she liked to get home.

"Before you leave, I almost forgot, I had so many bits and pieces left over from today I thought you might like to take them back to your dad." Janet reached underneath the counter into one of the cupboards, retrieving a small bag of carefully wrapped foil packages. Janet often sent Kiara back with a small bag of provisions, things that could be perceived as leftovers and not charity. Kiara smiled. "Thank you, Janet," she said, and wrapped her thin arms around Janet's waist, breathing in the perfume Victor bought her every year on their anniversary, a sweet sandalwood. Sometimes, Kiara would smell Janet's perfume lingering lightly on her skin after she had gone back to the trailer in the evening and her throat would tighten as she wondered what her own mother used to be like before she ran away from them, before she died.

Kiara stepped back and turned to give Mary a quick kiss on the cheek before grabbing the bag and heading out to go back to the gate in the fence. The smell of roses was heavy in the air, the night now a pure plush black with diamond stars gleaming above like the eyes of thousands of observers staring impassively down.

Kiara passed Shane and Melanie on the patio and didn't turn to say goodbye as she passed through the garden, thinking that they wouldn't notice her anyway. She kicked up the damp earth as she walked back through the trees to the trailer. She was tempted to stop and lie down on the ground with the pine needles and bury herself deep into it, becoming part of the earth beneath her feet.

She gently opened the door to the trailer and shut it behind her. Her dad was lying on the couch, his eyes closed. She walked to the small kitchen and put the bag of food into a cupboard, trying to be quiet.

"Whatcha got there?" Her dad opened his eyes, staring red-rimmed and bleary at her, his chin rough with stubble.

"Just some food daddy. You want some?"

He nodded. Kiara got a plate from the pile in the sink and wiped it clean. Unwrapping the foil packages, she put some chicken and potatoes on the plate, and carried it over to her dad. He eyed her warily.

"It's gone 8pm. Where you been?" he asked.

"Just at a friend's house." She started picking at a hole in the pocket of her pants, hoping he wouldn't ask her any more questions.

"Hmm. Those rich friends of yours." He took one of the chicken legs in his hands and bit into it, flesh separating from bone, the skin parted and hanging down as he tore the meat off.

Kiara didn't say anything.

"You know what kid?" He pointed the chicken bone at her in a jabbing motion. She shook her head.

"If you're lying to me about where you've been..."

"I'm not lying daddy," she said quickly.

He glared at her. "Don't interrupt me."

"Sorry," she whispered. The hole in her pocket was getting larger, her fingers scraping against the edge of her thigh, rubbing nervously.

"If I find out you've been hanging out with boys, whoring around like your mother, there'll be hell to pay," he stared at her, breathing noisily through his nose, the food churning in his open mouth. The smell of sweat, stale beer and chicken made Kiara's stomach tighten. He was in a bad mood. Whenever he was in a bad mood, he started talking about her mom and how she let him down, how she was unfaithful, how she had humiliated him.

"I promise daddy, I don't hang around with boys," Kiara said, looking at him in his tired eyes.

He blinked and grunted. "Good. Go to bed."

Kiara went to her room and quietly shut the plastic folding door. She lifted her t-shirt to her face and breathed in the smell of sandalwood and told herself not to cry.

Ten years ago

"Neglect," said Janet, thoughtfully. "Surely that would be good enough reason for us to take her away from that man?"

Moira looked at her younger sister and shook her head. Moira was taller than Janet, her bright silver hair cropped and fashionable, and she usually wore several oversized necklaces at a time, the beads always clacking together and becoming tangled. She had been married once, years before, but it had ended in a bitter divorce, though fortunately they had never had children together. She wasn't particularly maternal and felt no need to seek out another potentially painful partnership. She was happy on her own in Philadelphia working for a top law firm, and at fifty-one she had no intention of slowing down any time soon.

Moira was spending the weekend visiting, she didn't come often but Janet was always glad to see her, and just like when they were children they both slipped easily and naturally into their previous roles again – Moira advising and chastising Janet as the wiser older sister, Janet listening carefully. They were sitting on the patio in the early morning sunshine, sipping coffees, a light breeze sending the scent of the roses their way.

"No Janet, that's not really a strong enough cause. She's got somewhere to live, she has clothes, she goes to school." Moira leaned towards her across the patio table and lowered her voice. "You say there are no signs of abuse of any kind?"

Janet shook her head and sipped her coffee slowly, feeling its warmth run down her throat. "She can be fairly withdrawn but no, I don't think he's actually abusive towards her."

Moira leaned back and folded her hands together over her stomach. "Have you ever asked her if she'd like to stay with you permanently?"

"We've asked her a couple of times over the years, but every time she shuts the conversation down." Janet crinkled her eyebrows. She couldn't understand the child's loyalty to that man, or her refusal to talk to Janet and Victor about how they could help her. Kiara had gotten extremely good at cutting conversations dead, changing the subject, or shutting down entirely. It was as though there was some kind of emotional shutter she was able to slam down to keep everyone out. Her face would go blank, her eyes distant, a cold flat blue like the ocean on a grey winter day.

Janet had seen that reaction before from Victor, whenever he was asked about his family or his childhood. Shane had once asked him about the crumpled photograph in Victor's wallet, a black and white snapshot of a boy, Victor's younger brother Ned. Victor had simply shaken his head at Shane and walked away. Janet had tried to explain to Shane afterwards that there were things his dad just didn't want to talk about. He had never asked about Uncle Ned again.

"Then I'm not sure what you can do Janet. I don't think you have sufficient concern to force anything by law, certainly." Moira tilted her chin up to the sky and closed her eyes, enjoying the warmth of the sun in a languid, cat-like way.

Shane and Melanie walked out on to the patio. They had left college early to drive back to spend the weekend and see Moira. They walked hand-in-hand, a perfect match.

"Here's my favourite nephew," Moira said, getting up from her chair and giving Shane a hug, her many necklaces pressing into his chest. He was so much taller than her now that she had to lean on tiptoe.

"Favourite by default Aunt Moira," he said, laughing.

"So lovely to see you again Melanie," Moira said, as Melanie leaned in to kiss her powdered cheek.

Melanie liked spending time with Shane's family. They were nice people, polite, wealthy, and rather undemanding. Shane and Melanie ruled the roost whenever they were there. Dating an eldest son was always the best way to ensure the top position in a family, Alma had told Melanie, and she had paid attention to her mother's advice. Janet was always keen to make sure Melanie felt comfortable and included, nothing was too much trouble.

"Shane!" Kiara came bounding up from the back of the garden, arms waving, her red hair glowing like it had caught fire in the sunshine. She tackled him with a flying hug and he caught her, laughing, while Melanie looked on, lips pressed together.

It had been two years since Shane and Melanie had left for college. Kiara had helped him stack his car with boxes of clothes and books, making seemingly endless trips from his room down to the drive, thighs aching from the effort of walking up the stairs again and again. When he had driven away she had watched his car from the upstairs bedroom as far as she could follow it. He was only a few hours away but suddenly it felt as though the world under her feet had split apart and he was on one side and she on the other, the distance growing bigger every day. She missed his presence terribly. It wasn't that they had spent much time together, but she missed his easy kindness towards her, the way that he showed an interest in her music, the way he made her laugh.

Shane released her from the hug and she turned to greet Moira, with another enveloping hug, and Melanie, with a polite smile. Kiara knew Melanie didn't like her being around but she missed Shane so she put up with the icy rejection she felt coming her way from Melanie's barbed comments and tight smiles. No one else seemed to notice it except her.

"God, I barely recognise you," Shane grinned at her and shook his head. "Let me guess, you've got a job, got an apartment, graduated, and are getting married?"

Kiara giggled. Shane had always joked about her growing up, but this time he saw her it was true, she had lost a lot of her girlishness when before she had been all bony elbows and grazed knees. She'd finally grown taller, curves starting to appear.

Janet had given her some more of Sarah's old clothes, seeing that what Kiara was wearing was becoming too tight, too revealing. Kiara had blushed, embarrassed, and Janet had gently offered to take her underwear shopping. Kiara had felt almost sick with embarrassment as they went to the mall and a quiet store clerk measured her with a cool efficiency. She desperately wanted it to end, her armpits moist and her face glowing, sweat beading along her lower back, as Janet had tried to hold up different examples of bras to see what Kiara might like to try. Kiara had just stared at them awkwardly and shifted from one foot to another, blinking at Janet and whispering *"I don't know."* In the end Janet had bought a selection in her size, paid for them, and taken Kiara for a soda, where she had chewed on her straw and given monosyllabic answers till Janet managed to make her laugh by talking about the time Victor and Shane got lost on a camping trip.

"Have you had breakfast?" Janet asked Shane and Melanie. They shook their heads.

"I'll fix you something. Kiara, run and get Victor from his study, will you? Tell him Shane and Melanie are here and we're going to eat."

Shane and Melanie settled on the patio, and Janet headed into the kitchen to prepare warm croissants, more coffee, fruit and granola. Moira started to ask Shane and Melanie about college. Sarah was away at a school trip and wouldn't be back till later that day.

Kiara walked indoors into the cool shade, towards Victor's home office, on the other side of the ground floor of the house. She knocked twice, softly, on the wooden door and opened it just enough to peer round.

Victor was typing on his laptop, papers scattered around him. His agency had grown, the headquarters still in New York, but this time an entire building was his, with his office right at the top floor. He would come home and tell Kiara and Sarah the famous players and sportsmen he had spoken to or met that day and tell them stories about what they were really like. He would usually spend another hour or two in the evening in his home office, and several hours at the weekend too, Janet and Sarah bringing him a regular supply of hot sweet coffee.

"Victor?"

He looked towards the door to where Kiara stood, half in half out of the study, her fingers curled round the edge of the door.

"Hey, it's early for you today." Normally Kiara would stop by late morning or early afternoon. The Jacobs usually thought she was sleeping in but in truth she would spend the morning cleaning and tidying the trailer and try to fix her dad a sandwich or something to leave him for the day so he would have something to eat.

She smiled and nodded. "Shane and Melanie are here, and Janet's making some breakfast. You want some?"

"Sure thing, I'll be done in ten." He waved her over to the desk and showed her a document on his computer. "See that?" She nodded, not sure what she was looking at.

"That's a contract to take over another sports agency that's not doing so well. We'll get all their talent and it'll make us the biggest and the best." He smiled proudly, but Kiara could see the lines around his eyes and mouth, the streaks of steel grey running through his hair. The expansion of the business had come at a cost to him. His hope was for Shane to run it with him so they could share the load together, but he just had to hold on till Shane had graduated.

"Congratulations." She wrapped her arms around his shoulders and gave him a hug. She tried not to compare her dad to Victor. She used to when she was little, but it made her feel sad and frustrated, and then ungrateful to the man who had kept her alive, if nothing else, when her own mother didn't want her.

"Thanks kid. Tell Janet I'll be out soon okay?"

"Sure."

She walked back to the kitchen to help Janet prepare the breakfast. As she walked into the kitchen Janet wasn't there and Melanie was chopping the fruit at the black counter top, efficiently slicing kiwi, banana and strawberries, an acidic tang in the air.

Kiara hesitated. "Hey, um, Victor will be out in a few minutes," she said, awkwardly. Kiara wasn't afraid of Melanie, but everything in Melanie's actions and comments suggested a dislike of Kiara being around, and even if no one else picked up on it, Kiara was sure that Melanie would be happier if she weren't there.

"Do you need help?" she asked, eyeing the pile of fruit still to be chopped.

Melanie nodded and pointed her knife, sticky with green blobs of kiwi flesh, towards the other chopping board. Kiara grabbed it and found another sharp knife in the drawer. Peeling a banana, she sliced carefully in silence, adding it to the large fruit bowl that was now half-full.

"So, Kiara," Melanie said, taking another strawberry from the pile, "I hear you're auditioning for the school play."

"Yup," Kiara nodded. The juice ran down her fingers and stung a small papercut. Every year her high school put on a play and any student from sophomore year onwards could audition, so this year Kiara wanted to try. It was a musical called My Fair Lady. Kiara knew it was based on some book that she hadn't read, but she had looked up the story on the internet at the library. It was about a poor girl who is taken in by a rich man and trained to act like a wealthy person, and they needed a good singer to play the role of the poor girl. Kiara thought that she was both poor and a good singer, so she might have a shot.

"You're going for the lead role, right?" Melanie said, casually, looking at her sideways, a sliver of green glittering against her dark eyelashes.

"Um, yeah I think so."

"That's very brave of you Kiara. I mean, you'd be on stage in front of *all* those people. Everyone would be looking at you, hundreds of people."

The idea of performing on stage didn't actually bother Kiara. It was part of her plan. She wanted to be a famous singer, then she would have her own money, respect, and no one would push her around again.

Melanie continued, "And I remember that being part of the play is a pretty expensive thing. I mean you have to buy several costumes, and get your own makeup. And they rehearse pretty late at night too, sometimes till midnight. Still, it's *so* good you want to try."

Kiara's heart sank. "Really? You have to buy the costumes?" Melanie nodded, scraping another mound of chopped fruit into the bowl. "When I was in the play in my junior year it cost me a couple hundred bucks to buy everything I needed for my part, and I didn't even have a main role."

Kiara picked the green leaves off a few strawberries, and sliced them, thinking of how much money a couple of hundred bucks was, and how impossible it was she could get anything near that much.

Melanie carried on chopping. "I wasn't definitely going to audition you know," Kiara said, more to herself than to Melanie.

"You could always try another year," Melanie said, brightly.

"Sure," Kiara nodded without looking at her.

Melanie deftly tipped the last of the fruit from her board into the bowl, scraping along it with the knife, and wiped up the juice that had pooled over the counter, despite their best efforts. She grabbed the bowl of fruit and headed off for the patio without another glance at Kiara, who stood staring at the counter, counting the flecks of white in the marble and making impossible calculations in her head.

She was silent for the rest of the day and went home early in the afternoon with excuses of schoolwork, saying she would stop by the next day. When she didn't turn up for lunch, Shane wanted to go over to see if she was okay, but Victor stopped him. "Her dad won't like you stopping over there, believe me. Best leave her be. I'm sure she's fine."

***

Kiara headed through the crowded hall to her next class, swerving to avoid the groups of students. There was laughter, shouting, girls pairing off to go to the bathroom, guys shoving each other and showing off. A small crowd gathered round the noticeboard outside one classroom to see the list of the chosen few who had successfully auditioned for the play. Kiara averted her eyes and walked quickly past the throng, but she couldn't miss the delighted shriek of the girl who got the main role. Jade looked over her shoulder, laughing with her friends, her long dark hair shimmering over her shoulders. Kiara walked faster.

The interview

"As I got older, my dad's drinking definitely got worse. That's what killed him in the end," Kiara said, sadly.

Beth nodded, tilting her head sympathetically. "He died when you were twenty-one, right?"

Kiara looked down, chilled by the memory of her last visit to the trailer and what she had done. "Yes, just before I turned twenty-one."

She stayed silent and her gaze met Beth's. "Besides your dad, did you have any other family?" she asked.

"No. It was just me and him."

It was a lie, but Kiara couldn't talk about her cousin Rob. She had first met him when she was a teenager, he had come to the trailer for some unspecified reason, her dad allowing him to stay for a few days on the couch. She thought maybe he had been in some kind of trouble and needed somewhere out of the way to stay, but neither her dad nor Rob wanted to tell her what was really going on.

It had been the first time she had met anyone else who counted as family. Rob had a strange, lurking quality to him, as if he belonged in a shadowy corner like a spider. He had slept most of the time, drank beers, answered her questions in a flat voice with heavy-lidded eyes, his pale skin greasy and sallow with smatterings of acne across his chin. He told her about his apartment in New York and she asked question after question about life in the city.

Only Marco knew how important Rob had eventually been to her, and it was definitely something she didn't want to discuss with Beth Winters. Fortunately, Marco had agreed with her on this point.

Seeing that the family question was a dead-end, Beth moved on. "I'm curious, how did you go from your music lessons to the pop star you are today? When did that dream start to take shape for you?"

Kiara felt her heart stutter, just ever so slightly. She was getting to the point where she would have to unpack the memories of that night from where she had stuffed them down deep into locked rooms in her mind.

She breathed out slowly, trying to calm her pulse. "The first time I performed in public was when I was seventeen, at a high school talent show."

Eight years ago

Sarah shivered and drew her sweater round her. There was an autumnal chill in the air and the dampness from last night's rain shimmered on the ground in dewy halos.

She was visiting from college and her mom had taken her to a late birthday lunch at Crawford's. Sarah had decided she didn't want a big fuss this year, after all, her eighteenth last year was huge, and this year Shane and Melanie were busy setting up their new apartment and her dad seemed a little stressed with work. He had moved offices after the towers came down last year. He couldn't bear to be near the site of such death and destruction, where so many people had perished.

She stepped into the kitchen to fix herself some hot chocolate, and heard Kiara playing the piano. A sorrowful sonorous song came faintly through the doors of the dining room, and Sarah decided to offer to make Kiara some hot chocolate. Since she had left home for college the girl's presence in her family home seemed less significant somehow. Her friends at college didn't know Kiara, so there were no more jokes and jibes about her mom's 'charity project'. The only person who was really bothered by Kiara's presence was Melanie, her disdain was clear to Sarah, though seemingly not to anyone else, and not to Kiara either, she hoped.

Sarah opened the door to the dining room and walked to the piano. Kiara seemed lost in the song, bent over the keys, her white fingers pressing down firmly. She looked up when Sarah came to the side of the piano, caught by surprise. Sarah could see she had been crying, tear tracks ran down her face, moisture gathering under her chin and down her neck, her eyelashes spiked and stiff from the salty tears.

"Oh hey, what's the matter?" Sarah had never been particularly close to Kiara, the meanness of other girls had put an invisible barrier between them, and Kiara had known which side Sarah was on and it wasn't hers. It was an unspoken awkwardness, so it usually Shane or Janet who managed to coax Kiara to open up, but neither of them were here.

Kiara wiped her face with her hand. "Nothing," she murmured.

"Right, so why are you sitting here crying then?" Sarah said. When Kiara didn't answer, she tried again, "boy trouble?"

Kiara looked surprised, "No, nothing like that at all."

"So… what's up then?" Sarah really wasn't very good at this. She sounded impatient, hectoring, just like her dad did when people around him were too emotional. Her mom and Shane were so much better at sounding like they cared.

Kiara cleared her throat. "I'm nervous," she said, looking down at her hands, twisting them together on her lap, fingers pulling at each other nervously.

"Nervous about what?" Sarah said, pulling up one of the heavy wooden dining chairs, its dark wood chilly to the touch. She shivered as she sat down and thought of the hot chocolate she had abandoned making and felt annoyed that she instead found herself in a cold room trying to offer support to an emotionally shut down teenager.

"It's just the talent show, at school…" Kiara said, hesitantly. Sarah nodded. "Well, I'm singing in it," Kiara continued.

"Okay, good. You'll be great." Sarah's face softened as she saw the anxiety in Kiara's eyes. "You really are a good singer Kiara. Honestly – everyone will think so." Sarah genuinely meant it, the whole family all thought Kiara was brilliant. It was a mystery why it had taken her so long to perform in public.

"It's not the singing I'm worried about," Kiara shook her head and sniffed, look round for a tissue. Sarah grabbed a tissue from the box on the sideboard and handed it to her. "Thanks," she said, wiping her nose.

"What's making you feel nervous then?"

Kiara nibbled on her lower lip. "You know the other kids make fun of me, right?" Sarah nodded, guiltily. She knew and she had never helped, though she could have done that.

"I'm worried they'll say things about me or laugh at me when I'm on stage." Kiara looked at Sarah. It was the first time they had ever spoken about the way things were at school. It was like breaking an emotional dam between them, creating a space just big enough for some friendship and understanding to seep through.

"Kiara, you're an amazing singer. If they make fun of you, they're morons!" Sarah said, insistently.

"What are you planning to wear?" Sarah asked, suddenly thinking of something she could actually help with.

"See, that's another thing…" Kiara said, trailing off.

Sarah jumped up. "Wait here," she said, and hurried out of the room, heading for the living room.

Victor was watching a ball game, his legs up on the couch, half-asleep. "Daddy," said Sarah, striding into the room and standing in front of the TV, hands on hips.

"What do you want sweetheart?" he said, sleepily, trying to wave her out of the way of the screen.

"I need your credit card."

He laughed. "There's no way you're getting my credit card – I've learned my lesson after last time." Victor didn't believe in giving Shane and Sarah endless credit. They had healthy allowances, but credit cards were banned. Last year, Sarah had borrowed his card for her prom shopping and racked up a larger bill than he had expected on a variety of purchases, not all of them prom-related. He had been furious and made Sarah wash all the family cars, five of them including Shane's, as a punishment.

Sarah rolled her eyes. "It's not for me."

"Well, who's it for then?" he was trying to peer around her at the TV, missing the action.

Sarah stepped over to him and leaned closer, lowering her voice, though no one else was around. "It's for Kiara. I want to buy her a dress for her talent show performance."

Victor was surprised, Sarah had never shown much of an interest in Kiara before. He loved his daughter but he knew she could be a little selfish, she certainly didn't have that tender heartedness that her mother had, at least not that he had seen.

He nodded. "My wallet is in the study. Take the Amex."

She kissed him on the cheek. "Thanks."

Sarah bounded back to the dining room where Kiara was sitting shuffling through her music. "C'mon," Sarah said, grabbing her arm and pulling her up.

"Where are we going?"

Sarah half-dragged her down the hall in her new-found enthusiasm. "To the mall."

Kiara hated the mall, a vast shiny temple of things she couldn't afford. After her last disastrous visit with Janet to buy bras she had avoided it whenever possible. This visit was much more fun and, for the first time, Kiara felt like she had a girlfriend. Sarah drove her red convertible, top down despite the chill, the cold air whipping their faces and hair. By the time they got to the mall Kiara's curls were an electrified mess, and Sarah couldn't stop laughing as she helped her to comb them down.

They went from store to store, Sarah leading the way and picking out dresses she thought would suit her colouring and figure. Sarah was an expert shopper and had a great eye, having spent almost every weekend since she was ten at the mall with her friends. Kiara was happy to be told what to try on, and eventually Sarah decided the winner – a floor length, deep-blue gown with a smattering of tiny crystals that reflected the light and made the dress sparkle like a night sky.

Kiara couldn't stop smiling as they drove home and Sarah promised to do her makeup on the night of the talent show too.

"You'll come then?" Kiara asked, hopefully, as they breezed back home, the top thankfully up as the late afternoon rain arrived in splotches on the windscreen.

"We'll all be there. I'll make sure of it," Sarah replied. "I promise."

Kiara felt like her heart was full of light. It was the happiest she had been for a long time.

***

"You look perfect." Sarah snapped the lid back on the eyeliner and leaned back to check the final effect. It was a big transformation. Gone was the scrawny girl with the pointy limbs and the frayed denim. Kiara stood up in her new dress, red curls tumbling past her shoulders, bright blue eyes framed by long dark lashes, with a hint of blush and a sweep of eyeliner. The dress sparkled in the light like twilight, the perfect fit around Kiara's small waist.

Kiara had come over to get ready in Sarah's old room. It was still the same as before Sarah left for college, a huge room with a romantic white-framed bed, posters everywhere, beautiful curtains with entwined pink and purple flowers climbing up them, framing the large windows that overlooked the garden. The smell of vanilla perfume and hairspray mingled in the air. Sarah had been at work on Kiara for hours now, painting her nails, taming her curls, gently doing her makeup while they listened to music.

"Thanks Sarah," Kiara said, and quickly wrapped her arms around her in a hug. Sarah was surprised and felt a small rush of affection for her that she hadn't felt before. Sarah had to admit that she felt pretty good about helping her, knowing that there was no way Kiara's dad would have bought her a new dress for the occasion.

"Ready to come down?" Sarah asked.

"Sure, I'll just get the shoes on and try not to fall over." Kiara pulled on some strappy silver sandals that Sarah had found for her, and grabbed Sarah's arm to walk down the stairs, giggling as she wobbled on her heels.

Victor, Janet, Shane, and Melanie were waiting for her in the hall. There was a restless buzz in the house, like just before one of their parties or when it was someone's birthday. Mary trotted over to the hall. Since her stroke a few years ago she no longer worked for the Jacobs but she often popped by, particularly on special occasions like these. Kiara walked down the stairs with Sarah, where one-year earlier Sarah had walked down in her eighteenth birthday dress to family applause, where four years earlier Shane had bounded down in his tux to go to the prom and Janet almost had to restrain him to pose with her for a photo.

"Oh my god, Kiara!" Janet exclaimed, already teary-eyed. Kiara was smiling, cheeks dusted with pink, eyes glowing, as though someone had taken a spotlight and trained it right on her, lighting her up for the world to see. Victor gave her a hug and told her: "You're going to be brilliant."

Shane looked at her and shook his head in disbelief. "Wow Kiara. You clean up good."

"Thanks Shane," Kiara said, as he put his arms around her and whispered "you'll be great" in her ear.

Melanie smiled but it didn't reach her eyes. "You look very pretty Kiara," she said, as graciously as she could. "It was so nice of Sarah to help you with your makeup."

Kiara nodded. "Yes, this is all thanks to Sarah," she said, and glanced over at her, gratefully, while Sarah smiled.

The drive to the school had been a blur, Kiara sat in a nervous daze in the back seat while the conversation hummed around her. Kiara leant back in the buttery soft leather seats and stared at the passing streetlights, counting them in her head, her hands moist, her breathing shallow. They had parted at the school, the Jacobs to find their seats in the auditorium, greeting people they knew, while Kiara went backstage to prepare. Students who were performing were tense and excited backstage. The air had an electricity, a tautness to it like a thunderclap waiting to be released from the clouds.

The performers started and Kiara had to wait, as she was on fifth. She listened backstage to the acts and the applause, counting the seconds, the minutes dragging until it was finally her turn. She took a deep breath and walked on to the stage, concentrating on her steps, not wanting to stumble. The lights on her were bright but she could see the expectant faces in the audience, half-submerged in shadows. She knew where to look for the Jacobs – Sarah had told her where they would be sitting. Three rows from the front, towards the left of the stage, they were there as promised, smiling, nodding at her, Shane giving her the thumbs up.

The intro to her song started and she focused on the opening bars and closed her eyes. Her heart was fluttering in her chest, her hands sweating but steady on the microphone, which she gripped hard, an anchor in her hands. There was no trailer, no father, no school, no fear, just the notes, the beat, and her voice, floating in a dark peaceful place with no horizon.

She only came to her senses when the applause started, the Jacobs jumping to their feet, leading the claps, fast and furious. She took a moment to sweep her eyes around the room, not quite believing that there was no one laughing and jeering, but there was only clapping and cheering. She smiled, bowed and walked off stage, her feet unexpectedly sweaty and sliding in her shoes. Backstage there were people coming up to her to say congratulations, patting her on the back, and she felt that this was the beginning of a new life, one with dresses and applause and smiles, silver shoes and eye liner. It was perfect.

***

The Jacobs' house burned with bright lights and chatter, discussing the show, everyone agreeing Kiara's was the standout performance of the night. It was gone 9pm but she had told her dad she would be home late because of the talent show. He had stared at her blankly, dull-eyed and docile, his usual prickliness soothed by the glass of bourbon in his hand. He hadn't offered to go and watch her perform, he had just shrugged and drooped his head to take another gulp.

Tonight, she didn't care about anything. She felt giddy with joy, a happiness that felt like a bright light inside of her, warming every part of her soul. Janet had hugged her, tears in her eyes, saying over and over how proud she was. Victor was practically ready to start phoning record companies and jokingly walked over to his study to start 'negotiating contracts' before they pulled him back into the kitchen, laughing, for celebratory drinks. Janet poured out glasses of champagne and handed Kiara one, winking, saying that one small glass couldn't hurt. She sipped the liquid slowly, golden and crisp, and smiled the entire evening.

After a while, her cheeks and ears were burning and she felt hot and lightheaded, so she walked out the patio doors for some fresh air, leaving Mary, Janet and Victor in the kitchen. She had seen Sarah and Melanie take some wine and head off to Sarah's room, but she was surprised to find Shane sitting outside on his own on a lounger, staring at the pool.

"Hey! What are you doing out here on your own?" she said, sitting down on his lounger next to him. The winter wasn't quite upon them yet but the night was cool with autumn freshness.

"I just wanted some air, some time to think," he said, smiling at her, shuffling up to make some more room.

"Think about what?" she asked.

"Nothing and everything," he said, grinning.

"What does that mean Shane? Don't be so cryptic!"

He laughed, and then looked at her. "You were really amazing tonight," he said.

Kiara smiled. She wished she could take all the compliments from today and record them, to play them over and over again when things weren't so good, to remind her that life could have highs as well as lows. "Thanks Shane."

"No really, I mean it. You were definitely the best. And the prettiest, of course." He winked at her, though in the dim light she could barely see the features of his face.

She shivered as a breeze blew over her bare shoulders, and he put his arm round her to draw her into his warmth. She leaned her head against him and closed her eyes, breathing in the warm scent of his cologne. She could feel the solidity of his muscles through his shirt and found herself wondering what it would feel like to be with him, what it would be like if he looked at her the way he looked at Melanie. He had put his hand on her knee, his index finger softly tracing small circles around it. She closed her eyes and listened to him breathing, his pulse a steady rhythm next to her cheek. Suddenly she desperately wanted to be part of him, to merge his pulse and hers, to slide into his skin and be totally absorbed in him.

Kiara had never felt something like this before, the way she felt right this minute with Shane's arm around her, the peaceful night draped over them. It was like she had been plugged into an electric current and the switch had flipped, it was coursing through her skin and veins, waking up sensations both intensely wonderful and utterly terrifying at the same time.

Without even thinking, she leaned in and pressed her lips against his. His fingers tracing circles on her knee stopped and for a second, she felt him respond to the kiss, moving his lips against hers, his mouth warm, the scratch of his stubble against her chin, before he put his hands on her shoulders and gently pushed her back, breaking their connection. A cold river of disappointment doused the current that had been thrumming through her body just seconds before.

"Shane. I'm sorry. I, er, oh god, that was a mistake." Kiara stammered. Her face was red but he couldn't see it in the dark.

"Kiara, I can't. Melanie…"

"I know, I know. Seriously. Please let's forget about it," she pleaded, her voice quivering.

She stood up to go, wanting to leave quickly and pretend this minute had never happened and wouldn't change anything and everything.

"Kiara wait, you don't have to go."

"I better get changed and go home," she said over her shoulder, walking quickly back to the house.

Shane was about to follow her, but he decided to let her go. The kiss had taken him completely by surprise and there had been a moment when he couldn't think of anything except wanting it to happen. He could smell the warmth of vanilla rising from her neck, her curls dropping over his shoulder with a metallic hint of hairspray. The tastes of her, a hint of champagne, the sweet spiciness of the cinnamon gum she loved, the raspberry stickiness of her lip gloss, all so new on his mouth, sent a jolt of excitement right down his neck through his stomach. For a second, he had been desperate to pull her close and open her mouth with his, but then Melanie flashed into his mind and he knew he had to push her away.

His head was thrown into confusion, a thousand thoughts colliding in his mind, thoughts of Melanie and her husky laughter after sex, entwined in sweaty sheets, of Kiara as the skinny kid he teased endlessly, the sobbing teenager he had comforted, now the young woman he had stolen a first kiss from. He loved Melanie and had been thinking about marriage that evening by the pool before Kiara had come out. He put his head in his hands and breathed deeply. He would need to talk to Kiara about this tomorrow and try to explain, apologise, and hope it wouldn't change things between them, though it felt to him like something had irrevocably shifted that night.

In Sarah's room, Melanie and Sarah were sipping wine, talking about Sarah's college and the guy she was dating. He was nice, Sarah was saying, but rather boring. Sarah was lounging on the bed, legs tucked under a white furry throw, Melanie on a chair beside her, her ankles neatly crossed, her short black dress highlighting the paleness of her arms. She poured herself another glass of wine, and interrupted Sarah's description of her boyfriend's lacklustre bedroom performance. "Seriously Sarah, why did you bother giving that girl a makeover today?"

Sarah raised her eyebrows. "What do you mean?"

Melanie widened her eyes. "I mean, she lives in a trailer, what good does it do to get her all made up for one evening only for her to have to go back to her normal life right afterwards? Her dad will probably just sell the dress for booze money anyway."

"I thought it was a nice thing to do. She doesn't have a mom to help her, she doesn't even have any friends," Sarah said, defensively. She had been rather pleased with her philanthropy and hadn't thought of what would happen after this evening, about Kiara going back to the trailer, about how one perfect evening might just raise her hopes rather than solve her problems.

"I really don't know how you can stand her hanging around here, waiting for hand-outs from *your* parents. And the way she fawns over Shane is just pathetic. It makes him uncomfortable."

Sarah listened to Melanie, thinking her both right and wrong at the same time and not sure how to tell the older girl that Kiara was sweet and thankful, though Sarah herself had thought the same thing as Melanie many times, jealous and annoyed at the intrusion of the younger, needier child in their lives. As for Shane, she knew that it probably wasn't him who was uncomfortable but rather Melanie who didn't like the closeness he had with Kiara. But she stayed silent, nodding, unsure what to say, feeling hypocritical when she knew how many times she had willed Kiara to leave, and had turned her back on her when she could see and hear the bullying at school.

"Yeah, I guess you're right," she said, hoping to move the conversation on, "I just felt sorry for her, that's all."

She heard someone walk past the door and run down the stairs, a gentle shuffling, someone in sneakers. Sarah pushed back the white throw and padded to the door in her bare feet, dark red toenails flashing against the cream carpet, just in time to see Kiara at the bottom of the stairs heading for the kitchen, dress gone, jeans and sneakers back on. Sarah walked quickly to the spare bedroom next to hers, Melanie craning her neck curiously to watch her go. The beautiful blue dress was hung carefully on the closet door in the guest room, the dark blue swooshing down over the white wood like an inky waterfall, still swaying slightly, still warm, the silver sandals tucked neatly underneath.

Sarah felt her chest tighten and bit her lower lip nervously, hoping that Kiara hadn't heard their conversation. Sarah went back to her room and poured herself some more wine, distracted by guilt, Melanie showing her things in a magazine she hoped Shane might buy her now that he was working for his dad and earning good money.

In the kitchen Kiara kissed Janet and Victor goodbye, hugging them closely. Mary had already left, she got tired more quickly since she had been unwell. Kiara could hear Shane in the living room watching TV but she didn't want to face him just yet, so she headed out the back doors and started home. It had been a night of such brilliance but the high had lasted such a short time that she wished she could start it all over again.

The interview

Kiara clutched her hands together in her lap. She was getting increasingly anxious. The first part of the interview had been difficult enough, as she expected it would be. It was like dredging up an old seabed, disturbing things that had long since drowned, putrid bloated nightmares coming to the surface in a murky gloom.

On stage, in the studio, she was successful, beautiful, and desirable. She could control the nightmares and drown out the memories of who she used to be but right now this interview made her feel exposed for who she really was. She was trying to hold her legs still, to keep breathing in time with her heartbeat, clasping her trembling hands together, clutching at each other like two drowning souls on a dark night.

Beth had done enough interviews to know when her guest was uncomfortable. She felt sorry for this girl but she had to carry on. Her audience expected her to have the big reveals, the shock twists, the love child that no one knew about, the footage never seen. Whatever dirt her researchers revealed, she would expose it, and that would be the same for this young singer, regardless of her discomfort.

"Let me get this straight Kiara," Beth said, leaning towards her guest, "this family took you in, cared for you, treated you like one of their own. It's thanks to them that you had years of music and singing lessons, helping you to nurture your talents so you could become the star you are today."

Kiara nodded. Beth continued, raising an eyebrow, "But you say you don't speak to them at all anymore? What on earth happened?"

"I ran away," Kiara said quickly, the words tumbling out, feeling as though the heat of the lights suddenly multiplied on her.

"What made you run away?" Beth lowered her voice, her cool grey eyes unsettlingly still and unemotional.

***

The Jacobs watched in tense silence as Beth leaned towards Kiara, who looked stiff and pale and thin under the lights. Two garish red blooms began to creep up on her high cheekbones, her jaw clenched.

Shane steeled himself, took a breath and held it, wishing he could go into another room and not hear about that kiss, that messy and mistaken night when he watched her walk away and out of his life for so many years.

Sarah shifted in her seat, wondering if it was her fault and if Kiara would say so, not realising that Shane had his own guilty burden too. They both sat, awkward and nervous, hearts racing.

Victor held Janet's hand and gave it a squeeze. Janet remembered how afraid she had been for Kiara when days and months and years passed and she had never come back, never written, never told them she was okay. She had often thought of Kiara before she went to sleep at night, thinking of her in the dark with no one to help her or hold her.

After all those years of not knowing, of so many unanswered questions, now they might finally learn why Kiara had left their lives, and they all waited to hear it from her lips.

***

Kiara had pleaded with Marco not to make her do this interview. She had grabbed his tanned arm, begged him not to promise the show a big 'reveal all'. He had demanded she do it, then patted her hair, soothed her, and made the deal. He knew the story already, he had bargained for the right price, and she had to go through with it.

She looked at her shoes, strappy silver shoes, like the ones she wore that night, gleaming softly under the studio lights, and looked back up at Beth, who was waiting impassively, her eyes expectant like a sky before a storm.

"I was raped," she said.

Eight years ago

Kiara walked swiftly back to the trailer, the cool air whipping by her ears and her sneakers roughing up the dirt. The breeze whispered through the tops of the trees, a wordless murmur to the stars. Her head was full of Shane and that kiss, regret growing and spreading like mould in her stomach. She knew he was crazy about Melanie, so why did she think that he would want to kiss her?

Kiara knew she would have to go over tomorrow to see them, have to face him and Melanie with her smug white smile, while she would sit hot-faced and awkward, trying to find the way to say sorry when she could get Shane alone. She felt sick and giddy and was sure it couldn't just be the champagne Janet had given her. She took deep shivery breaths of the cold air as she reached the trailer and headed inside.

Her dad was sitting on the couch, talking intently to another man, whom Kiara had never seen before. He was sitting at the small table Kiara sometimes used for doing her homework, the thin wood feeling as though it could buckle and snap if you pushed just slightly too hard on its rough surface. The man smirked as she walked in, his reddened face partly hidden by a dirty beard straggling past his chin.

Her dad looked at her and frowned. "I thought you were staying at your friend's house tonight?" He sounded hoarse, a red-rawness to his throat that could be from booze-induced vomiting or a cold.

"No daddy," Kiara shook her head.

Bill shrugged his shoulders and turned back to his visitor. Kiara went to her room, snapping the plastic door across to its clasp, even though she knew it would never stay shut.

"Now Bill. I've been very patient, but you and I have a problem, don't we?" The visitor talked in a low grumble with a southern twang which would have sounded friendly if it weren't for the expression on his face, a sneer even the beard couldn't hide. Down by his legs he patted a smooth baseball bat as though it were a faithful pet waiting for instruction. His large hands were coarse, the short fingernails torn and dirty, with crimson splotches on the knuckles.

"You see, I want that money, my money, that you owe. I've waited long enough so I either take it tonight or I take something else from you. This trailer, your truck, your legs maybe?" He grinned, his face twisting to reveal stained yellow teeth, uneven like old tombstones rising from neglected grounds.

Bill was silent for a moment, swirling his bourbon in a glass smeared with greasy fingerprints. "You know I don't have the money," he rasped, finally.

The visitor smirked. "Hmmm." He tapped one of his dirty, bent fingers on his beard. "What shall we do Bill?"

Bill knew he was toying with him. He tried to think how to persuade the man to go away, to give him more time, but his mind was fuzzy from drink, like it had been packed with cotton.

The visitor gave a sidelong glance to the end of the trailer where Kiara had gone a few moments earlier. "You know Bill, you got a pretty little lady there." His thin lips curled up at the corner beneath his beard. "I'm sure some men would happily pay for some time alone with her."

Bill knew what his visitor was asking for and squeezed his eyes closed. That girl was always out, always taunting him with silence,

64

ungrateful, her mother's eyes staring at him, judging him, every day. And if the trailer was gone, what then for the both of them?

He opened his eyes, pink-rimmed, dark pouches underneath from alcohol and anger-disturbed sleep. "And what might that time be worth to you?" he asked his visitor, as if asking for the price of one of his trucks.

"Well," the visitor hesitated, and thought for a moment, turning his head towards Kiara's door. "You know Bill, as you're an old friend, we can make a good deal. I guess I could let this whole ugly situation go…"

Bill nodded, and took another sip from his glass, wincing as the heat of the liquor scraped his throat. "I guess we have a deal then." He drained the glass in one greedy gulp and tipped in more from the bottle by his feet, sloppily sloshing some on his sleeve.

Kiara was laying on her back on her narrow bed, not bothering to change out of her clothes, arms tucked under her head, the edges of this world becoming fuzzy as sleep approached, when the plastic door slid open. She was awake quickly, unused to any disturbance in her room after dark. Her father never came to her room, he never wished her good night, or came to check on her. She usually found in him in the morning where she had left him the night before, hunched on the sofa, his rough skin cold in the early morning air.

The man who had visited her father stepped in and pulled the door closed behind him. She looked at him, confused. "Are you looking for the bathroom?"

He shook his head, and in a quick movement had grabbed her shoulders and forced her down on the bed, one hand reaching down to tug at the zipper to her jeans. She yelped, gasping in shock, and he put one hand over her mouth. She could smell the sour stink of beer on his fingers, feel the skin scraping against her lips, pushing her jaw down and holding her onto the bed. She was trying to cry out, to yell, use her fists to beat against his body but his hand pulled her jeans down around her thighs as though she were made of paper, a blade of grass fighting against a hurricane. His weight against her pushed her into the thin mattress and it was like being encased in concrete, his legs on her legs, his hand on her chest, inside her t-shirt. Tears ran down her face onto his hand across her mouth, his splayed fingers digging into her cheeks wet with salt and saliva.

His greasy face lowered against hers, he forced himself inside her in one sharp thrust, pain spreading through every inch he touched. She breathed in sharply, the pain stopping her from fighting, and slumping underneath him she turned soft and pliable, waiting for it to be over. He finished with a groan, panting with his wet stagnant breath in her ear. He waited a few moments before he pulled out of her, breathing heavily, pulled up his pants, threw a blanket over her and walked away, leaving the brown plastic door half open, sagging on its track.

She lay there, breathing in and forgetting to breathe out till her chest ached, then exhaling violently, raggedly. Tears ran from the corners of her eyes into her hair, her pillow wet, a pain inside of her and a warm dampness seeping from her into the bed. She could still smell his hand on her face, his ashy breath, the sweat from his forehead.

She heard a creak outside her door and was suddenly terrified he might come back. Her father pushed the door open and looked in at her.

"Daddy," she whimpered, "something happened…"

Bill looked down at Kiara, her red curls in disarray around her pale skin, and in his drunken daze saw only her mother, leaning back against the pillows and looking at him with a disappointed air. He turned away and shut the door, and Kiara realised with horror that her father had allowed this to happen, that he had let that man force himself onto her and take something that she could never get back.

She lay stiff and silent until she was sure her father had either fallen asleep or passed out. Her head ringing, a white-hot pain beating behind her eyes and a dull ache in her stomach, she stood up slowly. She peeled off her jeans, her panties, her bra, her t-shirt, dropping them on the floor like dead rose petals falling after the autumn rains. She pulled on some clean clothes, intending to get out of the trailer and run to the Jacobs where she would be safe, but then her thoughts started to pick up speed, and she realised that she would have to tell them what happened. There would be questions, descriptions, investigations. A police officer asking her to describe where she had been touched, a doctor taking samples from her, her father arrested, a court case reported in the papers.

She had heard about a girl at her high school a few years ago who had accused another student of rape at a party, and the students had divided into groups of those who believed her and those who didn't, rumours abounding, casual gossip at lockers implying that she had made it all up for attention. Kiara couldn't face it – the kids at school already thought she was trash, now they would know that she was soiled, tainted, used, and that she was so unlovable that her own father had allowed it to happen.

The sense of shame turned her legs weak, and she sat down on the edge of the bed. She knew she couldn't do it, couldn't go there and tell Janet and Victor what that man had done to her, to say those awful words and share those wounds with those who were so hopeful and proud just hours before.

As she couldn't stay here, she knew there was only one place she could try. She reached under the bed and pulled out a jar, wrapped up in a t-shirt. Her savings jar, odd quarters here and there, money from the Jacobs for birthdays or Christmas, chore money for clearing leaves from paths in autumn and shovelling snow in winter from driveways bigger than the trailer she lived in. She grabbed the mix of coins and notes and shoved them into her pocket, hoping it would be enough to get her to New York, to cousin Rob.

She grabbed her school backpack, an old drawstring bag with a flaking black logo, and stuffed a few possessions inside, clothes, underwear, a comb, lip balm, a teddy bear Janet and Victor had bought her for her ninth birthday. She held it to her face and breathed it in, trying to will herself back there when she was nine and things were better.

Silently, she slid open the door and leaned out, looking to see where her father was. She couldn't see him on the sofa, so he must have gone to sleep in his bedroom. She walked softly towards the door and slid out into the night air, dark and damp, lustrous with stars. She started walking.

Part Two
Running

Eight years ago – Kiara

It was 2am and Grand Central Station was still humming with activity when Kiara had stepped off the train, trembling and glassy-eyed, trying to think through the next steps but forming thoughts that kept coming to dead ends.

She had only been to the city once, with the Jacobs, to go to a ball game where Victor knew most of the players. She had been amazed at the size and the intensity of the city, the energy of millions of lives all fighting for space and jostling for room. Janet had hurried them from the train, holding onto Kiara and Sarah, Shane helping to lead the way. Kiara hadn't paid attention to where they were going, happy to float along with them while she stared, distracted, at the swirling humanity around her.

Right now, she felt nauseous and dizzy, the ground gently rocking beneath her feet at though she had just gotten off a boat and was waiting for her body to adjust to dry land again. She realised she hadn't eaten or drunk anything for hours, apart from the glass of champagne at the Jacobs' house. What happened in the trailer just hours ago seemed like a spectre of a nightmare, a shadow floating in the back of her mind, a dull pain between her legs reminding her as she walked from the train.

She checked her pocket for how much money she had left over after buying her train ticket. A few crumpled bills lay furled in her hand. She was so thirsty, her throat tight and sore, and she still had to get to Rob's neighbourhood and find him. Feeling overwhelmed, she found a bench and sank down gratefully, watching the people move around her. She was so tired she found herself settling in to a trance-like state, slumped on the bench, and had lost track of how long she had been there when a voice punctured her daze.

"Are you okay?"

She sat up straight, whipping her head towards the sound. A young man had sat next to her, long hair down to his shoulders, his jeans ripped at the knee, smiling.

"Everything okay?" he repeated.

"Um yeah, yes, thank you," she stuttered back.

"Rough night?"

She nodded, realising she must look shambolic, her clothes thrown on in the dark and her hair wilder than usual. "I need to get to Hunts Point. Do you know how I can get there?"

"You take the six, that's the green line, it'll get you direct to Hunts Point," he said.

"Thanks," she said, pushing herself up from the bench and grabbing her bag, she walked away quickly, following the signs to the line she needed.

***

Kiara stumbled woozily up the steps of the subway exit, the red bricks glowing warmly in the streetlight. The rocking of the subway and her extreme tiredness had almost caused her to fall asleep, her head gently nodding on to her chest, then snapping back up again as she tried to stay alert, terrified of missing her stop or being robbed or worse.

She had gotten off the train, buffeted by the hot subway air, shuddering at the scuttling shadows of rats. She knew Rob lived in a building not far from the Hunts Point market, at least he did when he came to visit them two years ago. She had been desperately curious about his life in New York, imagining the glamour and the fun of living in the city, and he had scribbled down his address on a scrap of paper for them, in case they ever needed to get in touch. She hoped he still lived there.

She headed several blocks away from the subway. A young girl was hanging out on a stoop, casually draped over the steps, her long legs swinging. Kiara decided she would have to ask someone for directions at some point and walked over hesitantly. As she got closer she realised that the woman wasn't young after all, she was thin, her face lined and her hair patchy. Her lime green tube top revealed her bony shoulders and a tattoo of a rose on her upper arm, the red faded to a dusty pinkish-grey.

She looked up at Kiara as she approached, narrowing her eyes.

"Um excuse me? I'm looking for this address. Do you know where it is?" Kiara said, showing her the piece of paper.

The woman grinned at her, revealing dark terrible crevices where teeth should have been. "Over there darlin'." She pointed a finger with a long fake nail towards a large squat building made of dark brick.

"Thank you," Kiara said, shivering at the gaping holes in the woman's mouth, walking away towards the building where she hoped she would find Rob.

The building was a huge apartment block and although it was now gone 4am lights still blazed in some of the windows. Kiara walked up the steps to the entrance, a big wooden and glass door she assumed would be locked. But although there were rows of buzzers on the side for each apartment, the door swung open easily to the street.

The dim lobby was lit by a single bulb, filmy with grime, casting a grey-orange glow over the walls, like a sunset covered by a dust storm. Graffiti tags looped around the walls, careering energetically around the plaster, with a broken bike dumped in the corner of the lobby and a doll's body with one arm and no legs or head, abandoned on the floor. The sour smell of stale urine leeched from dark corners. Kiara shuddered, her head swimming, nausea rising in her throat, and checked the scrap of paper where she had scrawled Rob's address. She headed towards the stairs, the graffiti tags spiralling up the wall with her as she climbed.

She stopped on the third floor, breathing heavily. Rob was in number fifty-eight, an apartment near the end of the third-floor hallway. She walked down the hallway, counting down the numbers, and as she passed the doors she caught snippets of sound from behind some of them, a TV programme, a baby wailing, voices murmuring. Garbage littered the hall, with discarded chicken bones, a takeout box, a child's shoe, and an old mattress with burn holes slumped against the wall like a person who'd lost a fight.

As she walked on the smell of the building settled on her skin, a noxious fog of weed and stale cigarette smoke, boiling cabbage and diapers. She swallowed hard, an uneasy churning in her stomach, and knocked on door fifty-eight. She knew it was crazy to turn up here unannounced at 4am, not even sure if Rob were still living here, but he was her only hope.

Please, she begged silently, *let Rob be here.*

Rob opened the door. He stared at Kiara blankly, his eyes glassy, dark greyish-purple circles underneath.

"Rob? It's me, Kiara," she said, hoping to see some spark of recognition.

He furrowed his eyebrows together, tilted his head and narrowed his eyes, looking at her as though she were far away, then he nodded slowly. "Cousin Kiara? Uncle Bill's girl?"

"Yep. In the flesh." She smiled weakly, hoping he couldn't tell that her knees were shaking. Her fists were clenched at her sides to stop them trembling.

He opened the door wider, allowing her to step inside. "What the hell are you doing here?" he asked, rubbing the back of his neck and closing the door behind her.

The apartment felt cold, although Rob was only wearing a t-shirt and boxers, his feet bare and bony against the thin brown carpet.

"Um, I need a place to crash for a bit." She bit her lip and looked at him hopefully.

Rob pressed his thin lips together and exhaled slowly, nodding. Without saying anything, he walked through the hall into a room at the far end. The carpet was dusty, covered with flecks of fibres, hair, crumpled tissues and a jumble of socks. Kiara could feel the floor's grittiness under her sneakers as she followed him.

The living room looked out over the front of the street. There was a sagging blue couch, the stuffing springing out in patches, the fabric fraying, in front of a coffee table and a large TV. There was a mattress on the floor, yellowing and sunken, with darker brown patches spreading over the surface like scum on a pond. At the end of the room was a small kitchen area, the shiny plastic counter top covered with a mess of takeaway cartons, empty cans, bottles, and empty bags of chips strewn over the top.

"Wanna beer?" Rob said, as Kiara perched tentatively on the couch.

"Could I get a glass of water?" Her lips were sore and her mouth tasted sour.

Rob sifted through the detritus in the kitchen, grabbing a takeaway coffee cup and rinsing it in the sink, then filling it with water. He brought it to her and she took it gratefully, gulping the water down quickly, slightly tangy from the previous contents of the cup.

"You don't look so good." Rob said, leaning back against the couch, bringing one ankle up to rest on his knee, his thin arm extended along the back of the cushions.

"I'll be fine. I'm just tired."

"You gonna tell me why you're here at 4am?"

Kiara looked at him, unsure what to say, so she didn't say anything. She shook her head and looked down at the carpet.

"In some kind of trouble?" he prompted.

She shook her head again. She felt so tired that her chest ached when she breathed, she felt heavy and ponderous, her head trying to hold onto thoughts and failing, they vanished into the dark like water swirling down a drain in a storm.

Rob frowned. "Are the cops likely to come looking for you?" he asked.

She looked back at him, heavy-eyed, her vision blurry, and shook her head. "I could really use a rest," she mumbled.

Seeing that his cousin was in no state for explanations, Rob stood up and went out of the room, and returned in a moment with a green blanket. Throwing it onto the mattress near the couch, he pointed at it. "Knock yourself out, kid." Kiara nodded and stumbled over to the mattress, drunk with exhaustion, and crawled under the blanket. Sleep took hold in an instant, like full and swift submersion in a dark ocean.

Eight years ago – the Jacobs

"She hasn't come over today?" Shane took a sip of his coffee. He had been hoping to see Kiara, to talk to her about last night and explain. He wished she had a cell phone. They had bought her one last year, but it had gone missing after a few weeks. She always claimed that she had lost it, but he was pretty sure her dad had sold it.

Janet shook her head. "It was a big night for her last night, Shane. She's probably just sleeping in today, taking it easy, letting it all sink in."

They were in the kitchen, where a fresh pot of coffee was brewing and there was a hot sweetness in the air from cinnamon buns warming in the oven. It was 1pm, and Shane and Melanie were leaving soon to go back to their home in New York. Sarah had already left to drive back to college.

Janet carefully took the hot tray from the oven, laying it down on the counter to cool. When Shane didn't reply, she looked over at him, frowning at his coffee.

"You okay?" she said, raising her eyebrows at him.

He looked up and smiled his easy grin at her. "Yeah sure. I guess I'll see her another time." Janet took a knife from the drawer and started to separate the cinnamon buns, sliding one onto a plate for Shane and handing it to him with a fork.

"How are things going at the new house?"

"Great. Melanie's always picking out new things, inviting people over. I hardly have to do anything except pay for it all,"

Shane laughed. He and Melanie had bought a house in the city, with high ceilings, big windows, and dark wooden floors that creaked and sighed under their feet. Melanie had been busy decorating, comparing colour swatches and fabrics and hunting out interesting decorative pieces online, and Shane had been happy to sit back and let her furnish their home while he got to grips with the business.

He really wanted to see Kiara before he and Melanie left, but he would have to talk to her another time about that kiss. He felt deeply uncomfortable about the way he had pushed her away and wanted to make sure he hadn't hurt her feelings. Hopefully he'd get to see her soon and they could put it behind them.

Eight years ago – Kiara

Kiara's head was hurting, a dull ache in the back of her skull that throbbed with each heartbeat. She slowly pushed herself up from the mattress. The windows were bare, letting in the greyish light from a clouded sky over the city. She had no idea what time it was.

She got up stiffly, still woozy from lack of food and water, and walked down the hall, looking for the bathroom. She nudged one door open and was relieved she found the right room. Her fingers searched for the light switch and flicked it on. The room was filthy, the toilet a murky brown, the basin swabbed with various stains. The tiles on the floor had once been white but were now covered with a film of dirt and sticky under her feet. She shuddered.

She nearly cried out when she saw the blood speckled in her underwear, the starkness of the red against the white made her head swim with vivid memory. She was still sore from what had happened, the scene kept flashing into her mind before she tried to chase it away, squeezing her eyes shut. She desperately wanted to shower him off her, but she couldn't see any towels. She washed her hands, splashing her face with cold water, trying to ignore the scum around the rim of the basin and dabbing her face dry on her t-shirt.

There was no sound from the other rooms, so she assumed Rob was asleep. She went to rummage in the kitchen, looking for something to eat. She felt trapped, not wanting to leave the safety of the apartment and walk unknown streets looking for food, not sure where Rob was and not wanting to disturb him if he was asleep. There wasn't much to eat in the kitchen. *Just like home,* Kiara thought wryly. Eventually she found a half-empty bag of stale chips and washed them down with several glasses of water. It wasn't much to satisfy her hunger, but it helped. She sat back down on the mattress and waited for Rob to emerge.

She had dozed off again, lulled to sleep by studying the curves of paint across the ceiling, white arcs like rainbows with the colour sucked out, when Rob came into the living room followed by another man. He was tall and lanky, his white blond hair cropped short. Both he and Rob were in t-shorts and boxers, crumpled and creased from the night, their voices husky and rough from sleep.

Kiara sat up as the blond man slouched on the couch. He stared at her with piercing aqua eyes, his black tattoos curling out from under the arms of his faded red t-shirt and snaking down towards his wrists.

"Dan, this is Kiara, my cousin. Kiara, this is Dan, my roommate," Rob introduced them.

Kiara smiled a weak hello. Dan nodded at her.

"Kiara, are you hungry? We're going to order pizza." Rob was rifling in the kitchen, opening some beers for him and Dan.

"Yeah thanks Rob, I'm starving." She stood up from the mattress, Dan's eyes following her as she went to the kitchen.

"Hey um Rob, do you have any towels so I can take a shower?" she said.

"Sure, I'll get you one."

Rob set down his beer and handed one to Dan before going to another room and coming back with a scratchy, thin towel, frayed at the edges, damp and musty. He handed it to Kiara and flopped on the couch next to Dan, flicking on the TV. Kiara grabbed her bag and went to the bathroom.

The tub was filthy, with dark patches of mould gathering on the tiles and on the shower curtain. There was no shower gel, just a small bar of soap, cracked on the surface. She hesitated, then grabbed it and rubbed it vigorously between her hands to lather it up before pressing it hard on to her skin, desperate to feel clean again, standing under water almost hotter than she could bear.

She dried herself quickly and roughly with the musty towel and pulled on some clean clothes. She stuffed her bloody underwear into the bottom of her bag, her hands shaking. Suddenly she felt as though the walls were closing in, the damp foggy air felt heavy and threatening. She closed her eyes and sat on the edge of the tub, fingers gripping the cool porcelain, trying to fight off the thought of him inside her, of his rough hands on her face. She breathed in hard and lurched towards the door.

She could smell the pizza had arrived, a tomato tang in the air, wafts of oily cheese and spicy meat. She leaned against the wall, dizzy with the memory of movie nights with the Jacobs. She staggered down the hall, Dan and Rob eating the pizza on the couch. Rob nodded at the pizza boxes, there were two slices for her. She barely chewed, letting the mouthfuls slide down her throat, licking trembling fingers and watching the basketball game on TV with unfocused eyes.

Eight years ago – the Jacobs

Janet was pale as she placed the phone back into its cradle with a soft click. She looked over her shoulder at Victor.

"She's not shown up at school for two days," she murmured.

Victor stood up. "I'm going over there."

Janet nodded hopefully. "Maybe she's just sick?"

Kiara had always come to the Jacobs' house even when she was ill. Janet would make her tomato soup and crackers, hot lemon and honey, and tuck her into a warm bed, even if only for a few hours before she went home. It was so unlike her not to turn up that Janet had a cold tremor of anxiety running up her spine.

"Try not to worry, I'm sure she's fine," Victor said reassuringly, and patted her on the shoulder.

Victor headed toward the trailer, the fresh dark earth soft under his feet after last night's rain. There was a hint of cold in the air, a quiet threat of winter under the autumn breeze. He rapped on the trailer door and waited. There was silence apart from the birds in the trees, gently singing. He knocked again, this time harder and with his fist, the vibrations running down his wrist. Hearing shuffling footsteps inside, Victor stepped back slightly. Bill opened the door, gummy-eyed, wan-skinned and unshaven, smelling of sleep and stale liquor.

"What do you want?"

"I'm here to find out where Kiara is. She hasn't been to school for two days," Victor said tightly, his mouth pressed to a thin line, teeth clenched. Bill had always taken a rude tone with him and he had tolerated it for Kiara's sake but if anyone else had spoken to him that way, he would have squared up to them.

"She's gone."

Victor's stomach bundled into a sharp ball of nerves and he breathed in quickly.

"Where is she?" he said, his voice stretched and taut like a tightrope.

Bill gave a short hoarse bark of a laugh. "Damned if I know. Probably gone to her cousin's."

Victor wanted to grab the man round the neck and shake him hard. He stepped up to him, glaring at him directly in his eyes, the irises yellowed and shot through with thin red veins.

"You'll tell me when she left, and where she's gone Bill. You tell me the truth right now," he said, furiously.

Bill blinked, surprised. He was hungover and aching, in no state to stand up to Victor's sudden anger.

Glaring back, he said: "She left on Friday night. Told me she was going to stay with her cousin in Phoenix. That's all I know and that's all I care. She's almost eighteen, she can do what she wants."

Bill took some small pleasure in the control he had over Victor, that only he held the truth to what had happened and there was no way he was going to incriminate himself or his visitor that night. Bill didn't know where she had gone, he didn't remember Rob's address, and thought it best that she fend for herself from now on.

"What is her cousin's name? Where in Phoenix?" Victor said, his fists clenched, raging about how little this man cared for his only child.

"Rob Walker. I don't know where he lives in Phoenix – Rob told Kiara his address, and she took it with her when she left."

Breathing hard, Victor turned his back on Bill and walked quickly away back to the house before he did something he regretted.

***

"So, how come you called us over dad?" Sarah asked, forehead furrowed with concern.

Both she and Shane had received a call from Victor requesting they come over to the house the weekend after they had just visited. Sarah had a pit of anxiety in her stomach as she drove to the house, desperately wondering what it could be that had made her dad sound so grave and distant over the phone. When she arrived, her parents were both pale and reserved, her mom looking distracted and like she hadn't slept well at all. Sarah began to think the worst and was relieved when Shane finally arrived so they could find out the reason why they were there.

They sat around the table in the kitchen, Victor sombre and pale as he told them that Kiara had gone a week ago and there was no sign of her. Janet and Victor had held off telling Shane and Sarah,

79

hoping that Victor could track her down or that she would turn up one afternoon, bounding through the garden, as if she had never left.

Sarah put her hands to her mouth. "Oh mom, why would she leave?" Even as she said it, Sarah thought back to a week before and the conversation with Melanie that Kiara might have overheard.

Shane stared at the floor, mouth dry and heart thumping. He hoped desperately there was a simple explanation, that he wasn't to blame, and thought of Kiara alone and wandering somewhere. *Please let her be safe,* he prayed.

"What did her dad say?" Shane cleared his throat, breaking the silence.

"He said she went to stay with some cousin, Rob, in Phoenix," Victor replied.

"Arizona? Why the hell would she go all the way there?" Sarah asked, shaking her head, her blonde hair swishing.

"She does have a cousin called Rob. I remember her mentioning him," Shane said, thinking back a few years, "I don't remember him living in Phoenix though. At least, I don't remember Kiara mentioning that." He tried to remember where she said Rob was from but couldn't.

"I've contacted all the Rob Walkers in the directory there, but I guess he could be unlisted, or go under another name," Victor said.

"What about the police?" Sarah asked.

"I spoke to the police. We've reported her as missing, but they said as she's almost eighteen, and her father says it was her choice to leave and stay with family, they can't prioritise looking for her."

"She turns eighteen next week," Janet said, and bent her head forward, tears seeping down her face, leaving powdery trails.

"Maybe she'll come back?" Shane said hopefully, wishing that Kiara had a cell phone that they could try to contact her on.

"I hope so. I'm going to Phoenix to put up some posters and see if I can ask around if anyone has seen her," Victor said. "That hair of hers makes her stand out so hopefully someone will remember seeing her," he smiled thinly.

"I'll come with you," Shane sat up straight, energised by the prospect of being able to do something.

Victor nodded. They sat in silence and the air was heavy with their unspoken fears of what had happened to Kiara, where she was now, and if she was safe.

Eight years ago – Kiara

The air was thick with the smell of weed, and Kiara could taste it in her mouth, feel it settling in her hair. She was curled up on the mattress in Rob's bedroom, while Rob and a few other men smoked on the couch.

Every day there was a stream of people coming to the apartment, usually from the early afternoon, some staying to smoke, swallow or shoot up, others leaving after purchases were made and money exchanged. The visits carried on throughout the night, with some people occasionally staying till morning, collapsed on the couch or folded up on mattresses in the living room or bedrooms, like piles of old clothes. Kiara usually slept wherever she could find a space, preferring Rob's room to the living room, though she often woke up to find someone else splayed across the mattress with her, snoring, drooling, or barely conscious.

Rob and Dan took it in turns to deliver out, with one always staying in the apartment to see to visitors. Once or twice they had returned with bruises and black eyes from rough deals or upset customers.

Kiara didn't ask questions and didn't say anything, she just kept silent and hoped Rob would let her stay. Two nights after she arrived Rob had called her out on why she left home. He'd noticed her strange moods, flickering like a broken TV, one minute there and the next minute blank and muted. She hadn't told him the whole story, just that something bad had gone down with her dad and she could never go back.

He'd nodded thoughtfully and offered her some weed, perhaps in a gesture of solidarity or sympathy, but she refused. She'd always promised herself she would never smoke – knowing it could damage her voice, her most precious commodity. She accepted the vodka he gave her though, grimacing as she sipped it from a filthy glass smeared with fingerprints. "*It'll help shut the demons up,*" Rob had told her.

Kiara had never drunk before, except for the glass of champagne just a week before, but the vodka made her feel heavy and tired, wrapped in clouds, dulling the sharp nudges of nostalgia that kept haunting her. It helped her to sleep even when every light was blazing at 3am and Dan was vomiting in the bathroom and people were talking nonsense in the living room, tripping, their unhinged laughter echoing down the hall.

Dan was not happy about her being there and glared at her with resentful eyes. When he realised she was going to be there for more than a few days, he had laid into Rob, arguing with him about her and the cost of her being there. Kiara knew he was right – she couldn't keep on freeloading.

She started helping to answer the door, checking who the visitors were, tidying up in the mornings when everyone else was still too stoned or drunk or asleep, running out to do errands and buy food. She counted pills, weighed and bagged powders, checked the money. It wasn't enough to appease Dan but the regular visitors began to like her and Rob found her useful.

She found some kind of routine in the midst of the mess and noise of the apartment. In the late mornings Kiara checked on anyone who had slept over, that no one had stopped breathing or choked on their own vomit, she was used to doing that for her own father so the action had an almost comforting familiarity amongst the strangeness of her new life.

Rob usually gave her a few dollars to buy food and sometimes she'd run to the market, but the noise and the crowds made her feel uneasy, the articulated lorries in the street made her flinch as they ground past belching out noxious smoke. She preferred the small shops along the Avenue, their lights beaming out into the dark evenings and tinny Latino music from cheap radios echoing out from their doorways.

She'd stay up late, answering the door until 2 or 3am, then clutch a bottle of vodka to her chest and curl up somewhere, sipping it until sleep overpowered her. She quickly came to prefer the crisp, cold clarity of vodka over anything else – beer made her stomach churn, while the smell of bourbon and whiskey reminded her of her father.

The centre of her world had been the Jacobs' house, now it was this filthy apartment in a place where she knew no one. Dan disliked her and Rob only tolerated her, for now at least. Her horizons were now formed of the apartment and the streets around it, and the current day alone. She couldn't think of the future and wouldn't allow herself to think of the past except when drunk, for both its pleasure and pain made her sick to remember.

***

Apart from Rob, Dan, and regular clients, Kiara didn't know anyone in the city. She felt like a speck swallowed up in a vast sea of people, invisible and alone. She missed the Jacobs, was heartsick with longing for them, and lulled herself to sleep with vodka-infused daydreams of the times she had spent with them.

She was walking with her head down one day, looking at the floor, when she bumped into the young woman who lived in the apartment opposite. Kiara had been running out to fetch something to eat, and practically collided with her neighbour in the hallway.

"*Cuidese*! Careful!" the woman said, grabbing the wall for balance, teetering on extremely high heels, a brown bag full of groceries tucked under one arm. She had warm caramel skin with thick dark hair tumbling down her back.

"I'm sorry!" Kiara reached out a hand to steady her. "You okay?"

"*Si si si,*" the woman said quickly, nodding. "And you?"

"I'm fine," Kiara paused awkwardly. "I'm Kiara, I live next door."

Her neighbour arched an eyebrow. "I'm Betsabe." She grinned as Kiara tried to get the pronunciation right – Bet-Sah-Bay. "Call me Betty," she said, smiling.

She shifted the groceries onto her other hip and inserted her key into the door. "Would you like to come in?"

Kiara was surprised at the unexpected invitation and for a moment stood in silence, her back against the hallway wall, uncertain.

"*Venga nena,*" Betty said, waving at her to come in.

Kiara walked inside, the air perfumed by floor cleaner, baby powder, and something frying in oil. Kiara had gotten used to the general squalor of the apartment and even though she tried to keep it clean she knew she fought a losing battle. She had almost forgotten what a clean home should smell like.

"*Ya llegue,*" Betty shouted out, and shooed Kiara into the kitchen. There was another young woman there frying something on the stove and an older woman cradling a baby at the table.

"Who's your friend?" the young woman at the stove said to Betty.

"She lives across the hall," Betty said to her, dumping the grocery bag on the counter. "Kiara, this is my sister Veronica, my Aunt Suyapa, and Veronica's son, Isaac."

Kiara smiled and waved hello. Suyapa peered at Kiara and laughed, "*Qué pelo tan rojo! Como un fuego!*" The two women laughed with her. Kiara had taken basic Spanish at high school but couldn't remember any and thought maybe the aunt was worried about the stove catching fire.

83

They persuaded her to stay for fried plantain and Kiara nibbled on hot oily pieces, while listening to Betty's story of how they came to the US and ended up in Hunts Point all the way from Honduras, paying someone they referred to as a *coyote* vast sums of money to get them across Guatemala and Mexico and over the border.

"You ever heard of San Pedro Sula, Kiara?" Betty asked. Kiara shook her head – geography hadn't been her strong point at school, along with languages, maths, and just about everything else.

"Well, this Hunts Point is *nada* compared to San Pedro. Just death and killing all the time everywhere, guns in the street, always gangs fighting and killing people for nothing," Betty said, shaking her head.

Betty explained that they couldn't afford for their two brothers to come so they left them behind in San Pedro and were saving to pay for another *coyote* to get them across. It sounded like a terrible place and an awful journey and Kiara wasn't surprised they wanted to come to the States. She was just happy to sit and listen, being poured endless refills of soda by Suyapa who spoke almost no English and offered it every time with the words "*màs refresco?*" and never waited for her to answer. Suyapa was big and round and pillowy, her hair dyed a bright blonde with the same caramel skin as Betty and Veronica, but her teeth were rotten with a few black stumps remaining. She never stopped laughing and smiling as she played with Isaac.

Kiara avoided most of their questions about herself by asking them to tell her more about the life and family they had left behind in Honduras, and the journey they had survived to get here, which sounded epic and terrifying.

Eventually she had to go, reluctantly, as Rob and Dan might need her for something.

"Come back again," Betty said, as Kiara stepped out the door. "You're always welcome."

Eight years ago – The Jacobs

"There's been no contact from her at all?" Moira asked Janet, biting into her pastry and dabbing the corners of her mouth.

"No, not a thing," Janet said, looking sadly out of the window at the pale winter skies.

It had been two months since Kiara had left and Janet thought about her every day. Her heart still lurched with excitement if the phone rang, and she was always disappointed that it was never Kiara's voice on the line.

Sometimes Janet would dream of Kiara lying cold and white like marble on a coroner's table, accusing blue eyes staring at her and grey lips whispering for help, and Janet would wake in a sweat-soaked shudder, those words scraping at the edges of her consciousness like dry dead leaves on the ground.

Victor and Shane had no luck in Phoenix – there had been no sightings, and they couldn't trace Rob. Victor had come back from each trip more disillusioned and more tired, so Janet told him to stop and rest until the New Year, then try again. She had hoped and prayed for Kiara to come back for her birthday, then for Thanksgiving, and now for Christmas, but as each milestone passed hope receded further. She had bought her presents and stored them carefully, wrapped and ready in case one day she came through the door.

"Janet I'm so sorry. I know how much you cared for her, you all did." Moira's eyes dampened with tears to see her sister suffering.

Janet turned from the window and sat down at the kitchen table, taking a sip from her peppermint tea, the steam from the cup curling gently into the air. "Shane and Sarah are in bits about it. They phone every couple of days to see if we've heard anything. Ted and Mary phone all the time too, but I have no updates, no news to tell them."

She sighed, looking at Moira, her eyes red-rimmed and lined with tiredness. "I feel so helpless."

Moira took her hand and held it, not knowing what to say.

Eight years ago – Kiara

"*Feliz navidad*!" Glasses clinked around the table as the clock chimed midnight on Christmas Eve. Betty, Veronica, Suyapa and Kiara were crammed in knee-to-knee in the warmth of the kitchen, a roast chicken nestled on the table, shiny under the lights, and Isaac sitting plumply on Suyapa's lap.

Kiara was so grateful to have somewhere to go for Christmas. Rob and Dan were partying hard, Kiara could hear the music throb through the wall from their apartment. She had been desperate to avoid it, knowing from their previous party what sorts of things might happen. Fortunately, she had the Martinez family waiting for her across the hall. It was customary in Honduras to eat a huge feast at midnight on Christmas Eve, and they wanted to keep the tradition, happy for her to join in.

Despite being jammed in amongst her new friends, her mind kept wandering away to the Jacobs. She could picture them staying up late with a toast, Shane with his arm around Melanie, maybe Sarah had brought home a college boyfriend this year. She wondered if they missed her.

She had been considering getting in touch with them to wish them merry Christmas, but then thought of the rush of questions that she would have to handle about why she left and where she lived now, and she just couldn't face it, couldn't face telling them about the rape or about the life she now led.

At first, she hadn't thought too much about what Rob and Dan were involved in and, terrified they would ask her to leave, she didn't mind what she had to do to stay. In a few short months she had become part of a world she had never known and she couldn't unsee or unhear the things she had experienced here – the hookers coming by straight from working the corner, counting out crumpled bills with shaky hands, smelling of cheap cologne and sweat and desperation, the Russians raising their heavily accented voices in terse negotiations with Rob, the groups of young men Dan hung out with, looking at her, brushing up against her in the hallway, sucking on their teeth as she walked past.

She never felt safe anymore, anywhere. At night she would lay down and a sense of dread would creep into her heart, and the only way she could find peace was to keep sipping from a bottle till her racing thoughts came to a shuddering stop and the world fell away. She couldn't imagine what the Jacobs would think of her now.

She knew she had wandered off into her thoughts for too long and tried to force herself back into the present, to hold on to the smells and sounds and the way the plastic chair felt, sticking to her legs, the silky fatness of Isaac's arm rubbing against hers, the scent of red wine plummy and rich in her glass.

"*Y tu familia joven*?" Suyapa asked her, smiling her toothless smile.

"She's asking about your family Kiara," Veronica said, trying to swipe Isaac's mouth with a damp washcloth.

"I don't have any family, apart from Rob," Kiara replied, feeling bad for lying to her friends but not wanting to unpack the whole mess for them here and now. She had told them that she didn't have any family before but Suyapa always asked and Kiara couldn't tell if she had forgotten or if she didn't believe her.

"*No tiene,*" Veronica translated for Suyapa, who stood over Kiara and wrapped her arms around Kiara's shoulders, pulling her into her chest and stomach, soft and warm. Kiara smiled and looked up, and Suyapa laughed. "*Qué ojos!*" she exclaimed, walking away to the counter to grab more drinks to refill glasses. Kiara giggled, Suyapa was enchanted by her blue eyes and was always tugging on her red curls.

"Hey Betty," Kiara leaned in to Betty while Suyapa was getting drinks and Veronica was trying to mop up a wriggling Isaac, "can I give you guys something towards this, a few dollars?"

Kiara didn't have much money and relied on small handouts from Rob when he was feeling generous, so a few dollars was all she owned but she would happily give it to the Martinez family. They gave most of their money to *coyotes* to pay off their own debts and hopefully one day pay enough for their two brothers to make the journey over, plus they had Isaac to feed and sent money home to Honduras regularly. As a result, they too had very little, though they were extremely generous with what they had and always happy to share with Kiara, to invite her over for coffee or pour her glasses of soda while she had a spare thirty minutes to stop by and say hello.

Betty shook her head, "No *amiga*, the tips have been good this week, people are pretty generous around Christmas, so it's okay."

Kiara thanked her and took a newly clean Isaac onto her lap to give Veronica and Suyapa a rest. He was six months old, with rolls of fat on his arms and legs, squidgy as a marshmallow. Kiara kissed him on one plump cheek, his sticky hands grasping at her hair and face, holding on to one curl tightly, and Kiara thought about her own mother, and how she had left when Kiara wasn't much older than Isaac was now. She must have been a very unlovable baby for her own mom to leave her behind.

She hugged Isaac close and kissed the top of his head, the dark wisps of hair damp and hot, the scent of the washcloth lingering on his skin. Veronica adored her baby boy – her whole face lit up when she looked at Isaac, and she kissed and petted him incessantly. Kiara ached to see that sort of fierce and enduring love and wondered what it felt like to be the object of such affection.

Kiara stayed with the Martinez family that whole night as they feasted and opened presents. They went to bed around 2.30am, Suyapa giving up the couch for that night so Kiara could sleep over, the throb of the party across the hall still pounding. She had forgotten to bring anything to drink herself to sleep and lay awake, thoughts of the Jacobs, her mom and dad, the apartment, and the trailer, crashing and churning in her mind. Laying down to sleep was when thoughts like these came crowding in on her, rudely intrusive and taunting, and usually the alcohol dulled her brain so she could rest and not have to actually feel the unbearable sadness pressing down on her. *How did it all go so wrong so quickly?* she thought, staring at the ceiling.

She had turned eighteen just a few weeks ago and spent the day in the usual routine, not wanting to tell anyone it was her birthday. Dan had a filthy hangover, retching in the bathroom most of the morning and early afternoon, emerging red-eyed and raw-throated, glaring at her and pushing her out of the way in the kitchen. The bathroom was a mess, vomit splattered on the basin and puddled on the floor, foul-smelling and streaked with bile and blood. Dan knew she would clean it up.

The day had started badly and ended badly, with Kiara walking in on a hooker giving Rob a blowjob in the bedroom that night. He hadn't noticed, his head held back and eyes closed, low moans through his mouth, and she had turned on her heel and propelled herself out the door as swiftly and silently as she could, cheeks burning, not wanting to go back to the living room where Dan was dealing with a number of clients, and unable to go into Dan's bedroom, because he never let her. Dan's bedroom was where they stored all the money, the drugs, the equipment for weighing and bagging. His bed (the only bed in the apartment) lifted up from the mattress on a hinge, revealing an empty frame underneath with plenty of space for storing it all.

Without alcohol, Kiara knew sleep wouldn't come easily, even though she felt safe in the Martinez apartment. She lay on the couch, the Christmas lights wound around the plastic tree blinking silently, like colourful eyes winking at her in the darkness, and eventually the dark of the night began to fade and a pale dawn light seeped in and it was Christmas day.

Seven and a half years ago – Kiara

Kiara shivered as she shoved cartons of instant noodles and bags of chips into the cupboards from paper grocery bags. It was mid-February and a cold front had swept the city, the temperature plunging. The sky outside was slate grey with the peculiar back-lit glow that only happens when the skies are getting ready to snow again on an earth that already stood white and frozen and hard as iron beneath them.

The apartment was freezing, neither Rob nor Dan were particularly good at keeping the heating working or paying any bills on time. Dan had crashed out in his room an hour before, warning Kiara to watch out for any visitors and wake him if anyone stopped by. He was sick, with a swollen throat and streaming eyes, clutching a blanket round him, otherwise he wouldn't normally sleep in the afternoon. Rob had gone to drop off some purchases to a client of his and was due back any minute.

Kiara had just curled up on the couch, tucking her cold feet up under her, rubbing them to get the blood moving, when she heard the key turn in the front door and steps shuffling down the hall. Rob lurched in, one hand clutching his face, the other his ribs, his knuckles grazed and blood dripping from between his fingers, his coat speckled with clumps of melting snow.

"Rob! Oh my god, what happened!" Kiara yelped, leaping up from the couch and running to support him. He leaned on her and together they staggered forwards, pitching from side to side until Rob collapsed onto the couch, letting out a heavy groan that ended in a high-pitched whine of pain.

Kiara ran to fetch ice and a towel, which she pressed with shaking hands onto Rob's face, now a patchwork of purple and red bruises, blood spatters, and dark tears in the fabric of the skin. He held the cool cloth to his face while she dabbed with tissue at the leaking wounds. Her heart pounded at the bright crimson stains on the paper-white tissue, bringing back memories of how she had bled after the rape. She shook her head to force away the wooziness that rose up on her suddenly, and asked Rob again gently, "What happened?"

He winced as she wiped his wounds, his eyes moist with pain. "Just the usual bullshit. Argument over costs, who owed what. I stood my ground but there were three of them and they kicked the shit out of me."

He groaned as he tried to move, clutching his side. "Fuuuuck that hurts."

"Lay down and don't move," Kiara told him. There was no point in asking if he wanted to see a doctor, Kiara already knew he wouldn't. Dan and Rob avoided anything that could draw attention to themselves, and that included doctors, hospitals, parking tickets, or dodging fares on the subway.

"Get me something to help the pain – anything – whatever's to hand," he told her.

She nodded and ran to the kitchen, pouring a full glass of whiskey and handing it to Rob, who opened his mouth wide and tipped it down his throat in one swift movement. "More," he gasped, and downed the next glass, while she popped painkillers from a packet, which he gulped down dry as she freed each one from its foil blister.

Leaning back, panting, he squeezed his eyes shut.

"Getcha anything else?" Kiara asked, perched on the edge of the couch next to him.

He opened his eyes, "Nah, I'm good." The shock, the alcohol, and the painkillers were beginning to kick in, his breathing slowed and his eyes glazed a little, lids drooping.

"Did you know it's my birthday today?" he said after a few moments of silence had passed.

Kiara shook her head.

"I'm twenty-three-years-old and what have I got? What have I got for those twenty-three years?" he laughed, a rasping breathless laugh that made Kiara shudder.

"I'm sorry Rob," she half-whispered, unsure what to say, thinking how Rob was the same age as Shane but seemed so much more fragile, wizened, and vulnerable.

He looked at her with dark brown eyes that looked almost black, his expression unreadable. "Why are you still here?" he slurred slightly. "It's been months. Why haven't you gone home?"

"I can't go home Rob. I won't go back." She stared at him defiantly and curled her hands into small fists at the very thought of returning to see her father, knowing what he had allowed to happen to her. She would rather die out here in Hunts Point than go back to that man.

Rob's head lolled backwards and then jerked forwards onto his chest, fighting sleep. "You don't want this Kiara, trust me," he slurred incoherently. He rested his head back against the couch and his breathing deepened and slowed as he fell asleep.

Kiara covered him with a blanket and sat on the floor with her back to the couch, listening to him breathe, counting the seconds between each breath. Selfishly, she knew she couldn't lose Rob as he was the only one she had left now. She was entirely dependent on his tolerance, which was all the more surprising given that their relational connection was tenuous at best.

Rob's mother, Lizzie, was only her dad's half-sister, and the half-siblings hadn't grown up together. Rob had drifted in and out of foster homes after his mom died in a car accident when he was thirteen, his father unknown and untraceable. Bill hadn't wanted to take him in, barely able to look after his own child, so Rob had been shunted into a series of unsuitable placements where he proceeded to lash out violently at everyone trying to help.

Rob knew what it was like to feel unwelcome and unwanted, intruding on someone else's family life and trying to pretend it was your own. Maybe that's why he allowed her to stay – he was the only one who knew what it was like to feel utterly alone with no home as an anchor, to feel like a lost ship using all its energy to stay afloat with no regard to trajectory or destination.

The TV was on in the background with no sound. Kiara flicked through the mute channels, not really focusing on anything, content to just keep the picture reeling from film to commercials to music videos. She stopped on a press conference where a sportsman was addressing the audience, cameras flashing and hands waving with questions. Her thumb hovering over the remote, she was about to carry on channel hopping when she froze and inhaled sharply as the camera zoomed out. Beside the sportsman sat Victor and Shane Jacobs, nodding and smiling, speaking into the microphones in front of them, laughing with the sports star. A red news banner across the screen announced – "Basketball super star signed to Jacobs Sports Management."

Tears spilled from her eyes. She couldn't put the sound on for fear of waking Rob but what they were saying wasn't as important as seeing them there. She cried soundless, shoulder-shaking, chest-compressing sobs, tears running down her face and neck and dampening her sweater, fingers pressed to her mouth to stifle the sound of her ragged breathing. Shane. Victor. She mouthed their names over and over again, rocking gently before the TV long after they left the screen.

Seven and a half years ago – The Jacobs

"You did so good sweetie!" Melanie squealed as Shane walked in the door that evening. She jumped into his arms and he lifted her off the floor in a bear hug, laughing.

The business was going from strength to strength and after two years Shane was helping his father with record-breaking deals to secure the top athletes and taking part in regular press conferences. He got such a high from it, working more and more hours, his office lights blazing till 10 or 11pm at night, long days fuelled by nothing more than coffee and the absolute certainty that this was what he was called to do and driven by the pride he had in delivering for his father.

Melanie was delighted in his progress as they toasted every deal and every raise. There had been a worrying few months where Shane was listless and preoccupied, flying off to Phoenix every weekend, turning down projects, dinners, and parties, unable to take his mind off Kiara. Melanie had cajoled and distracted him, had tried to help him understand that she was probably fine and with her cousin or friends somewhere, and not some damsel in distress that he needed to rescue. Four months after Kiara left he finally seemed to be getting over it, Melanie thought, accepting that Kiara was gone and turning his mind to more important matters.

With Shane's earnings Melanie could afford to live at her own leisure, filling the time with shopping, lunch dates, and spa treatments, determined to make those hours full of comfort, fulfilment and satisfaction. In return, she made sure Shane had all the support, love and encouragement he needed, always returning to a clean home and a beautiful wife.

Shane kicked his shoes off and followed her into the living room of their beautiful New York townhouse that she had so tastefully decorated. She handed him a beer from the fridge and stroked his arm. "Is your dad pleased?"

"Yup," Shane grinned. "It's going so well that he's decided to take some more vacation time this year to go to the beach house and get some rest, and I'll be in charge so he won't have to worry about a thing."

Melanie nodded. She knew it meant he would be away long hours but that didn't bother her.

"I imagine he needs a rest," she said, running her nails up and down his sleeve.

Shane nodded, "He really does."

Victor had busied himself with searching for Kiara, but it had taken a greater physical toll on him than on his son, and he took to bed for five days with a raging fever in late January. It was the longest time Shane had known him to be sick. They had taken it in turns to sit by him, bringing drinks and medicine and watching over him.

In the depths of the fever he had sobbed in sweat-soaked sheets, calling out for his brother Ned. He had rambled to Shane, eyes wide, telling him over and over that it wasn't his fault that Ned died, that he had tried to save him, had pulled him from the river and tried to breathe life back into him, but his father had still held him responsible, beat him senseless and never forgiven him. Victor had moaned and torn at his hair as Shane had tried to comfort him, helpless and afraid to see his dad finally let down his emotional barriers.

After that, Shane, Janet and Sarah had held a family meeting and decided to stop going to Phoenix every weekend, and try to wait in peace for news or contact from her. They were all struggling, emotionally empty and physically ground down. It was the worst kind of emotional limbo, dealing with the fears, the guilt, the unanswered questions, and happy memories became sad ones simply because she was in them and they missed her.

Shane hadn't wanted to stop looking for her, but he knew it was right to allow hope to burn each day with a small but steady flame rather than a raging fire that consumed everything else. He still thought of Kiara every night, often turning over that kiss in his head, sometimes waking up thinking she had returned or never even left, but the deepening silence and the slow glacial passing of the winter months made it feel more and more that she was lost to them forever.

"Don't forget we have CeeCee's wedding at the weekend," Melanie said, scrunching her bare feet into the soft white rug in front of the couch. Melanie was chief bridesmaid for her best friend's wedding and never ceased to drop it into conversation, with little hints about wedding dresses and engagement rings. Melanie and Shane had been together a long time now and she felt the time was right, if not actually overdue, for the next step.

"Sure, looking forward to it. Did they ever sort out the whole seating chart debacle?" He asked, and they both laughed. Derek and CeeCee had a long-running dispute over the famously complicated seating arrangements for their various family and friends, and Melanie had kept Shane filled in on all the various arguments and disagreements she had been privy to as bridesmaid.

"They did, finally. I hope our wedding won't be as stressful or complicated," she smiled at him.

"I'm sure it won't be," he put an arm round her and leaned back, grateful for all he had in his life, and wishing that only one thing could be remedied.

Seven and a half years ago – Kiara

Rob's cell phone beeped, the buzz from the vibration making Kiara jump. It was the day after Rob had returned in a bad state, and he was still bleary from painkillers and alcohol, lying floppily on the couch, taking calls and leaving most visitors to Kiara to handle as Dan was still sick in bed, barely aware of what had happened to Rob as he was feverish and sleeping most of the time.

Kiara didn't mind, she could count out the bills, dole out what people asked for, and write down what people wanted for Rob to get from various dealers he knew.

Kiara was sometimes astounded at the amount of money that flowed through the apartment like a paper river, only ever passing through as the money disappeared as quickly as it arrived. Kiara often overheard conversations between Rob and Dan, their lowered voices frantic and tense, about people they owed. Kiara wasn't sure where the debts had come from, but she guessed it was the reason why Rob and Dan had got into this kind of thing in the first place.

They had been teen runaways from the same children's home, got into some kind of trouble and did what they could to work themselves out of it, still owing an unknown amount to a mysterious web of creditors and dealers and never quite able to untangle themselves. They were fiercely loyal to each other, as close as brothers.

Rob leaned over wearily and grabbed his cell, checking the voicemail and sighing as he hung up the phone.

"Kiara, I need you to do something for me."

Kiara was sitting on the floor watching a game show on TV, her back to the couch but alert in case Rob needed anything. She twisted her head to look at Rob and raised her eyebrows, waiting.

"You've got to deliver today," Rob said, grimacing as he did so. "I'm sorry, but Dan's too ill and I can't go out like this, so you have to help out. Think you can handle it?"

Kiara nodded, her heart sinking, nerves rising in her chest like battery acid.

"I'll tell you what to do, okay?" Rob said and, pushing himself up on his elbows, gave Kiara her instructions.

Dan and Rob had a variety of means of getting around the city depending on what they were delivering and where to, and they didn't tend to go far, but Kiara didn't know her way around the city like they did, having barely left Hunts Point since she arrived. She was terrified of getting lost in the mass of people in the city and being alone on the cold streets by herself.

Rob knew he couldn't ask her to get there by herself, and it was still snowy on the ground with an icy chill in the wind, so he called her a cab. She was to take the cab to an apartment building on West fifty-sixth street and tell the guard that she was there to visit Mr Daniels of apartment thirty-three. If he asked her name, she was to say "Marianna". She was to hand over the delivery to Mr Daniels and take the money, counting it carefully to make sure it was all there. She was to leave immediately, hail a cab on the street, and come straight back again. Rob gave her Dan's phone to carry with her in case she needed anything.

Kiara counted out the bags of blow and pills, shoving them into a backpack Rob gave her. He looked at her as she put her sneakers on. "You look like a student. No one would suspect you of anything."

"Good," she said, not really hearing him, her mind running over the instructions again and again, terrified of forgetting what she was supposed to do, or making a mistake, or getting arrested and going to jail.

Rob's phone chirped. "The cab is down the street – I didn't want him coming to this building. Mr Daniels knows to expect you." Kiara leaned her head out of the window and could see the cab waiting for her down the street, facing away from their building so hopefully he wouldn't see which apartment block she came out of.

As Kiara turned to walk down the hall, Rob called out behind her – "Stay safe!"

The cab smelt like stale kebab and body odour, a humid wave that made her feel nauseous as she slid inside from the frozen winter air. The heat was on full blast, and before long, her armpits were starting to sweat, her hands clammy. The cab turned corners sharply, Kiara sliding along in the backseat from left to right, her head spinning and her stomach starting to churn. Reflections of the city slid along the windows, black and glittering against the grey sky, the Hudson gliding by to her right, flat and gloomy in the pale winter light.

Eventually the cab stopped outside an apartment building, a steel and glass tower rising up from a snow-speckled sidewalk. Kiara handed the driver his cash and slid out, mentally checking the name of the building twice before she shoved the revolving doors to the lobby, which glided round with a soft swoosh.

The concierge looked at her, raising his eyebrows under his bottle green hat. "Who are you visiting please?"

"Mr Daniels, apartment thirty-three," she replied.

"And you are…?"

"Marianna."

The man gave a bored sigh, and phoned apartment thirty-three, waving her over to the elevator when all was cleared.

She punched the button for the third floor and let out a long shaky breath when the elevator doors thumped shut and it began to rise. She suddenly felt desperate for the bathroom and squeezed her thighs together, hoping she wouldn't be here for long.

When she tapped nervously on the apartment door, Mr Daniels opened it quickly and gestured for her to come in. The apartment was like the building, hard shiny surfaces in black marble and steel, with a pristine unused kitchen and huge glass windows looking out onto the city. Her customer was youngish, in his thirties perhaps, with dark hair. He motioned for her to sit on the couch, which was bright red and low-backed and clearly more for show than for comfort. She perched on the edge and laid out the delivery on the glass-topped coffee table in front of the couch – cocaine, Oxy, Adderall.

"As you requested Mr Daniels, it's all here," she said, glancing at him nervously.

He grinned at her, flashing perfectly straight white teeth. "You can call me Andrew," he said, counting out crisp bills and handing them to her.

He looked at her as she checked the bills. "You're Rob's helper? Looks like you should be in school."

She paused and met his eyes which were a deep ocean blue. "I'm older than I look," she replied, tucking the bills into her pocket and standing up.

"In that case, wanna stay for a drink? You can sample some of this with me if you like, Marianna," he extended out the last 'a' of her fake name and smiled slowly. The whiteness of his teeth and the deep blue of his eyes plus the smooth glass façade of the apartment made Kiara feel like she was trapped in a shark tank. She shook her head and walked for the door, remembering Rob's strict instructions to get back straight away, even though she still needed the bathroom.

Andrew let her out with a smile and said: "Make sure Rob sends you next time."

Leaving the apartment block, Kiara felt giddy, her hands shaking and floppy-legged, it took her ages to hail a cab and she started to walk in the hope of finding a passing one more easily. She trudged along the sidewalk, taking big gulps of icy air, hurting her chest with the cold. She felt lighter and freer without the drugs in her backpack.

The recent snow flurries had melted into filthy slush, and piles of black-stained snow and puddles of freezing water gathered at the edges of the sidewalk. Her feet were beginning to numb in her sneakers, soaked through to her socks, when she finally managed to flag down a cab.

The driver was an Indian man in his fifties who had a plastic ceremonial sword swinging from the mirror, and he tried to make polite chat with her as they passed through the city back to Hunts Point.

"Are you working today dear? What is it that you do?" he asked.

I'm a drug dealer, Kiara thought in her head, suddenly wanting to laugh at the absurdity of it, because it couldn't possibly be real and yet here she was, the dollars in her pocket proof of what she had done and who she now was.

"I'm a student," she said, settling back into her seat, watching the passing buildings slip by on her way back to Hunts Point.

Seven years ago – The Jacobs

"A toast, to the happy couple," Victor raised his glass and smiled at Shane and Melanie.

"To the happy couple," echoed the large group of people who had gathered around them. Glasses clinked and champagne was sipped as they celebrated their engagement just a few weeks after Melanie's twenty-third birthday.

It was a perfect August day, with sultry heat and cloudless skies, the scent of roses perfuming the warm air as the sun beat down on the white patio and gleamed off the pool.

Janet buzzed through the crowd, greeting everyone, delighted at the happy news and the wedding yet to plan. Sarah was cooing over Melanie's ring, a large diamond solitaire, princess cut, reflecting a thousand sunbeams from its glittering depths.

"It's gorgeous Mel," she said, "I can't believe my brother actually chose this for you."

Melanie laughed, her dark hair straightened and glossy and a light tan brightening her complexion. "I know! I was getting tired of waiting. I'm so glad he finally asked!" She laid her hand on Shane's arm and rested her head on his chest with a triumphant smile.

Shane bent down to kiss her on top of her head, her dark hair warmed by the sun. "Mom is so happy – look at her," he said, nodding in Janet's direction as she laughed gaily and waved her hands around as she talked with the guests. It was the happiest they had seen her in months, since last October.

Sarah followed his gaze. "I'm so glad you guys did this. Not just for mom of course, but it's great to see her so excited. We all needed some good news, something positive to focus on," she said thoughtfully, chewing on her lower lip.

Sarah's eyes flickered to the gate in the fence then back to Melanie again, who was talking about wedding plans, but Shane saw her glance and he knew they were both thinking the same thing, both wishing Kiara would stroll through the gate, the last ten months just a simple misunderstanding.

"Sweetie?"

"Hmm?" he turned his head back to Melanie, who was looking at him quizzically.

"You with us?"

"Sure, yeah, sorry," he said, nodding. Jade arrived shortly afterwards and after giving Shane a brief hug she grabbed Melanie and Sarah to refill their drinks and talk about the wedding next year. Melanie had wanted to get married sooner but Shane had insisted they wait at least a year so they didn't have to rush, but in reality, he was hoping that Kiara might come back before the wedding.

Seven years ago – Kiara

The city was enveloped in a fog of smoggy heat, a yellowing cloud sitting astride the buildings, smothering the people below. Kiara was tired out, sweating and sticky, and gratefully sipped from a glass of water filled with ice.

Kiara had stopped by to see her friends on the way back from a round of deliveries. She tended to do a few in the late afternoons, Rob preferred her to do the ones in daylight while he took care of the later ones, although sometimes they switched it up depending on what requests came in and who the clients were. Some of the clients now only wanted Kiara to do their deliveries.

She had traipsed downtown to Manhattan in the smog and fumes, traffic snarling through the streets, agonisingly slow, and she was glad to get back safely. She always left the apartment with a deep pit of anxiety in her stomach, even with clients she knew well. It felt good to relax in Betty's living room for a few minutes with the windows wide open, though the stagnant summer air barely moved through them.

Isaac toddled up to her, reeling and lurching, on the cusp of falling with every step, until he grabbed her knee and banged his mouth wetly against it, leaving a damp patch on her jeans. She giggled and grabbed his hands.

"Hola Isaac!" she said, jiggling his hands and making him laugh, while he swayed from side to side like a small drunk.

Veronica laughed and scooped him up, kissing his cheeks. He squealed happily, and Betty grinned at him as she curled up on the couch next to Kiara.

"*Qua pasa Kiara?*"

"*Nada,*" Kiara leaned back against the cushions, glancing at Betty and smiling. "I'm just tired out today. It's too hot."

"Have you got any more work to do today?" Veronica asked, swivelling her head round from where she sat with Isaac on the floor, cartoon music jingling merrily from the TV.

"Maybe I'll get called out again, but more likely I'll stay in this evening and see who stops by," Kiara replied. "What about you two? Shifts tonight?"

Betty nodded. "We're both working tonight. There is air con at the club but maybe people won't come out in this heat."

Betty and Veronica worked in the Treasure Chest club a few blocks away. They made pretty good money, especially when the tips were generous, enough to pay for the apartment, pay the *coyotes,* send money home and save for their brothers. More than once they had offered to introduce Kiara to the club, believing dancing to be safer than drug delivering, but she had refused, unable to bear the thought of taking her clothes off in front of men. Her body still didn't feel completely her own since the night she had left, she still remembered the pain and the humiliation of being touched by that man who felt he had some kind of right to use her for his pleasure against her will. There was no way she was willing to submit herself to that feeling again.

"I better get going," she said, always sad to leave her friends. Their apartment was like a beacon of normality, the only place where she felt a sense of being 'at home' since the Jacobs' house. She often wondered what the Jacobs were doing, and she had passed by the JSM office several times on her deliveries. She had stood opposite the building once, a darkening evening not six weeks before, when white fluorescent lights were still burning out from several offices. She knew one of those lights might be from Shane or Victor's office. They were so close that she could almost imagine their voices over the city din. She had allowed herself just five minutes to linger then had to move on, back to Hunts Point.

"See you soon," Veronica called over her shoulder as Kiara left, still sitting with Isaac in front of the TV. Betty waved goodbye.

Kiara walked across the hall to open the door to apartment fifty-eight, but the door was already gaping open. Her shoulders tensed, knowing that Rob and Dan never left the door open. She paused for a moment then gently pushed the door, feeling instinctively in her heart that something was very wrong.

Seven years ago – The Jacobs

"To the bride-to-be," Melanie and CeeCee clinked their glasses, trying not to spill their deep-red raspberry martinis. The setting sun sent warm fingers of orange gold over the roof terrace of the bar, a perfect summer evening for catching up, gossiping, and flicking through wedding magazines.

CeeCee tapped one of the pages. "I like this one Mel," she said, pointing with a pink fingernail to one of the dresses, an ivory gown which was low-backed with a long train.

"Let me see," Melanie pulled the page closer, then shook her head. "I'm not keen on the neckline. I want a sweetheart neckline, like…" she paused, flicking through the pages, "that one. But not in that colour and definitely not fishtail."

CeeCee nodded thoughtfully. "You'll have to try some more on. When you find the right dress, you'll know."

Melanie sipped her martini, tart and refreshing, and her phone hummed in her purse. She leaned down to grab it and read the text that had come through.

CeeCee raised an eyebrow. "Mel?"

"Hmmm?" Melanie was smiling, distracted.

"Another declaration of love from the man of the moment?"

"Yup." Melanie slipped the phone back into her purse and grinned at CeeCee. "He's obsessed with me."

"And what about Shane? You're marrying him next year. When are you gonna call this off?"

Melanie shrugged. "I'm allowed a little fun, aren't I? I mean, Shane's working *all* the time. I get lonely, you know," she pouted.

"If you play with fire…" CeeCee waved a finger at Melanie, giggling as she did it.

"Look, I love Shane. I like his family, we've got a great house, lots of money, the wedding will be beautiful, it's just…" Melanie sighed dramatically, "this guy is amazing. I can't help myself, honestly, I can't CeeCee. But I don't want to hurt Shane and I do plan to call it off, soon."

Melanie appreciated the life that Shane gave her. She loved the comfort and security, the ease of his family life, and how happy her parents were that she was marrying him. He had prospects, was stable, kind, and gave her anything she wanted. She had often fooled around with other guys when they were dating, reasoning that she was just blowing off some steam, having a little fun, and had never thought much of it.

Then shortly after they had bought the house and Shane was working longer and longer hours, she had met a man in a bar, flirted a little, and ended up in his apartment. She had never intended to carry on seeing him, but the intensity of their affair left her with a craving she could never quite satisfy. She loved Shane, but she fantasised about Kyle, seeing him every few days, especially when Shane was working late. Shane was her safety net, but Kyle was her drug, although he couldn't offer her anything lasting or secure as he was just starting out in his financial career and was nowhere near as wealthy as Shane. Melanie wasn't stupid and wasn't going to throw away the life she had made for herself. She knew she would probably end things with Kyle before the wedding.

"Here's to the bride," CeeCee said, raising her glass.

Seven years ago – Kiara

Kiara crept silently down the hall, her heartbeat reverberating through her chest. Debris was strewn over the apartment. In the living room, the chairs were upturned, cheap imitation bamboo legs split in half, couch cushions thrown to the floor and ripped open, the TV overturned, the screen shattered. She turned on her heel and went to Dan's room. The mattress sagged against the wall and the bedframe underneath, where they kept everything, was empty, where only a few crumpled plastic bags remained.

Kiara stood with her hands over her mouth, breathing hard, her fingernails digging in to the sides of her cheeks. There had been thousands of dollars of drugs there, plus all the money Dan and Rob had, now all gone. Kiara reached out to lean against the doorframe, gasping, when she heard a low moan from Rob's bedroom.

"Rob! Dan!" she called out, running into the room.

Dan was lying on the floor, half-covered by an overturned mattress. Kiara grabbed the edges of the mattress and leaned backwards, slowly pulling it off him but struggled to grip it properly, her knees bumping into the thick fabric. She slipped several times but finally got the mattress off Dan, who had been badly beaten, his face swollen and caked in blood, his torso a patchwork of red and purple stains.

"Dan? Can you hear me?" Kiara knelt beside him, cigarette ash and glass pressing into her knee from the worn carpet. Dan squinted at her through puffy eyes and made a gurgling sound, drool mixed with blood seeping from the edges of his mouth. Kiara went to the bathroom and rinsed a washcloth in cold water, returning to Dan and wiping the drool and blood away from his mouth and nose, swiping the cloth gently over his bruised cheeks and forehead, where a deep gash trickled blood down the side of his face. He moaned again and closed his eyes.

Kiara sat beside him for what felt like a long time, though it could have only been twenty minutes or so, listening to his laboured breathing punctuated by low groans and unsure what to do, when Rob came in.

"What the fuck?" he dropped to his knees beside Kiara. "What the hell happened?"

"I don't know Rob, I just came back and found him like this, and all the stuff gone and…"

"Stuff gone? What stuff gone?" Rob interrupted, eyes widening in panic.

"Everything!" Kiara started to cry.

Rob's face went a waxy grey, and he lurched up from his feet and lumbered into the next room. Kiara could hear him through the wall as he saw the emptiness beneath the bed and let out a series of ragged groans, muttering "no, no, no, no, no" again and again.

It took him a few minutes to return to Kiara, his eyes red, his mouth a thin line. Without saying anything he helped to pull Dan onto a mattress, Kiara carefully taking his feet and Rob hauling him by the shoulders. Dan didn't wake up.

"I'm going to buy painkillers and booze. He's going to need them when he wakes up. Stay here, don't let anyone in, and clean up the fucking living room," Rob was talking to Kiara but not really looking at her, his eyes flickering around the room, briefly resting on her then scanning around again. She nodded and as Rob turned and left, she went to the living room to start clearing up.

Kiara was glad Rob wasn't gone long as she was afraid to answer the door and deal with people who would drop by. She knew there would be lots of people coming by that evening, some to see what they could get, others who had orders in. A wave of nausea passed over her in a sickly shudder, and she had to stick her head out of the window for air, though the summer haze seemed to have stolen all the oxygen in the atmosphere, leaving only a hot welter of fumes hovering over the buildings.

She and Rob sat silently in the living room after he returned.

"What are we going to do?" she whispered.

He looked at her and shook his head. "I don't know," he said, and tears began to track down his face. He wiped them away roughly with his sleeve and grabbed the bottle of JD he had bought.

"Fuck it," he said, and slugged from the bottle, passing it to Kiara. She gulped it down and they passed it back and forth between them until they couldn't move and the sky had darkened and they could no longer hear the pounding on the door.

***

The following afternoon Kiara was lying on the floor, her head pounding and her mouth dry. She had been drifting in and out of sleep, but the alcohol had finally worn off and the sharp edges of a hangover were stabbing her in the stomach. Shuddering, she raised her head. Rob wasn't where he had fallen asleep last night, but she could hear murmuring in the other room from two male voices – hopefully that meant Dan was awake and okay.

She went to the faucet and stuck her mouth directly underneath, gulping the water down, feeling the cold shock as it streamed its way into her empty stomach. She dry-heaved into the sink a few times, spit gushing into her mouth, until she could finally raise her head. She closed her eyes and took a few deep breaths. Normally her nightly drinking didn't affect her too much the next day, but she wasn't used to drinking whiskey and especially so much of it on an empty stomach.

She padded softly towards Rob's room where they had left Dan last night. She listened outside the door – Rob and Dan were listing what they had lost, what quantities had been stolen, and who might have done it.

She pushed open the door tentatively. Dan was sitting up, leaning against the wall, Rob next to him on the mattress with a piece of paper and a pen. Dan's face was like a bruised berry – swollen purple and black, his aqua eyes tiny spots of light in the middle of the raw flesh.

"Dan, it's so good to see you up and talking," Kiara said, as she sat down slowly on the floor in front of the mattress, curling her legs underneath her. "How are you feeling?"

Dan nodded at her and mumbled through his puffy lips – "I'm okay. Pretty sore."

Kiara looked at Rob. "Do you guys know who did this?"

"It could have been anyone. Sometimes when you get a big delivery from a dealer, they tip someone off to steal it back and split the profits. We'd just had packs of coke two days ago, so it could have been arranged after that, but I guess we won't find out and there's nothing we could do even if we did." Rob shrugged and looked at Dan, who nodded at him as if to urge him to carry on.

"Listen Kiara, we're in a bit of trouble," Rob continued, interrupted by a snort from Dan. Rob glared at him, "Fine, a lot of trouble."

Turning back to Kiara, he carried on. "We owe to lots of different people, and that stash was worth a lot of money, plus they took all our cash."

He sighed and looked at the floor. "Basically, we're kind of fucked."

"What are you going to do?" Kiara said, the floor gently swaying under her as her head pounded in time with her heart, pain pulsing in the left side of her skull.

"We can do a few things, call in a few debts, maybe stave off the demands for another day or two, but we have to move fast or," Rob paused and looked at Dan, "or the people we owe will do a lot worse than this. To all of us."

The pain in her head pulsated faster.

He leaned towards her. "Kiara, we need to make more money, we need more cash coming in if we're going to catch up and keep the guys we owe sweet." Rob's tone was more urgent, business-like. "We need you to start bringing in money of your own, do you understand?"

Kiara's eyes flickered from Rob to Dan and back to Rob again. "I'll go out and look for a job," she said quickly. She remembered that one day when she had been delivering she had seen a man with a guitar singing on the sidewalk outside one of the subway stations, people dropping some coins into his case as they passed. "I can sing on the street, that might make some money?" she added, hopefully.

Rob frowned. "You're not getting it are you? I'm not talking about twenty bucks here and there Kiara, that won't make a tiny fucking difference. You need to earn proper money."

Kiara was starting to panic, her voice lowered and eyes towards the floor, staring fixedly at the smear of blood dried into the thin carpet, she said "What is it you want me to do?", picturing the women drifting on the streets at night, leaning into car windows as they rolled by, and she silently prayed, *please not that, anything but that.*

Dan gave an annoyed sigh. "Do we need to spell it out?" he slurred.

Rob put a hand on her shoulder and gave her a nudge. She looked up at him, tears streaking down her cheeks. "Please," she whimpered, "I can't have sex for money, I can't be one of those hookers on the street, please."

"It's not that bad. You could get at least $50 for a blowjob, probably more, and they only last a few minutes," Dan said, twisting his pulped flesh into a grin.

Kiara gazed at him, horrified. Dan glared back at her. "You can't freeload forever. You've got to pay your way."

Rob interrupted. "Shut up Dan. I'm not sending her out on the street corners, okay?"

Kiara looked at him mutely. "Listen, your friends work in a club, right?" She nodded. Rob's voice had softened, gently cajoling her. "They can get you a place there, can't they? It's just dancing. You can do that, can't you, to help us out?" She nodded again, her mind wheeling, unable to speak.

"Good." Rob turned back to Dan. "Okay?"

Dan shrugged. "Sure. Let's get back to the real business. We've got a lot to do."

"Kiara – go talk to your friends now." Ordering her out, Rob turned back to the piece of paper and he and Dan started working out what they could get and what favours they were owed.

Kiara uncurled her legs, stinging with pins and needles, and went to the bathroom to wash her face and clean her teeth. She sat on the toilet seat, lid down, and pressed her hands over her eyes, trying to stop the tears. Her mind frantically running through all her options, she tried to think of what she could do. She had nowhere else to go and no one else to turn to. Betty and Veronica had no room with Suyapa already sleeping on the couch, and she couldn't ask more of them than they had already given.

Could she go home? She took a few deep breaths and tried to think about contacting the Jacobs. She knew that she would have to tell them why she ran away in the first place, they would make her talk to the police and she would have to relive all over again what that man, and her father, did to her. And then the police would start asking questions about where she had been these past ten months, Rob's name would get dragged into it, and they would go to jail. She saw herself, pale-faced and dressed in an orange jumpsuit, Janet and Victor disappointed, Shane unable to bring himself to visit her in jail, and the other women would gather round Janet and tut and shake their heads and tell her that they were right all along about Kiara Anderson.

Kiara put her hands on her knees and steadied herself. She knew what she had to do. She headed to Betty and Veronica's.

Six years ago – The Jacobs

The music pounded in the air and leapt out into the night sky, lights sparkling like gem stones around the rooftop bar, surrounded by the city skyline.

"Happy birthday!" Sarah's friends shouted out as her favourite song came on. They danced in a group on the dance floor, purses in the middle, laughing and singing and trying not to fall over. Sarah raised her arms and whooped happily. Celebrating being twenty-one and surrounded by her best friends, in one of New York's hottest rooftop bars, she felt that life couldn't get any better.

Her friends got her more drinks and the music thumped on into the night.

Six years ago – Kiara

Kiara's feet were aching, the balls of her feet burning, as she shifted from one foot to another and counted out her tips for the night. It had been a fairly good night and only one client had been an asshole, but security was always on hand to haul the clients out if they got rough.

The lights had come on and the girls were gathering their purses and jackets to leave. Betty walked up to Kiara. "Ready to go?"

Kiara nodded. "Sure."

They headed out of the club, saying goodnight to the doorman, the 4am sky still dark and the sunrise still only a distant glimmer on the horizon.

"My feet are killing me," Kiara said, hobbling slightly.

Betty laughed. "I know. Mine always hurt too!"

They linked arms to hold each other up, talking tiredly as they walked home together. Kiara didn't know what she would have done without Betty and Veronica's help. They had introduced her to the club's owner, who didn't even bother checking her real age, and Betty had given her clothes and shoes to wear for her first few shifts.

Betty and Veronica had taught her what clients wanted, how to make them stay and keep tipping. Kiara had listened to them in frightened silence and seeing her discomfort they tried to help her prepare before her first shift. When they had asked if she was a virgin she had turned bright red, stammering that she'd had sex, "just the once." She didn't tell them the experience had been forced upon her.

Even though she had been there a while now, the club still made her skin crawl, with its faux-leather seats, cheap carpet, and the cloying smell of perfume and sweat. She tried to pretend she was someone else when she was there and called herself Krystal. On her first night she had been terrified, awkward and trembling, spilling a drink on one client, too shaky to move with ease in her heels. The other women in the club had laughed at her but Betty had taken her arm, whispered encouragement in her ear, and picturing what Dan had wanted her to do gave her the strength to plaster on a fake smile and try to summon some enthusiasm. She knew that acting like she enjoyed it was a way of boosting her tips, so she laughed and flirted with clients even while her stomach was clenching and she wanted to flinch away from their stares.

Lots of the men were pretty docile and she was surprised how many had wedding rings on. Most of them just wanted a dance, although there were a few who had paid her to sit and talk to them, seeking what Veronica called the "girlfriend experience". Kiara guessed they were just lonely and she felt sad for them, but she was glad to take the money from them without having to dance.

Rob and Dan were pleased with the money she had started bringing back. She gave most of it to them and kept a little so she could buy her own clothes, shoes and makeup and not have to rely on Betty and Veronica for those. They had scrabbled around for a week or so, gathering up unpaid debts, borrowing money, appeasing the clients who had lost out, and making up for it so they didn't lose business. Things were still fraught, and Rob and Dan were much more tense than usual, but they were getting by. She had no love for Dan after what he had suggested but she was grateful to Rob for all he had done, and glad she could help him.

She left Betty at her apartment and let herself in to Rob's place. Dan was chilling in the living room with a friend of his, high and languid on weed. He looked at her through narrowed eyes as she came in, giving her a lazy grin. "Here she is," he said, nudging his friend with his elbow.

"Hey, how much for a dance?" his friend said, and they both laughed.

"Go to hell," Kiara said, grabbing a bottle of vodka from the fridge and heading for Rob's room, where he was splayed out on one of the mattresses, deep in sleep. She sat on the other mattress and leaned up against the wall in the dark, prising off her heels, and covering her legs with a blanket. She swigged from the bottle several times, holding it close to her, then drank some more, willing sleep to come soon.

She didn't like to close her eyes until she felt sleep already coming over her, for she saw too many faces in her imagination, her father, Shane, Victor, the men in the club, and worst of all, the face of the man who raped her, and he was always laughing. She forced her eyes open till her lids dropped like weights and the faces melted away to nothing.

Five years ago – The Jacobs

"Tomorrow's the big day. Nervous?" Victor grinned at Shane. Shane was staying over at his parents' house the few days before the wedding while Melanie finalised arrangements and had her bridal party gathered together. It had taken them two years to plan the wedding in the end, but Shane had been happy to leave Melanie to make most of the arrangements.

"Nope, can't wait," Shane smiled, and leaned back with a glass of single malt that his dad only opened on very special occasions. "Were you nervous before you married mom?" he asked.

Victor laughed. "Terrified. I just couldn't believe she was going to marry me till she actually said, 'I do'."

"Did your dad talk to you about it the night before, like we're doing now?" Shane said, cautiously. He never usually asked his dad about his past, but he was desperately curious and thought this might be a good time for his dad to open up.

Victor was silent for a moment, the hands of the clock in his study gently tapping away the passing seconds. "No, I didn't invite him to the wedding," he said, finally. "Come to think of it, he wasn't around for anything that was important in my life, and if he was, he was too drunk to remember it," he continued thoughtfully, swilling the whiskey around his glass, the amber liquid flashing in the lamplight.

Shane nodded.

"Just like Bill Anderson," his dad added.

They sipped their drinks in silence.

"I wanted to make it better for Kiara than it was for me," Victor said. "I guess I failed," he sighed heavily.

Shane shook his head. "Don't dad, don't blame yourself. We don't know why she left," he said, thinking of that moment by the pool when he watched her walk away.

"Do you still have a place for her in the seating chart?" Victor asked.

"Yep. Melanie was not impressed." Shane laughed. "She doesn't want an empty place."

"I wish it weren't going to be empty."

"Me too."

Victor looked at his son and raised his glass. "To absent friends."

Four years ago – Kiara

The fall skies were clear over the city as Kiara woke in the early afternoon. She stretched out on the mattress, her knees sore from her shift the night before and her head tired and heavy from the remnants of last night's vodka. Now that she was working, she didn't help Rob and Dan so much with their side of things, although they still asked her to from time to time if they really needed her. She tended to get home around 4.30am, and sleep till noon at least, then go out to buy food. Customers always came and went from the apartment, and she tidied up around them while Rob or Dan dealt with them. She often stopped by to see her friends across the hall in the late afternoons, and usually either Betty or Veronica was on shift with her so they would walk together to the club in the evening.

Yawning, she walked to the kitchen and poured herself some coffee, smiling at Rob as she entered.

"Hey Kiara, a word?" he said to her, running his hands through his lank and greasy hair.

She sat next to him on the couch, blowing gently on the hot coffee. "What's up?"

"Listen, I have some news for you," he began, awkwardly. She looked at him expectantly, eyebrows raised.

"Your dad died," he said softly, looking at his knees.

Kiara froze, her fingers tightening around the burning porcelain cup in her hand. "When? How do you know?" she said, ignoring the heat starting to tingle on her hands.

"A guy I know was passing through near there and I asked him to see if the old man was still around. Turns out he died just a few weeks ago. I guess no one knows where you are to tell you."

Kiara let out a long slow breath. She supposed she should feel sad but all she felt was a sense of relief. He was gone. She wondered if at any moment he had thought about her or had any regrets. Now she would never get the chance to find out, not that she ever intended to talk to him again anyway. Even though she knew he was dead, there was still an icy flame of hatred in her heart. She couldn't forgive him for what he did, but at least he had taken her secret and her shame with him. Now there was only one other person in the world who knew what had happened in her bedroom that night and she had no idea who he was.

After a few minutes of silence, Rob nudged her with a skinny elbow. "You okay?"

"Yup," she nodded.

"I'm sorry."

"Don't be," she said, shrugging her shoulders. Turning to meet Rob's eyes, she said: "Does your friend pass by there often?"

"Nope, but it could be arranged…"

"Could he take me?" she asked.

"I'll take you myself if that's what you want."

They arranged it for two night's time, Rob procuring a car from a friend, Kiara arranging a free shift, and Dan agreeing to cover the apartment.

***

They drove in silence at 1am, the radio turned low, Kiara watching the river drop away, the glowing city spires lit up behind them as they wound their way through suburbs. As they got closer her nerves grew and she slouched low in the seat.

"Did you want to go to the cemetery?" Rob glanced over at her.

"Nope. Just take me to the trailer, if it's still there."

Rob drove past the driveways she remembered from only a few years before, gated enclaves to cut-off worlds, the Jacobs' driveway flashing by before they were ascending the dirt path up to the trailer. Rob cut the lights and drove slowly, rolling up gently besides her childhood home.

"Want me to come in with you?"

"Nope. I won't be long." She shut the car door softly. Before she went to the trailer, she headed down the path to the old gate and opened it just enough to poke her head round to gaze at the Jacobs' house. All the windows were darkened. She doubted that Shane and Sarah lived there anymore, but perhaps Victor and Janet still did. She could smell the roses on the fall air, breathed it in and smiled, remembering Ted and Janet's constant fussing over those plants. She shut the gate and walked back to the trailer where Rob was standing outside with a cigarette, puffing out long white streams of smoke.

Heading inside, she went straight to her room. It was empty. The bastard had literally thrown away everything that she had ever owned or touched. She rested her head on the plastic doorframe. No matter how far in time she travelled away from what had happened that night, the memory always threatened to break back in from where she had locked it away. She moved on and checked her dad's room, where there were a few dirty sheets on the bed and a pile of clothes on the floor. She didn't stop to explore further. Just the smell of the place made her head reel with memories and she felt tears threaten the backs of her eyes.

Blinking hard, she took off the backpack she had brought with her and began pulling out what she needed. She stood in the doorway of her father's bedroom and squirted lighter fluid over the sheets, the bed, and the clothes on the floor. She walked through, draining the first bottle and starting the second, finishing the third bottle on the couch, then she disconnected the gas in the kitchen. Walking outside she grabbed the gas canisters from underneath and lugged them away from the trailer, Rob helping her unquestioningly when he finished his cigarette. She wanted the place to burn, but she didn't want to create a massive explosion near the Jacobs' house.

She nodded at Rob and he got back in the car and started the engine, ready to go. She held a match to the couch and the flame jumped and burned hungrily, tearing through the cheap fabric, black smoke rising, the fire dancing down the length of the carpet as she shut the trailer door and got in the car. Rob drove her away quickly, an orange glow throbbing behind them as they zoomed back to the city.

Four years ago – The Jacobs

"The police said it was definitely deliberate," Janet said, passing round the asparagus.

"Good grief." Alma paled beneath her makeup and fanned herself gently. "I hope they don't strike anywhere else."

"The weird thing is that the police said the gas canisters were all removed before the trailer was set on fire and the gas was switched off in the kitchen too. They said it was strange for the person who did this to be so careful. Normally arson is spur of the moment, quick and unplanned," Victor said, swirling red wine round his glass.

"Anyway, can we talk about something more pleasant please?" Melanie frowned.

"Of course, darling, like celebrating your first anniversary!" Alma replied, smiling at her daughter, her bright coral lips widening.

"Congratulations!" Jade lifted her glass and clinked it across with her sister's. The rest followed suit – Jade, Sarah and her fiancée Tim, Alma and Kent, Victor and Janet, and Melanie and Shane.

They started eating, Victor and Kent discussing the latest issues at the local golf club, Janet and Alma reminiscing about the wedding last year. Jade, Sarah and Melanie chatted about Sarah's upcoming wedding in the spring of next year – the next big event.

Shane was silent, frowning at his plate. "It doesn't make any sense."

Melanie looked at him in surprise. "What do you mean? Duck goes perfectly with asparagus."

Shane shook his head. "Why would they remove the gas canisters if it was some random act of arson? And it's a bit of a coincidence isn't it, just two weeks after Bill died?"

The table fell silent and Shane looked around. "I mean, what if it was her?"

Sarah nudged him. "Shane, it's just something that happened. Why would Kiara come back and burn down the trailer? She wouldn't do that."

"How the hell do we know what she would and wouldn't do? We still don't know why she left!" Victor put up a hand to stop him, but he raised his voice and continued. "It's been years. She could be a completely different person by now, for all we know."

Janet leaned across the table and spoke to him softly. "We'll talk about this later Shane."

Sitting back upright, she smiled brightly at her guests. "More wine?"

***

"Are you going to tell me what that was all about?" Tim asked Sarah, as she emerged from the bathroom adjoining her old bedroom. The room was still pretty much as she left it before she went to college. Tim looked out of place sitting shirtless on her childhood bed, where she had spent many hours giggling with girlfriends about boys.

Sarah sighed as she sat on the bed and started rubbing lotion on her arms. "You remember that girl I told you about? The neighbour we used to look after a lot?"

Tim nodded. "Sure. The redhead in the photos, right?"

"Yeah, Kiara. Well, the trailer she used to live in was burned down a few days ago."

"I understood that. I meant I didn't get what Shane was talking about. I thought Kiara was dead." He looked at her questioningly.

"Oh. Why would you think that?"

"Well, she's clearly not around anymore, and you guys always talk about her in such a weird way, I just assumed…"

Sarah moved on to moisturising her legs and feet and, after a moment, she turned to Tim with a sigh. "We don't know if she's dead or not. She ran away years ago when she was seventeen. We never knew why and we've never heard from her since." She shook her head, sadly. "I don't like to talk about it. It's too awful."

"I'm so sorry. That's terrible." Tim wrapped his arms around her and pulled her close, kissing her on the neck. She smelled of jasmine and honeysuckle, warm and summery.

She rested her head on his chest. "Shane is still convinced she's alive."

"And you?" Tim murmured into the top of her head.

"I don't know. I want to think she's still alive. But…" she sat upright to look at Tim. "I'm afraid to think of what might have happened to her."

"A scary thought," he nodded.

"Let's go to bed," she said, not wanting to think about Kiara anymore. When Kiara had first left she had spent nights kept awake by what ifs and dark imaginings, running over that last night and thinking that she could have made a difference if she hadn't gone off with Melanie, if she had just hung out with Kiara and shown her how much she mattered to them. With the passing of the years she had tried to let the thoughts of Kiara fade out of her mind. The sadness and the guilt were too exhausting.

***

Shane leaned back and stared at the glittering expanse above him. Slowly and methodically, he picked the label off his beer, peeling shreds off and adding them to a small papery pile on the side of the pool lounger. He knew he was grasping at straws, but his instinct whispered louder than his logic and told him Kiara had been there. He had been to the trailer site later that evening – roped off by police, it was a hulking black shell of ash and ruin, the trees and the earth around it scorched and burnt. He had looked vainly for any sign that she had been there. He didn't know what he had been hoping to find, and he found nothing anyway.

Shane looked up as he heard heels tapping towards him.

"Shouldn't you be with Melanie?" Janet said, smiling, and sat on the lounger next to him, kicking off her nude heels.

"I'll go up in a minute."

"Thinking about Kiara?"

"Yup," he nodded.

"Me too. Sometimes I almost forget how long it's been and then I remember." She looked over at him. "Four years this fall since she left." She dabbed at the corners of her eyes with her index finger, blotting away the tears.

Shane didn't reply, and glumly continued to peel the label until only a sticky residue remained on the bottle where it had once been.

"I went to the trailer after Bill died," Janet said.

Shane looked at his mom in surprise. "You did? What for?"

"I wanted to see if there were any clues to where she might be. I thought maybe she might have written to him and he just didn't tell us, or maybe he had an address somewhere written down."

"And?"

She gave a short laugh. "Nothing."

They sat in silence for a few moments. "I did make sure to clear out her things though. There wasn't much there, but what there was I took," she said.

"Wow mom, good thinking." Shane nodded in approval.

"I know I probably shouldn't have done that," she shrugged, "but I want to make sure someone who loved her has her things."

"What was there?"

"Oh, almost nothing. A few old clothes, a few books, school stuff. But I did find her notebooks. Did you know she used to write songs?"

He grinned. "Yeah. She told me some of the lyrics sometimes. I used to sing them back to her in a stupid voice to make her laugh."

He smiled at the memory, Kiara holding her sides, shrieking and giggling, begging him to stop.

"I still think she might come back for them one day. But until then, you need to focus on what you have in the here and now Shane. So, go upstairs to Melanie and enjoy the rest of your anniversary. Mom's orders." She winked at him and walked back to the house.

Once inside, she went to the spare bedroom, flicking on the light and closing the door behind her. She opened up the closet. The blue dress Kiara had worn on the night of her performance still hung there, patiently awaiting another outing, hopeful and vanilla-scented. Underneath there was a small bundle of gifts, carefully wrapped for Christmas and birthdays but never opened.

She reached in and took out a small plastic bag with a few meagre possessions inside. When she had gone to the trailer she had hoped to find something more but, like Shane, she had been disappointed. If this were a film there would have been clues, someone smart would have found something to lead them to her, but this wasn't a film and she found nothing to tell her where Kiara might be.

She flipped open one of the notebooks. There were pages of lyrics, scribblings, crossing-outs, corrections, doodles, and rhymes, some good, some bad, then a whole page of hearts with only one name written inside them. She smiled and closed the notebook. She had thought about showing it to him, but even with Kiara gone, it still wasn't her secret to tell. Maybe Kiara would come back one day and tell him herself.

Three years ago – Kiara

"Kiara," Veronica hissed in her ear, "there's that customer who likes you." She nodded in the direction of the bar.

Kiara scanned the room and saw one of her regulars sitting at the bar. Cherise was already talking to him, but he was shaking his head, waiting for Kiara to be free. She strolled over, giving Cherise a glare.

"Thanks Cherise, I'll take it from here," she said, and leaned on the bar next to her customer, a thick-set, balding man named Roger. He had walked into the club a few months ago looking completely lost and clearly uncomfortable, and Kiara had been one of the first to walk up to him. It turned out all he wanted was some company. Now he came in once or twice a week to see her, to sit and talk, buying drinks and tipping her generously for doing pretty much nothing.

At first, she had thought he was a creep. She got enough of them here, middle-aged men who tried to run their hands over her body or start touching themselves, and she would see the club lights shining off their wedding rings and sometimes think that there were no truly decent men.

Roger, newly divorced and deeply depressed, was a dream customer compared to them, and he liked to sit with a whiskey sour and talk to her about sport. Kiara kept up with sports news obsessively – she knew who was represented by Jacobs Sports Management and was always rooting for Victor and Shane's sign-ups to do well.

She had seen Victor and Shane on TV more than once. The first few times she saw them it had felt like a cold slap in the face, but after that she found it oddly comforting to see them both smiling, successful, and well. Betty used Facebook and Kiara had once asked her to check if Shane and Sarah had profiles. Kiara scrolled down their feeds, her heart aching, hungrily soaking up their lives, the birthdays, Shane's wedding, Sarah's engagement, vacation photos. She didn't ask Betty again, content just to know they were all okay, and not wanting to torture herself further.

"Drink?" Roger asked her. "Sure, a vodka soda would be great thanks," Kiara nodded, and perched on a stool next to him at the bar. She knew the bartender would just give her soda. She never drank while she was working – you could easily lose control of a situation if you didn't have your wits about you.

"How are you doing?" she said, smiling at Roger, sipping her drink.

"Well, it looks like my divorce will leave me with almost nothing. Apart from that, it's going great," he said, voice laden with sarcasm. He rubbed his eyes wearily.

"Tell me your thoughts on this year's Yankees line-up Krystal," he said. She nodded. JSM had a few Yankees players on their books, so she had been following their progress through the season closely.

"How old are you?" Roger interrupted her and leaned forward, squinting at her in the dim lights.

"How old do you think I am?" she said, coquettishly. Roger shrugged and frowned a little. "Too young to be here, that's for sure."

She shook her head, keeping a smile on her face.

"Seriously. How old are you? How'd you end up here?" he demanded. He sometimes got a bit personal when the drink kicked in, although he was never rude, just too curious for comfort.

"Now Roger, you don't want to know about my boring life, do you? Let's talk about you." She smiled and giggled flirtatiously, trying to put him at ease.

"I'd say you were nineteen, perhaps twenty," he said, still squinting at her face.

She sighed. "I'll be twenty-two this year, alright? Now quit asking me questions Roger, you know it's not polite." She mock-scolded, waggling a finger at him, and he grinned and relaxed. "Yeah, sure, sorry, sorry," he said, holding up his hands in apology.

They talked for a while, but the club was starting to fill up and Kiara wanted to move on. She didn't like to spend too long with one customer when there were others waiting, as they could get fed up and leave. She hopped off the stool and waved him goodbye, collecting the money he tipped her and thanking him. She worked the room, a few floor dances, one private. She had a quick break, then more dances.

She and Veronica left the club together after closing, comparing their take for the night, when Kiara heard her name being called.

"Krystal!" It was Roger, walking quickly after them, huffing a little, though they weren't going fast.

"*Dios mío!* Creep, creep!" Veronica whispered in her ear. Kiara tensed, glad she was with Veronica. This had happened before, and just in case they always carried pepper spray in their purses. Her hand found the cylinder in her purse and she curled her fingers round it, ready.

Roger wheezed up to them. "I'm sorry, I don't, I mean…" he puffed, trying to catch his breath.

Veronica tightened her fingers round Kiara's arm.

"Krystal, sorry to chase after you. I just… listen, I work in a hotel, well you already knew that, and…"

Kiara raised an eyebrow. Maybe this guy was trying to ask her on a date or perhaps he thought she was a hooker as well? She bit her lip nervously, glancing at Veronica, who was staring at her with a pained expression on her face.

"We're looking for bar staff, and, well, that's why I wanted to know your age, you see, you're over twenty-one, so I thought maybe you might be interested?" Roger burbled nervously and waved a hotel card at her. Kiara took it, surprised. "I could put in a good word for you with the manager, you know, as a thank you for listening to me all these months," he added, hopefully.

Kiara opened her mouth, but all that came out was a soft "oh". Veronica spoke for her, "That is so sweet of you, thank you, now we have to go. Goodnight," she span on her heel and yanked Kiara with her, practically pulling her off balance.

"Call the hotel and ask for Roger Miller if you're interested!" he yelled after them.

***

"Oh my god, that didn't happen?" Betty threw back her head and laughed. Kiara had stopped by the following afternoon to say hello and Veronica had recounted the story in dramatic fashion. Kiara couldn't stop laughing, holding onto her cheeks as they ached.

"It was nothing like that Veronica!" she shrieked, alarming Isaac, who was playing with his toys, and he looked up at them with wide dark eyes.

It took them a while to calm down. Betty and Veronica were in good moods as the journey for their brothers had finally been arranged. They were waiting to hear from them when they reached Guatemala and headed towards Mexico.

"Kiara, are you going to call him?" Betty asked, when they had finally stopped laughing.

Kiara wrinkled her nose. "What? No! He's probably a serial killer who wants to make drapes out of my skin. No way."

Veronica started laughing again. Betty turned the hotel card over in her hands. "C'mon Kiara, it's a real hotel, I've heard of it. Maybe you should give them a call? He obviously wants to do you a favour and maybe you should take it."

Kiara took the card back, a tasteful black background with white cursive script on the front. Hotel Leighton, on the Upper East Side.

"I just… I don't think this is for me. I don't know anything about bar work, I have no references, and my only experience is delivering drugs and being a stripper, so my resume doesn't exactly scream 'classy bartender' does it?" she said, unhappily.

"Yeah but he said he would put in a good word for you! Maybe he can pull some strings," Betty said, enthusiastically.

"And for what in return?" Veronica said, making a face. "No guy is going to offer a stripper something without expecting something back."

Kiara nodded. "Exactly. He'd definitely want me to sleep with him, at least once. If not more."

Betty shook her head. "Don't be so negative. Call him and at least see what happens. *Quién sabe?*"

She grabbed Kiara's cell phone from her purse and shoved it across the table. Kiara sat there, tapping a fingernail against the shiny table, hesitating. "Fine," she said, grabbing the phone and dialling the number.

"Hotel Leighton," a woman answered, sounding tinny and distant. Kiara pressed her cell to her ear. "Ermm good afternoon, can I speak to Roger Miller please?"

***

"Hey Rob, can we talk?"

It was a warm evening and the windows were open, street murmurs and car horns outside rising up in the darkness. Rob had just finished with a few clients and was settling down with some weed. Dan was out delivering and Kiara had been helping out.

"Sure," Rob said, and offered her the weed, but she shook her head. "Still not into smoking anything huh?" he smiled at her refusal. Kiara shrugged, she'd kept to her determination not to smoke and ruin her voice, not that she did much singing these days. Aside from depending on vodka to help calm herself to sleep every night, she had managed to avoid most of the drugs in the apartment, though Rob always offered, and she had tried acid and coke with him a few times.

Coke was a great pick-me-up for when she had a shift and the night before had been a bad one, riven with nightmares that even the vodka couldn't stave off, when she would wake up screaming and chilled with sweat. Those nights exhausted her and a quick bump of coke brought her right back, crackling with energy for her shift. She was determined not to do acid again though – one bad trip had freaked her out for days afterwards and intensified her nightmares.

She sat next to Rob. "I've been offered a job in a hotel bar."

He pressed his lips into a thin line, "Hmmm."

"It doesn't pay anywhere near as much as what I'm getting in the club, but it's a proper job, in a decent place where I won't have to take my clothes off or get grabbed at. And I can't let this chance go by," she said quickly, looking at the ground and wanting to get out the words she had mentally rehearsed in the bathroom.

She couldn't quite believe that anyone would offer her a proper job, with her lack of experience and references, but Roger had been as good as his word, arranging for her to meet the bar manager and giving her tips on what to say. The manager, a short and gruff man named Hal, loved to talk about sports, and was thrilled to find a female bartender who could discuss it with him, as well as being a pretty face for the customers. She had misjudged Roger too, who asked for nothing in return, who just felt sorry for her working at the club and wanted to do something to help her out. He wasn't surprised when she told him that Krystal had been a fake name either.

Veronica and Betty had been thrilled for her. She knew they would leave the club too if they didn't need so much money right now. Hopefully when their brothers arrived they would be able to move on, like her, to something better.

Rob breathed out a cloud of smoke. "You know Dan'll be pissed, right?"

"Listen Rob, you said it was just while you guys got yourselves sorted after that robbery. Well, it's been years I've been working in that club and I've given you both thousands of dollars. You're doing okay now and I want to get out of there. Period. I'll still pay rent,

I'll pay for food, I'll help you guys out when I can, anything you need. But I want to get out of that club."

Rob nodded, smiling at his cousin who was no longer so meek and afraid. "Okay. I'll square it with Dan. You do what you need to do."

She grinned at him and wrapped her arms around his thin frame in a quick hug. "Piss off," he said, laughing.

Three years ago – The Jacobs

Jade kissed her sister on the cheek. "How's it all been Mel? I bet you're exhausted, right?"

Melanie glanced over at the bassinet as she heard the baby stirring but he stilled and she turned back to Jade with a smile. "So tired. But Janet and mom have been around so much to help." She took a sip of hot tea. "I'm so glad you could come and visit."

Jade had flown in from Milan, where she lived with her husband, a wealthy Italian art dealer. She rarely visited but was glad to make a quick trip back to see her new nephew.

"How's Shane adjusting?" she asked, folding her legs up onto the leather couch in Melanie's tasteful living room.

"He's good. He's great with Joshua, completely crazy about him." Melanie smiled, running her crimson fingernails through her dark hair, cropped into a shiny bob with fashionable bangs falling over her green eyes.

"Can I hold him now please?" Jade said, holding her arms out, grinning. She had no intention of having children, but she was happy to have a quick cuddle with her nephew while he was still cute and small.

Melanie reached into the bassinet and gently passed the baby to Jade. He screwed up his mouth and fists as if to cry, face reddening, but then relaxed again, wriggling slightly as Jade took him. He half-opened his eyes, a flash of dark green, and a blond wisp gently poked out from underneath his baby hat as it slipped slightly to one side.

Melanie sighed. "Life's just perfect."

Three years ago – Kiara

Christmas lights flashed in the bar, lighting the faces of customers red and green. It was extremely busy in the bar leading up to the holidays. Kiara had shifts every night and loved the incessant buzz and the freedom she felt from having to offer up her body. She finished in the early hours of the morning weary but peaceful, sitting on the subway back to Hunts Point with a sense of calm, a slight darkening of dread only entering her mind as she walked down the Avenue to the apartment.

She never quite knew who would be there or what would be happening when she got home, if Dan would be high or shouting angrily as she walked through the door, or if Rob would be there to give her a lazy smile and a nonchalant shrug of his thin shoulders to welcome her back. Still, she paid her way, gave them as much as she could, and tried to keep a little for herself tucked into a slit she had torn in the mattress she used in Rob's room.

The bar regularly hosted live singers. She stared jealously at them as she served customers, the bright-faced red-lipped singers, talented young women her age, scraping by in the city on a performer's wage, but there in the spotlight and radiating joy with every beat. Every chord awoke a longing in her heart to feel the piano keys under her fingers again, to lean into the microphone, to soar away with the key changes to some better place that she had tasted briefly that night performing at high school. She would give anything to get that feeling back again – better and stronger and purer than any drug Rob could get her. But instead she whipped round the bar as customers pressed in to shout their orders at her, their hot breath and cologne in the air, the residue from drinks making the bar sticky and transferring to her fingers, her palms tacky with soda.

Two weeks before Christmas, the bar was packed with after-work drinkers, their shirts opened at the collar, ties loosened. Hal walked in with a face set like stone, tension gathering around his mouth, and slammed an empty glass down on the counter.

"Fucking band. Double-booked," he huffed angrily, his thick grey eyebrows drawn down over his watery brown eyes, a red tinge creeping up the back of his neck.

Jess, another bartender, raised her eyebrows at Kiara and turned away to serve another customer. They both knew to avoid Hal when he was annoyed, as he could be brutally caustic, taking his anger out on any staff close by. Michael brushed by Kiara, whispering "red alert!" in her ear.

Kiara liked her new colleagues. They were around her age, some were students doing a shift here and there for extra cash. They made her laugh, bought her a round of drinks on her twenty-second birthday, and invited her out with them on nights out. She never went but felt a tiny bit of normality transferring from them to her

121

when she was with them, though that feeling of normality wore off as soon as she returned to the apartment.

Kiara glanced at the stage and at Hal. There was an opportunity – an empty piano, a silent microphone. Drawing a breath, she stepped to his side, ignoring the customers trying to catch her eye.

"Hey Hal?" she said, speaking loudly into his ear.

"Be quick," he said.

"Want me to sing tonight?" The words tumbled out, quick and slippery, no taking them back.

Hal looked at her incredulously. "Have you gone insane? I hire you to serve drinks, not to do low-rate karaoke. Get back to the customers before there's a riot."

Kiara nodded and moved away, but went straight back to Hal again, compelled, unwilling to let the chance to chase that amazing feeling pass her by so easily.

"Let me do two songs. If they don't like it, or you don't like it, I'll come straight back off," she said, hopefully.

"No!" Hal roared back at her, making her jump. Some of the customers laughed, and a few looked at her uneasily, gave wanly sympathetic smiles and waved their credit cards at her.

Kiara hurried back to the bar, her face burning and eyes prickling. Breathing hard, she served with extra energy and a wider smile than before. Jess put a hand on her shoulder as she passed behind her, giving her a squeeze of solidarity.

Two hours later, the bar was settling into a smoother, slower late-night rhythm, drinkers stumbling outside for taxis home, or bracing the cold to go to a club, when Hal came up to her.

"Go on. If you're shit I'll fire you." He nodded his head towards the stage, where the piano sat alone and gleaming at her.

She grinned and hopped up. A few of the staff watched with interest as she adjusted the piano seat. She looked down at the keys and felt a tremor in her hands, a flutter in her chest. What if she couldn't do it anymore? It had been years since she played or sang, except when she sang nursery rhymes to Isaac and Suyapa would sigh that she had the "*voz de un ángel*".

Softly, she began to play the chords for a song she had practiced often and hoped would flow back to her as her fingers moved across the keys. November Rain, one of Shane's favourites. She pressed into the solidity of the keys, feeling the notes rise around her, vibrating through her, and sang it her way, gentle and slow, with a sonorous vibrato in the lower register.

The applause when she finished was enthusiastic, Jess whooped from the bar and even Hal nodded and smiled. She carried on. She loved the older classics that she used to listen to with Janet, like Bill Withers, Randy Crawford, and the British and rock bands that Shane had favoured. She had practiced them over and over, spending hours alone in the Jacobs' dining room when other kids were out with friends. Closing her eyes, she could almost imagine she was there now.

She played until the lights came up in the bar, the last few customers drifted out, and she gently closed the lid on the keys. Hal came up to her. "Good job Kiara. Maybe I'll let you play again sometime."

Two years ago – Kiara

"You ever thought about being a singer for real?" Jess asked Kiara as they stacked empty glasses at the bar.

Kiara shook her head. "Maybe when I was younger, but not anymore."

She waved goodnight to Roger, who was leaving for the night. He often stopped by the bar and sat quietly with a whiskey sour. Kiara always comped him a drink and made time to have a chat before he left, ever grateful for the job he got her.

She wiped down one of the tables, sweeping across the puddles of drinks and fragments of nuts with a warm damp cloth, the smell of cleaning fluid mixed with the sweetness of soda and stale alcohol.

"How come?"

"How come what?"

Jess sighed and rolled her eyes. "How come you don't want to be a singer?"

"Ermm, just not something I've thought about really." Kiara frowned. She would still love to sing but since she ran away her main thought had been self-protection and survival, rather than chasing childhood dreams. Too much had happened for her to think it was even possible now, and she especially didn't think any record company would be interested in a former stripper who lived with drug dealers.

"But you're really good," Jess interrupted her thoughts, smiling.

"She's right!" called out Wendy, another one of the bartenders.

Jess fished in her pocket and pulled out a crumpled, shiny poster. "Look Kiara, there was this guy here earlier listening to you, and he had to get going but he gave me this to give to you when you finished."

Jess shoved the poster at her. "See, this amazing club is holding open auditions to form a girl group for performing there. You definitely should try out – that guy seemed really keen for you to come along."

She shoved the poster at Kiara, who smoothed it out. "What guy?"

Jess sighed. "I don't know. Some customer – dark hair, really good-looking."

Kiara paused and read the poster. "They're looking for singers who can dance," she said.

"So? Try anyway, it can't hurt."

Kiara bit her lip and carefully folded the poster into her pocket. Maybe she would think about it.

They finished cleaning the bar, stacking away the hot glasses fresh from the dishwasher, a soapy steam rising from them as they stood on the bar. Kiara said goodnight and headed home, staring at the poster on the subway the whole way, her mind arguing back and forth about whether or not to audition.

***

The following week she was standing in line outside the club doors at 11am, forty girls in front of her, applying lip gloss, tossing their hair, shifting on high heels, chattering and laughing. She stood silently, nerves lingering in her chest as she folded and unfolded the poster and thought about leaving. Singing and dancing in a group was so far out of her comfort zone, she wouldn't even know where to begin.

She took a deep breath and made up her mind to leave, starting to turn on her heel to walk away, when she was tapped on the shoulder by the person behind her, a stunning black woman with gleaming skin and a riot of black curls crackling round her head. She wore ripped denim shorts and a bright beaded top. She looked confident, comfortable and perfect for a girl group, and Kiara felt completely lost and inadequate standing there in front of her.

"Yeah?" she said, staring wide-eyed at the girl.

"Do you have gum?" the girl asked, and smiled, a big bright smile that lit her up like the sun.

"Sure, only cinnamon though," Kiara dug in her purse and handed her a stick of cinnamon gum.

"Thanks!" The girl unwrapped it and popped it in her mouth. "I'm Alicia."

"I'm Kiara."

Kiara stood awkwardly for a moment before she realised the line of girls had moved in front of her, a gap opening up.

"You gonna move up?" Alicia said.

"Um, yep." Kiara shuffled to close the gap. She was still thinking about leaving when Alicia started chatting away to her about how nervous she was, and how her family weren't sure that she was doing the right thing, but here she was, ignoring their advice. She was disarmingly honest and open, talking without expecting a response except for the occasional nod from Kiara.

"You nervous?" Alicia asked her, seeing her shuffling from one foot to another.

Kiara nodded. "I've never auditioned for anything before. I'm not sure if I've worn the right clothes," she said, miserably. Looking around she felt that she wasn't dressed quite right. Her short skirt and tube top looked like stripper clothes, they were too cheap, too shiny, too clingy, her heels too high, the earrings Betty lent her too big.

Alicia looked her up and down.

"Um, don't worry too much about that. Just sing and dance your best and who knows!"

Kiara nodded and listened as Alicia carried on talking as they moved slowly forwards.

***

"What do you think Marco?" Anna leaned across the table as the five girls waited patiently on stage for their decision.

They saw groups of five girls at a time, each with a chance to sing separately, then dancing for a minute at the same time. Marco, Anna and Frank were looking to replace the club's previous group as two of the girls refused to work together anymore and the other had gotten pregnant.

Marco placed his fingertips together and studied the girls. "I like the black girl, blondie in the pink shirt, and the redhead. No to the dirty blond and the brunette – they can't sing."

Anna shook her head. "I don't like the redhead."

Marco looked at her, surprised. "She's the best singer – I saw her at a bar in a hotel. She's really good."

"She dances like a stripper," Anna replied.

"I can work with that," Marco shrugged and grinned.

"It's up to you Frank." Anna and Marco looked at him expectantly. Frank removed his glasses and wiped his nose and called out to the girls, who were waiting anxiously.

"Alright. Black girl, blonde girl in the pink and red girl. You three stay for this afternoon please."

***

Kiara cracked open a can of soda and took small nervous sips. Her next audition was in twenty minutes. She hadn't eaten lunch, her stomach churning over and around inside her, making eating impossible. If she just had to stand there and sing, she would be okay, but being asked to sing and dance that morning had left her legs rubbery and her hands shaking.

Alicia bounded up to her, her hands wrapped round a huge rye sandwich, mustard dripping onto the brown paper bag around it. She sat next to Kiara, stretching out her long legs in front of her, and took a bite.

"Want some?" she offered the sandwich to Kiara, who shook her head.

"I can't believe they asked me to stay," Kiara said. Alicia raised her eyebrows and spoke between mouthfuls of salt beef.

"You've got a great voice, probably one of the best. You're not a trained dancer, are you?"

"Nope."

"Exotic?" Alicia asked.

Kiara looked surprised. "Yeah. Could you tell?"

Alicia laughed merrily, curls bouncing. "Sorry but yeah."

"Oh god, what shall I do?" Kiara bit her lip, flushing.

Alicia swallowed and screwed up the paper bag into a ball, wiping her hands on her shorts and thinking for a moment before replying. "Too much tits and ass."

Kiara gaped at her. "What? What am I supposed to do about that?!" and then started to sputter with laughter, despite her nerves.

Alicia started laughing with her. "I mean, don't dance so much with your tits and your ass, sticking 'em out and winding so much. Tone it down and make your movements smaller, sharper, more controlled."

"Ah okay, I get it." Kiara said, doubtfully.

Alicia jumped up. "C'mon, I'll show you what I mean." Seeing Kiara hesitate, she said, "Do you want to get through the next audition?"

126

She grabbed Kiara by the hand and hauled her to her feet.

***

"Get your shit together Anderson!" Megan yelled.

"Ahhh sorry! Can we try that again?" Kiara put a hand to her forehead, bathed in sweat, the back of her neck hot and wet, her hair damp. Marco stopped the track.

Alicia stretched her arms above her head, breathing heavily. "Don't worry about it Kiara. We'll try again." Michelle nodded, returning to her start position without saying anything. Sierra and Megan exchanged looks.

"Right girls, again from the top please. Kiara, focus. This has to be ready by Friday night or I'll kill all of you," Marco called out and none of them believed he was joking.

The track started again. Their heels scraping across the stage, the five girls walking forward in unison, clutching water bottles in place of mics.

Anna strode in and sat beside Marco, her arms crossed, watching with a raised eyebrow. He clapped his hands together when they finished. "Take ten ladies," he said, and turned to Anna.

"What do you think?" he asked.

She stood still for a moment, head titled to the side as she watched the girls lie down on the floor, breathing hard. "They're good. Will they be ready for Friday?"

Marco nodded. "They will."

Anna looked over at Kiara, who was sitting stretching one leg out in front of her, panting hard.

"Still sure we've got the right mix of girls?"

Marco grinned. "Chill out. They're going to be great," he said confidently, leaning back with his arms folded behind his head.

Anna laughed at him. "You're so damn smug Marco. I'll tell Frank that they'll do their first performance on Friday night then, and we'll see if you're right."

Marco looked over at the girls. "I'm telling you Anna, this could be a winning combination. I'm already thinking about them being much bigger than just the club."

"World domination?" she asked, smiling.

"Yep."

"Well, they need a name first. You got one yet?" she asked, running a hand through her short blonde bob.

Marco opened a notebook beside him and flipped it open to a page of pencilled scribbles, then turned to Anna.

"Femme Fatale," he said.

Part Three
Pretending

Two years ago – Kiara

Kiara took another swig of vodka from her mug and felt it warm her chest, though her bare feet were cold on the kitchen floor.

"Kiara, are you going to sleep? It's 3am," Sierra padded into the kitchen, her blonde hair tousled and tied back, and poured herself a glass of water.

"Sure, yeah, in a minute," Kiara murmured. Sierra sat down at the table, stretching one leg out onto an empty chair.

"Tonight was insane," she said, grinning.

Kiara grinned back. "I know."

It had been another packed night at the club. Celebrity VIPs tended to come on Saturdays, tucked away in the alcoves, dark leather booths shrouded by filmy white gauze, away from the gaze of the other guests but visible from the stage where Femme Fatale performed night after night. Anna's PR had created a buzz around the club and the girls, making it the current New York 'hot spot'. Four months in and there had already been numerous magazine articles and newspaper reviews of the club, with Femme Fatale getting a few press mentions. Anna was worth every cent of her eye-watering salary.

Marco took care of the girls, setting them up in a small apartment near the club, ushering ordering and cajoling them through endless rehearsals, new songs, new routines, vocal training, dance training, and clothes fittings. He had a background in the music industry and Frank trusted his decisions for the group, as did the girls themselves.

Sierra sighed. "I can't believe Justin Timberlake was there tonight and I missed him! I've been in love with him for years. Can you believe it?" She shook her head sadly.

Kiara laughed. "Maybe he'll come back."

Kiara's phone buzzed on the table. She checked her messages and showed Sierra the photo from the text.

"So cute! Who is that?" she asked.

Kiara smiled down at the screen. "Isaac. Son of a friend who lives down in Florida," she said. Kiara texted Betty back. "*Tus hermanos?*"

Betty's message pinged back straight away. "*Nada*". The family were still waiting to hear from the brothers, who had set off from San Pedro Sula a while ago. The situation wasn't promising. Kiara had heard about people who set off across Mexico only for their escorts, the *coyotes*, to take all their money and leave them for dead. She hoped that wasn't the case for Betty and Veronica, who had moved down to Florida recently to be near a second cousin of theirs, tired of Hunts Point, sick of the slush and snow and the strip clubs. Kiara missed them terribly.

"Night Kiara," Sierra swung her leg back to the floor and wandered back to her room that she shared with Megan.

"Goodnight," Kiara replied, still frowning at her phone.

Kiara downed the rest of the vodka from her mug then, making sure no one was around, poured herself another mugful, quietly replacing the bottle in the cupboard, and going to the bedroom.

Alicia and Michelle were already in bed, Alicia sleeping on the top bunk and Michelle tapping along to music on her headphones on the bottom. She glanced at Kiara and smiled, mouthing 'goodnight'. Kiara slid into bed, carefully placing the mug on the floor beside her, then flipped off her bedside light. She settled down in the sheets and picked up the mug from the floor, fingers gently scraping for it in the dark, and drained the mug in one go, tilting her head back, feeling the comfort of the sting in her throat and the blurriness it quickly brought to her mind.

She lay back quietly, listening to the gentle breathing of the girls in the room and the tinny sound of Michelle's headphones quietly straining against the silence.

There was no banging on the doors, no one high in the living room, just a flat quiet, punctuated by the occasional tapping of footsteps from the street, passing cars, or a distant siren. The doors were locked, she was safe. Turning on her side, she sighed heavily and closed her eyes.

Two years ago – The Jacobs

"*Have a great night! Luv u x,*" Tim's text popped up on Sarah's phone.

"The husband?" Sasha asked, leaning in close to shout in Sarah's ear over the pulsing music.

"Yeah!" Sarah smiled and flipped her golden hair back over her shoulders.

Amber slid through the crowd and gently set down a handful of glasses on the table, sloshing some of the drinks over the side.

"A toast to the birthday girl! Twenty-five today!" Amber grabbed her glass and raised it, the group of girls whooping over the music as they clinked glasses together.

"I'm so glad you booked ahead and got a table!" Sasha yelled at Nicole.

Nicole nodded enthusiastically. "I wanted one near the front so you can see the group perform. They're so hot!"

Sarah laughed. She loved that Nicole had gone to such an effort to organise her birthday and booked a table in the hottest club in New York. There was a huge buzz about the place, celebrities photographed stumbling out drunk and bleary-eyed on Saturday nights, plus a fierce girl group called Femme Fatale who performed there every night to wild reviews. She couldn't wait to see them.

Two years ago – Kiara

Kiara shoved through the crowd to the bar.

"Hey!" a short and perky brunette put her hands on her hips and huffed as Kiara squeezed through to the front.

"Sorry!" Kiara yelled, and pressed herself against the bar, waving to get the attention of Jess, whom she had managed to get a job there.

"Kiara! What do you need? Aren't you going on soon?" Jess yelled.

"Not for another thirty minutes!" Kiara said, leaning over the bar. "Can you get me a vodka and orange?"

Jess nodded and whipped off to mix the drink, returning in moments with a tall glass.

"Thanks!" Kiara swung round and began to sidle through the crowd sideways to get back to the dressing room.

She took a sip of her drink to stop it spilling over the sides, pausing for a moment in the middle of the crowd, and heard a group of girls whooping and clinking their glasses, shouting out "Happy birthday!" Kiara shuffled a little closer to take a look as the group liked to call out birthdays for customers. She edged her way past a group of guys, twitchy and damp with perspiration, and then she froze.

Sarah Jacobs was in the club, surrounded by a group of friends, her blonde hair gleaming, glittering in a sequinned dress. Kiara turned and pushed through the crowds, urgently moving away, throwing the vodka down her throat in a gulp, choking on the acid from the juice.

She was already dressed for the performance, her black corset top holding her ribs in and, all of a sudden, she couldn't breathe. Running with her hands in front of her, she burst through the doors to backstage. Wide-eyed and gasping, she staggered on her heels through to the dressing area, where the other members of the group were busy with makeup and curling irons, a cloud of perfume and hairspray heavy in the air.

"Kiara! What the hell happened to you?!" Alicia looked alarmed and stood up to grab her arms as Kiara wheeled around, a frightened energy flashing in her blue eyes.

"I'm, I'm... not well. I can't do it. I'm going to throw up."

Kiara sat heavily on a plastic chair and put her head between her legs, her hair tumbling down, and stared at her black heels.

"I'm going to get Marco," Michelle ran out of the room, heels tapping urgently on the wooden floor.

"You have to perform. You're the lead singer!" Megan said, her voice tense and shrill with anxiety.

"No, no, no, I can't do it." Kiara held her head in her hands, feeling the sweat bead around her hairline and down her back.

Alicia knelt down in front of her, rubbing her arms up and down and murmuring soothingly.

Marco strode in, followed by Michelle.

"Kiara! What's up?" Marco shoved Alicia out of the way. "Look up baby doll. Hey, tell me what's wrong."

Kiara raised her head. "I'm sick. I'm not going on."

"Come on, don't cry," Marco said, as she blinked streams of tears down her face. "You'll smudge your makeup."

He frowned and leaned in close so she could smell the peppermint on his breath. "Have you been drinking? Or taken something else?"

Kiara shook her head. "One drink, that's all, I swear."

She grabbed his shoulders and stared into his dark eyes, pleading. "Please Marco, please I can't do it."

Marco stared back at her for a moment, then stood up and turned to the rest of the girls. Sierra folded her arms expectantly. Megan's mouth bunched into a puckered line, her eyes narrowed.

"Listen up. You'll have to go on as a four tonight," Marco said.

"But she's the lead..." Megan interjected.

"Well Megan, you're always complaining that Kiara's given all the lead vocals, now's your chance to prove that you're just as good, okay?" Marco stared at her, then turned to Kiara. "Go back to the apartment. I'll be over to check on you soon."

Kiara nodded and, without raising her eyes to look at the other girls, she grabbed her coat and left the room.

***

Marco found her in the apartment later that night, face down on the table, her hands clutching a mugful of vodka, tears pooling on the cheap wooden table. Her corset was still cutting into her breathing, her head dizzy.

"Right Kiara, I need an explanation." Marco sat next to her and tapped her on the shoulder. "You're not sick and I'm not stupid. Something's up."

She raised her head slightly from the table. "I'm not feeling well Marco."

He pulled her head back by her hair. "Ow!" she yelled, sitting up and glaring at him. She wiped a hand across her cheeks, smearing black trails of mascara across her blusher.

Marco frowned at her and threw her a Kleenex. "You're a mess. Wipe your face."

He sniffed at her mug and raised an eyebrow. "No wonder you feel ill. What is this?"

She wiped her cheeks with the Kleenex and looked at him incredulously. "Vodka."

"Cheap shit." Marco shook his head. "Where's the bottle?"

She tottered to the cupboard and reached behind several cereal boxes to where she kept her stash in a paper bag and plonked it down unceremoniously on the table. Marco grabbed a mug and poured himself some, wrinkling his nose as he sipped.

"So, what happened?" He leaned back in his chair and folded his hands over his torso.

Kiara shrugged. "I saw someone in the club that I knew, and it kinda freaked me out."

Marco raised an eyebrow. "Ex-boyfriend?"

Kiara laughed at the thought, given she had never dated anyone. "Nope, just someone I used to know. It brought back too many memories, and I, I couldn't handle it."

"Hmmm." Marco sipped his vodka, grimacing. "I don't know how you can drink this neat."

They sat in silence and Marco leaned forward, placing his mug on the table.

"Kiara."

She looked at him, eyes bleary from tears and alcohol. "Are you going to fire me from the group?" she asked.

He pressed his lips together. "I won't but I need you to be honest with me."

"About what?" she asked.

"About everything. You've barely told us anything about who you are or where you come from. You drink yourself to sleep every night, you have terrible nightmares." He held up a hand as she tried to interrupt. "Did you think we wouldn't notice? You share a room with two other women!"

"Listen," he said, rubbing his temples and lowering his voice. "I advocated for you to be in this group. Anna didn't want you, but ever since I saw you singing at that hotel bar I've believed in you. I need you to trust me and tell me everything so I can help you and protect you."

"From what?"

"I think Femme Fatale could be really big. But if that happens, then the press will start to ask questions, people will want to know about who you are and where you come from. You'll need help to handle that, but I can't help you if you don't tell me."

She looked at him quietly.

"Didn't you ever think that this would happen? That at some point that voice of yours might get you noticed?" he asked her, surprised.

She looked down at the table and traced a finger round a spill, her sharp red nails gleaming, blood-like.

"I guess I never really thought it was a possibility," she muttered.

"Well, it is," Marco smiled at her. "And as my most talented singer, I demand you tell me everything."

"How long have you got?" she replied.

While the group performed a lacklustre set in the club, Kiara laid it all out for Marco, telling him about the Jacobs, her father, the bullying, the rape, running away, delivering drugs, stripping, explaining that she drank at night to stop the nightmares or at least blur them from her mind so she could sleep.

Kiara told him reluctantly about Rob, unsure whether she should, but she couldn't think of a way to explain away those years and she knew that she had to be honest in order to gain Marco's help and guidance. She didn't want to tell anyone about Rob – she knew she owed him a debt that she could never repay for having taken her in when she had nowhere else to turn.

When she had auditioned for the group Rob and Dan had been scornful, thinking her foolish. To them she was just a runaway, a dead-beat like them, a vodka-soaked stripper who cried at night on a mattress in the corner, and they had never heard her sing.

When she told Rob she was leaving she cried, because he was her only family and out of all the family she had ever known, he was the one who hadn't abandoned her. He'd used her, but he'd also protected her too. She had hugged him and, seeing the concern in his eyes, she had told him that she would never mention his name to anyone, that his secrets were hers, that she would guard them as much to protect herself as to protect him. Yet here she was telling Marco everything she knew, risking him calling the police and turning them all in, although somehow in her heart she knew he wouldn't.

"So, there you are Marco," she said, draining the last of the vodka in her mug and messily pouring herself another cup. She glanced at the clock on the wall, 1am. The girls could be back in an hour or so, unless they stayed on till the club closed, which they often did, when they would be home closer to 4am.

Kiara leaned her head heavily on her hand, her pointed nails digging into her cheek.

Marco exhaled slowly. "That's quite an experience you've had for a twenty-one-year-old."

"Twenty-two," Kiara corrected him. "I'm twenty-three in November."

"Right." Marco looked at her and she couldn't read what was in his expression, whether it was sadness or pity or even disgust. Her eyes were heavy and she could feel the world peeling away at the fuzzy edges of her vision.

"Go to bed. I'll say you had food poisoning." Marco pushed back his chair and walked out.

"Oh, and Kiara?" he turned towards her and she sleepily lifted her head in his direction.

"Hide the drinking better, okay?"

She nodded and he walked out.

Two years ago – the Jacobs

Amber swayed on her heels as she leaned down to slide into the cab, squishing into Sarah and Nicole. Sarah leaned her head on Nicole's shoulder.

"Thank you so much for my birthday treat," Sarah said, affectionately and peacefully drunk.

"It was great, right?" Nicole smiled. "Though the group weren't as good as I remember them."

The cab glided off into the New York night, back to Sarah and Tim's apartment.

***

Sarah winced as Melanie's phoned chirped, and the family laughed.

"Another Advil?" Victor said, nudging her.

The family had gathered at the Jacobs' house to celebrate Sarah's birthday with a lunch. The trees had turned smoky reds and browns, aglow with the fall sunshine. The roses were starting to droop a little, their heads downturned, saddened by the loss of summer.

Janet passed around bowls of steaming potatoes, melted minted butter sliding down the skins, and crisp vegetables glazed and roasted in honey with flecks of sea salt. Victor doled out slabs of moist chicken and roasted ham.

Sarah was feeling slightly delicate after her birthday celebrations the night before, and gazed at her plate, her appetite dampened with nausea. Tim squeezed her arm, "Poor baby." She smiled and leaned into him.

Shane spooned mashed potato into Joshua's mouth, most of which ended up around Joshua's face, in his golden hair, on his hands or on his highchair. He giggled and slammed his hands down on the creamy mess. Shane looked dismayed. "Only five minutes and it's everywhere," he sighed to Melanie. She was frowning at her phone.

"Mel? Maybe put the phone away now? It's been going off all morning," Shane turned back to Joshua, patiently wiping his face and hands.

Melanie shut her phone with a soft click and slid it into the pocket of her jeans.

"Everything okay, Melanie?" Janet said, looking concerned.

138

Melanie smiled brightly. "Everything's fine Janet, thank you. It's just my friend CeeCee, always some marital crisis or another."

Sarah laughed. She had heard many tales of CeeCee's mishaps from Melanie.

After lunch they all sat in the living room, sipping coffee, Sarah grateful for the caffeine, when Janet came in waving a big brown photo album.

"Oh no mom!" Sarah grimaced and covered her eyes with her hands, but she laughed. Her mom's tradition of trotting out their childhood photos on their birthdays every few years embarrassed Shane but secretly Sarah loved it. Janet sat between Tim and Sarah, beckoning Shane and Victor over. Melanie was in the bathroom upstairs cleaning up Joshua.

Sarah leafed through the photos. "I forgot about this one," Sarah said, eyes shining as she turned the page to a large print of Sarah, Shane and Kiara, all piled on a sun lounger by the pool, skin reddened from the sun, wide grins over their aching cheeks. "How old are we all there, mom?"

"Let me see," said Janet. "I think Shane is fifteen, you're twelve and Kiara is ten."

"Great picture," Sarah said, smiling. "Can I get a copy to frame?"

"Sure," Janet nodded.

Sarah carefully removed the photo from the sticky plastic covering, peeling it back and putting the photo on one knee. "I miss her," Sarah said, tracing Kiara's face on the photo with her fingertips.

Janet sighed, "We all do." Shane nodded, silently.

"Keep going. I want to see the awkward teen years," said Tim, flipping over the page, and they started to laugh again at Sarah's experimental fashion, the awkward makeup, the years passing with the turning of the pages. Here and there the red-haired girl with the bright eyes appeared, and then she was gone. Shane and Sarah carried on growing older in the pages that followed as Janet added more and more photos of engagements and weddings and parties. Sarah wondered what Kiara would have looked like now, six years on from her last photo, the night of her performance at school, her and Sarah pictured at the bottom of the stairs, arms around each other, Kiara looking dazed with happiness in her blue dress.

"She will be twenty-three this year," said Shane, thinking the same thing as Sarah lingered on that photo a few moments longer than the others.

"Let's just hope that she's safe and happy, wherever she is," Victor said, as they carried on leafing through the album, hope and memories all that they had left of her.

Two years ago – Kiara

The girls gathered in Frank's office in the club. They squeezed onto the dark blue couch together, Alicia draping a leg over Kiara, giggling, Sierra and Megan linking arms and Michelle perched on the side.

Frank was sitting behind his desk, Anna leaning on the side of it, her crisp white blouse tucked into a brown leather skirt, her cropped blonde hair pulled messily back into a chignon. She looked at her phone as the girls chattered.

Marco strode in. "Sorry," he said, "had to finalise a few things."

He stood in front of the girls in his usual uniform of a black t-shirt and jeans, deeply tanned, his black hair gelled back. "I've got some exciting news girls."

Two years ago – The Jacobs

Melanie flicked through the pages of the magazine, feeling the heat of the conditioning treatment warm her scalp.

"Another coffee?" the assistant asked.

Melanie smiled. "That would be lovely thank you."

Melanie scanned the pages of the magazine.

New girl group Femme Fatale to tour with Gem Rivers

The hit group from New York's hottest club will be supporting international superstar Gem Rivers on her US tour next year.

Lead singer Kiara told Star News – "We're thrilled to be invited on the tour. We love Gem and can't wait to get out there and perform our hearts out."

"Right, let's get you over to the basin." Melanie was interrupted by the assistant, smiling politely, her hands clasped in front of her. Melanie slapped the magazine shut and dropped it back into the pile for customers as she walked to the sink.

Two years ago – Kiara

"What's the best way to play this out?" Marco asked Anna.

She stared at him coldly, her arms crossed. "You should have told me," she snapped at him.

He met her gaze impassively. "I knew you would want to get rid of her, so I waited till it was too late to do that. Now it's your problem too and you need to help me deal with it."

Anna huffed and walked around the desk to stand over him. "Marco, what the hell were you thinking? She's got a messy past and a drinking problem. This is going to blow up in our faces."

Marco shook his head, folding his hands in front of him, knitting his tanned fingers together. "Listen, you need to trust me on this. You guys hired me to manage the group because I have experience in the industry. I know talent, she's got it. The group is not the same without her."

Anna tapped her nails on the desktop, a strand of blonde hair gently resting over her ear. She dropped her head and looked at the floor, frowning.

"Plus, she's not an alcoholic," Marco added.

"What?" Anna snapped back.

"She's got it under control. It's like a comfort blanket, something to help her sleep at night. No big deal, okay?" He held up his hands. "Honestly, I've seen people with less talent and bigger addictions in the industry. This is not going to be a problem."

Anna threw her hands in the air. "Great, my fears are allayed," she said, sarcastically.

Outside the door, Kiara sat on the floor in the hallway, listening to the murmurs in Marco's office. She felt a swell of gratitude run through her body as she heard him defending her.

Anna exhaled slowly, putting her hands to her head. "Okay. Okay. You're right. We're stuck with it for now at least. So, here's what we're going to do."

Marco later explained to Kiara the things they would do to help make sure some of her secrets stayed buried for now, and though she had already heard everything through the door she nodded eagerly and acted as though it were new to her ears.

Anna had some suggestions for making sure the focus was on the group as a whole rather than on each individual member. Reporters would only be given the girls' first names, and no ages, and Kiara wasn't to do any interviews on her own. Marco, Anna and the PR team would deal with journalists who were a little too intrepid, feed them false information, stonewall them with silence or bribe them with exclusives to keep them sweet. This would work for a time, but there would come a point when she would need to answer some questions, Marco warned her, and they would need to find the best way to do that.

Marco couldn't guarantee that the Jacobs' name wouldn't be linked with her eventually. There would be people from school who remembered, probably someone could dig out a photo somewhere. There was less to link her with Rob – no photos, no real evidence she had ever lived with him, and the people who knew about it wouldn't want to draw attention to their connection with Rob either, so the team hoped that part of her life could remain largely hidden.

Kiara felt relieved. It was hard to imagine anyone realising who she was, up on the stage in the bright lights, but she knew she would be recognised at some point, maybe even the Jacobs would see her in one of the magazines. In a way, she wouldn't mind them seeing her as a success, making something of herself, and she thought maybe they would be proud. She was more worried about the time in Hunts Point – the drugs, the stripping, and the rape – those were the things she feared being made public, and those were the things she relied on Marco to help her protect, for now at least.

She would do anything Marco said to keep it that way.

One year ago – The Jacobs

Shane sat swirling a glass of JD round and round, his fingers wet with condensation, looking at the pile of papers in front of him that demanded his signature.

Divorce… division of the assets… custody

He drained the glass and picked up a pen.

***

"How are you settling in?" Janet ran her hand along the kitchen counter in Shane's apartment.

Boxes were strewn around the living room, precarious piles of cardboard containing everything from the minor to the most important, his life stuffed into storage and turned into debris.

"Um yeah, good thanks." He rubbed his eyes wearily, and searched for the coffee pot, hidden under a newspaper.

"Let me Shane," she said gently, taking the pot from him and rifling through the drawers for a spoon.

Shane sighed and rubbed a hand over his chin, unshaven and rough.

"How's Melanie and Joshua?" she asked, not looking at him, busying herself with making the coffee.

"They're fine," he said, gruffly.

Janet glanced at him and he shook his head. "I really don't want to talk about it."

Nodding, she turned back to the coffee pot and sought out some cups in a cupboard overflowing with random items, shoved in without thought or order. Shane sat at the kitchen counter, watching her, wondering how things had turned around so quickly. One moment he was married with a son, a wife he adored, the perfect couple in the perfect home. Now he was in this soulless apartment, the blank glass windows staring out onto a city he felt adrift in, steel and black surfaces reflecting only his own sad face back at him.

He had begged Melanie not to break up their life together, not after so many years of happiness. He had choked out apologies for working so hard and so late, for when he wasn't there for her, for when he hadn't paid her enough attention. He would try harder, be better, try anything to make her stay and not take his life away from him. She had been cold, adamant, and determined to end things, an icy bolt from the blue, a shock to him like falling into arctic waters. She had been matter-of-fact, curt and exacting, while he floundered without a clue.

And she was now happily ensconced in their house, their home, and seeing someone else. It felt as though the very ground under him had fallen away. Joshua was toddling around their beautiful home and bumping into someone else's shoes, hearing another man's laughter in the bedroom they once shared so happily.

It was unbearable, both the imagination and the reality, the day-to-day confusion of waking up without her and his son close by. He was so angry at her for tearing their lives up like this yet he knew he would run back in a second if she asked him to return, still in love with her, missing her soft pale skin, her steady breathing in the night next to him, the sounds and sensations of her, the only woman he had ever wanted.

Janet handed him a black coffee and he took it thankfully. "How is all the paperwork coming on?" she said, deliberately avoiding the word divorce, not wanting to distress him further.

"It's moving along. I'm not contesting," he said, looking down at his coffee.

"Oh Shane," Janet sighed. "I can't believe you won't contest it."

"I know, but what can I do? She wants a divorce, I can't oblige her to stay married because of the way the legal process works. I may as well get this over with as soon as possible."

"Still," she hesitated, "won't admitting fault just make the settlement better for her and worse for you, even though you've done nothing wrong?"

He shook his head. "We agreed that if I made things easy and didn't contest, we could agree terms and find a way forward."

"And anyway," he added, "I really don't care about the money. She can have half. All I care about is seeing Joshua."

Janet nodded. "That's the most important thing." Looking around, she smiled at the mess. "Just like your bedroom when you were a teenager," she said.

Shane laughed. "I haven't quite sorted things out yet. I've been staying late at work most days."

"I know, your father told me," she replied. Victor had suggested Shane take some time off to get himself settled, but Shane had refused, needing the distraction of work. He would be there in the office till late, gazing blankly at emails, leaving voicemails for people past 10pm, preferring his office to his empty apartment.

"Why don't I come over one day while you're at work and help to sort things out?" she suggested.

Shane shrugged. "Up to you mom. I'm fine either way."

She patted him on the shoulder. Clearly, he was not fine, but there was very little she could do. She was devastated when he told her and Victor that Melanie had asked for a divorce. They were stunned and confused, certain that it must be a phase or a mistake, but it was neither.

Now all Janet and Victor could do was watch their son tackle a divorce and hope to see their grandchild when they could. She felt helpless watching him go through this and not knowing how to help except by making coffee and offering to sort his apartment for him. He had only gotten worse when he found out about Melanie seeing someone else. She couldn't understand how that woman had been happy to date again so quickly, and she had wanted to go over there and shake her and demand an explanation, but of course, she hadn't.

One year ago – Kiara

Kiara shivered in her thin robe, linking arms with Megan as they tottered around the hotel suite trying not to trip over the thick black cables that were twisted over the floor like a nest of snakes. The balcony doors were wide open, a thudding summer storm outside turned the air damp and cool, the skies over Los Angeles a murmuring and ponderous grey.

Sierra was standing by the window in the suite, arms bent behind her head, pouting in to the camera, mouthing to the track playing in the background. She leaned into the camera and ran her hands up her thighs. The stylist had chosen a deep crimson bra for her to wear with a matching thong. The deep red set off Sierra's tanned skin, and they had straightened her long white-blonde hair so it swooshed down her back and over her shoulders in pale waves.

"Gorgeous!" yelled the director.

"She's really good at this," Megan leaned into Kiara.

Kiara nodded, the nerves starting to rise in her stomach. She breathed deeply through her nose and clenched and unclenched her fist.

Alicia bounded up behind them and wrapped them both in a hug, squeezing them affectionately. "I'm done!" she announced, as they examined the stylist's work. Her curls were an energetic crowd around her head, her eye makeup a golden sheen across her dark skin, her lithe body shown off by cream and gold underwear.

"Oooh you look amazing," Kiara grinned. "Is Michelle still in makeup?"

Alicia nodded. "I can't believe we're doing this! Our first music video! I could literally die!" They laughed and Sierra walked up to them. They all applauded her, exchanging hugs.

It had taken Kiara a while to get used to the intensity of being part of a group of women who lived and worked together, day and night, sharing rooms, bathrooms, toiletries, shoes, meals. They were all very different people, but their shared success kept them bonded, consistently amazed and surprised by the new experiences on offer to them as they adjusted to their new world, which Marco, Anna and their new team guided them through with both patience and persuasion.

They were told where to go, what to wear, how to act, what to say. The times they were left to themselves they lounged together in pyjamas, rubbing aching feet, making meals, laughing endlessly, and yawning constantly as early mornings and late nights took their toll.

They had fractious moments, like any group would. Alicia and Michelle argued constantly about cleanliness, Sierra was frequently impatient with Kiara's lack of dance skills, and Megan was often annoyed by the insistence that Kiara take the lead on most vocals, especially when Kiara was asked into the studio to record the demos

145

first and the rest of the group had to fit around her part. But they also formed close friendships, and the lack of time they had to visit friends or family meant they became each other's family, toasting their birthdays on tour buses or in hotel rooms.

At first, Kiara had felt claustrophobic and smothered, but she soon relaxed into the group, feeling part of a family for the first time since the Jacobs. She spent hours talking to Alicia during late nights lounging in hotel rooms on the tour and whispered conversations in the back of the tour bus. Alicia told Kiara about her parent's disapproval of her career, Kiara in turn timidly opened up about her childhood, mentioning her father's alcoholism and the problems at school, but she kept most of the details of what had happened to herself.

Interviewers were light on detail about the girls' backgrounds, preferring to ask about the group dynamics, their styling, their personalities, any feuds. Journalists were fed details about their families and careers, and were told Kiara's parents were both dead.

Kiara got better at hiding her night-time drinking. She decanted vodka into water bottles and mouthwash bottles in her bag, taking swift large gulps in the bathroom with the tap running, cleaning her teeth immediately afterwards.

"Kiara, your turn please," the video director was calling out her name. The girls wished her luck and she made her way over to the filming area.

"Right Kiara, we want some shots of you on the bed first, you'll be singing these lyrics here, okay?" the director said, pointing at the lyrics on a screen.

Kiara nodded, unsure. He raised his eyebrows at her. "You'll need to remove the robe, Kiara."

She untied the robe, feeling exposed in just a sapphire blue bra and lace panties, her curls defined by styling cream, her eyes framed by cobalt eyeshadow and huge dark lashes.

The first scenes were of her lying on a bed, looking up at a camera, mouthing along to the lyrics. For other scenes, they had her standing with her back against the window, with the rain running down the glass behind her, tilting her head back and sliding down it. Then the other girls finished their individual shoots and they shot some together as a group.

Kiara had been used to taking her clothes off for men in the club, but this felt different. Here, no one was touching her or making demands, she felt safe and confident, surrounded by women who were enjoying themselves. There was no client to chase after and only the camera to please.

"That's all ladies, amazing," the director announced at the end of the two days. They whooped excitedly and danced around before they had to get changed and ready for more work.

Ten months ago – The Jacobs

"She's alive," Janet said, wide-eyed with shock and her eyes glistening with tears, when Sarah finished playing them the YouTube video.

Victor sat silently, hand over his eyes, as Janet began to cry next to him, her shoulders shaking with sobs interspersed with quakes of laughter as she looked at Shane and Sarah. Sarah was smiling joyfully and Shane was shaking his head, dumbfounded.

"Alive, and a famous singer!" Sarah shrieked happily. "They've been in magazines too," she said, fishing out a large pile of shiny magazines from a bag at her feet.

"I never normally read stuff like this, but Tim has them in his waiting room for patients, so I picked one up the other day and flicked through and found this," she stabbed at a page with her finger. There was a two-page feature on Femme Fatale, each member pictured with their "vital statistics", their likes and dislikes.

Shane looked over the page. "Look here," he said, tapping his finger on Kiara's photo and short bio underneath with snippets of unrevealing information, except for one fact. "It says both her parents are dead." He looked at Sarah, Janet and Victor.

Sarah shrugged her shoulders. "So?"

"So, Kiara knows her dad died."

The fact settled in the air, his unspoken questions hovering silently.

Victor sighed and responded, "I don't really see why that's confusing Shane."

Shane stood up and waved the article at them. "She knew he died! How? Did she come back? Was he in touch with her all along and he didn't tell us? I don't get it." He looked exasperated, feeling that even though they knew she was okay, there were still so many questions, so many things they didn't know. He felt a flash of anger at Kiara then, while they had worried themselves sick with sleepless nights and fruitless searches she was out there working towards her dream of fame and fortune, without a word to them or anyone.

"She's been okay all this time and she never got in touch. Why? What happened?" he raised his voice and realised his throat was closing up. He sat down and put his head in his hands.

Janet put an arm around his shoulders and leaned in close to him, speaking softly. "Shane, let's just be glad she's okay for now. I'm sure that one day Kiara will help us to understand when we're back in touch with her."

He nodded, feeling exhausted from the sweet rush of euphoric relief and fierce pride at seeing Kiara alive and living her dream to feeling an intense angry urge to force her to tell them why she had left and finally confirm that he was to blame so he could tell her he was sorry.

They sat in silence for a moment, trying to understand this new reality. Just as they had struggled to accept her sudden departure they now had to deal with her unexpected entrance back into their lives.

"So," Sarah began, "I guess we get in touch with her management company?"

Janet nodded. "I'm sure that we can get a message to her."

"No," Victor stood up and folded his arms, his eyes turning thoughtfully around the room before turning back to his family. "We won't contact her."

Janet widened her eyes. "Victor, you can't mean that?"

"Daddy!" Sarah said, indignantly.

"We don't know why she left but we do know that in the last seven years she has chosen not to contact us. It has to be her choice to get back in touch, when she's ready."

Victor looked at his family and said, quietly but firmly, his voice leaving no doubt of his determination, "Promise me you'll do this my way."

Stunned, they nodded. He turned and walked away to his study and shut the heavy wooden door with a soft click.

***

Janet came to see him later, when Shane and Sarah had left. She shut the door behind her and leaned back against it. Victor was sat in his office chair, thrumming his fingers on the dark mahogany desk before him, his desk lamp a soft halo of light in the deepening evening.

"What's on your mind?" she asked him.

He pursed his lips for a moment. "Do you remember when we met?"

She nodded, still leaning against the cool wood of the door, a comfortable solidity behind her back.

"It had been seven years since I had left home when I met you. Seven years of silence between my father and I."

Janet remembered. She had been twenty-three, Victor twenty-five, and they had fallen in love quickly and easily, a joyful peaceful union. He had met her family, loved them as they had loved him, but he had refused to talk about his family at all. He didn't invite his father to the wedding, and he had died a few years later, the silence between father and son extending into the afterlife. Victor hadn't gone to his funeral either.

Victor continued. "When I left, I had good reasons. I felt those reasons were good enough to never contact my father again. It was all too…" he paused, narrowing his blue eyes, "ugly."

Janet walked over to him as he hung his head, and held him as she stood, his head against her stomach, her hand smoothing his iron-grey hair.

He looked up at her. "Kiara has her reasons. I think she'll come back to us if she can."

Janet nodded, dabbing away tears from her cheeks. Inside, she was burning with frustration, wanting to tell Victor that he was wrong, that it wasn't the same, that they had loved Kiara and loved her still and Kiara needed to know that they were waiting for her with open arms, desperate to see her again. But she kept quiet and stood holding him as the night deepened around them.

Nine months ago – The Jacobs

Shane wrapped his hands round Joshua's waist and kissed the top of his head, breathing him in.

"How are you doing?" Melanie asked him, warily.

They sat in the living room of the home they once shared but now Shane felt like an intruder in the house he had worked so hard to buy. There was another man's coat in the hallway, a different aftershave lingering in the air, different shoes, different books, the coffee *he* liked in the kitchen. Shane's jaw clenched.

"Good. And you?" he said shortly, jiggling Joshua to make him laugh, and staring only at him, avoiding Melanie's gaze.

"I'm good, thanks Shane."

An awkward silence settled between them as she packed a few things for Joshua into a bag. "Where are you off to this weekend?" she asked.

"I'll be taking him to my mom and dad's," he replied, resentful that the short time he had with Joshua had to be shared with anyone at all, even his parents.

"That's nice," she murmured, searching for Joshua's favourite toy, a soft colourful caterpillar Jade had bought him when he was only a few months old and Shane's world had been complete.

"You know Kiara is okay?" he said, suddenly, as he stood up to leave, lifting Joshua easily with him.

Melanie crossed her arms as Shane took the overnight bag from her. "Oh?"

"Yeah. Singing in a famous group. She's in all the magazines and newspapers."

"Well, that's good news." Melanie pressed her lips together, her eyes sliding down to her arms, checking the time on the new watch Kyle had bought her.

Shane took the hint and walked to the front door. He turned briefly back to Melanie. "I'm surprised you didn't see her sooner actually, given how many of those gossip magazines you read."

She shrugged as she shut the door behind him.

One month ago – Kiara

The single had been huge – number one all around the world. The girls were suddenly catapulted into a new realm of fame. Appearances and performances were now global, Paris, Madrid, Cape Town, Sydney. They slept on tour buses and planes, their exhausted heavy heads bent forward on aching necks, raw throats soothed with lemon and honey.

Kiara loved the constant movement, the noise, the thrill of performing. There was no chance to settle or think as they went from one thing to the next. Sometimes sleep crashed in on her rudely without the vodka, on other days the buzz after a performance was so intense none of the girls could sleep at all and they stayed up bleary-eyed with ears ringing and trembling hands, feeling high and shivery and ecstatic. They downed Red Bull, forced sore feet into heels, mainlined coffee, and threw food down their throats when they could.

They were thinner than before and needed more makeup to cover their lack of sleep, but each of them felt it was worth it. Michelle suffered the most from the lack of schedule and the irregular hours. She would retreat quietly to the back of the bus or her hotel room with frequent headaches and jumpy from the caffeine highs. Alicia took it all in her stride. Sierra and Megan moaned constantly but loved every moment. Kiara was happy to be there with them, and still couldn't believe the speed with which things had changed.

She often got messages from Betty and Veronica with updates on Isaac, and one brother had made it to them, unscathed physically. The other brother had been lost on the train journey across Mexico and they feared the worst. They waited without news, heartsick and anxious. Kiara once thought that this was perhaps how the Jacobs felt when she disappeared without saying anything and they didn't know she was okay, but she quickly pushed the thought away.

With the increased fame came increased media attention. The girls were constantly interviewing as a group, but the questions became more personal. A magazine did an individual feature on Alicia, talking about her family and their disapproval of her dream. The girls were voted into the list of the world's sexiest women, with Kiara at number nine.

Kiara knew the time would come when they had to be upfront, especially as she was the lead singer, and the interview requests were being turned down constantly now, which was making people curious. Several times Anna and Marco had woken her up with an early morning phone call or called her late at night about potential stories, so when Kiara's phoned buzzed late one night she assumed it was them.

She was chatting to Michelle in their hotel suite after another day of promotions. The other girls were watching a movie, except for Megan who was taking a bath. Kiara had grabbed her phone to glance at it while still chatting with Michelle, but the message was from a number she didn't recognise.

"This is Dan. Rob is dead."

Kiara froze in horror at the stark black words on the bright screen. She had always made sure Rob had her cell phone number even when she moved out to live with the girls, just in case he ever needed something, but she asked him not to keep it saved in his phone, for obvious reasons. She walked off from Michelle, who was still speaking, grasping her phone, panting through her mouth, and texted back.

"What happened?"

Her phone beeped in reply.

"Shot. Bad deal gone wrong."

"When?"

"2 days ago."

Kiara put her hand to her mouth and bent over double, her vision blurring with tears, a vice tightness in her chest stopping her breath. She gasped and whimpered, holding on to the doorframe of the bedroom in the hotel suite. Sierra swung her head round from the couch where she was lounging over Alicia.

"Hey, what's wrong?" she said, alarmed, as Kiara sank to the floor.

Michelle came running over and Sierra and Alicia jumped off the couch. Kiara shook her head, too overwhelmed to speak, and cried there on the floor, Alicia stroking her hair, till Kiara leaned away, weak and exhausted from emotion, murmuring about the death of a friend. The girls helped her up and into one of the bedrooms, where she lay on the bed, and checked her phone again as she was curled up with sobs. Dan had replied.

"Police investigating. I'm leaving tonight."

Kiara hesitated before responding, then punched in the letters.

"Where is he?"

Dan's reply pinged back straight away.

"City morgue. Getting rid of your number now, as agreed."

Kiara hesitated for a moment. There was no love lost between her and Dan, but she was grateful he was doing as she asked. She didn't know what to say and she had no help to offer him. Eventually she texted back.

"Good luck Dan"

Kiara put her face between the swollen pillows of the hotel bed and wept into the soft cotton, dampening the fresh sheets with sorrow. The following day she called Marco early in the morning before they left for the next city. He came to the door of the suite five minutes after she called, still rumpled from sleep, his jet-black hair ruffled and a shadow of stubble grazing his chin.

"What's up?" he looked concerned as soon as he saw her, red-eyed and pale, her eyes creased and shadowy from lack of sleep.

Kiara invited him in, checking the girls weren't up yet, and sat on the couch.

"My cousin is dead," she said flatly, her throat dry and scratchy from crying, her chest tight.

Marco nodded, and put his arm around her.

"The drug dealer?" he whispered in her ear.

She nodded.

"How?" he asked, rubbing her arm.

"He was shot, I think it was a drug deal gone wrong," she replied, leaning into him, comforted by the warmth of his closeness.

"How did you find out?" he said.

"Dan texted me. He said he was leaving the city last night and the police are investigating."

Marco drummed his fingers on his knee. "Dan has your number?"

Kiara nodded, Rob had it in the apartment written down and tucked away, but they had always agreed that, should anything happen, the number would be destroyed so she couldn't be linked with anything Rob and Dan had done. She knew they used burner cell phones and that Dan would cover his tracks to protect himself.

Shortly after she had been accepted in the group and moved in with the girls, she had gone to Hunts Point for the last time, the last time she saw Rob alive, and she had given Rob and Dan a chunk of money she had saved up. She knew there would always be a risk that they would come back to her, especially with this unexpected fame, but they never had, and she didn't think Dan would contact her again.

"He's disposed of my number now," she said.

"Can he or Rob be linked to you?" Marco asked, an urgent edge to his voice, though he was trying to speak softly.

She leaned back and faced him. "I don't know Marco, but I don't think so. Dan will be long gone by now anyway."

She bit her lip. "Rob's body is in the city morgue."

Marco shook his head. "Don't even think about it Kiara. You can't go to see the body, you can't go to any funeral. You cannot be linked with him, do you understand?"

When she didn't reply, he spoke more sharply. "Do you understand?"

"Yes, Marco."

"Good."

They could hear the other girls starting to stir. Megan padded out of one of the bedrooms and stopped, surprised to see Marco there so early. She raised her eyebrows, looking at Kiara. "Everything okay?" she asked.

"Everything is fine Megs," Marco replied.

She looked at Kiara, who nodded in agreement, and closed the bathroom door behind her.

"Get yourself ready and packed up. We've got another long day today," he said. He tugged on one of her curls and ran his thumb across her cheek to wipe away a tear that had lingered that she hadn't even felt fall from her eyes. "You look like shit."

She smiled. "Thanks Marco."

"Anytime." He grinned back and left the suite.

Kiara sat there for a moment in silence. Her last remaining family member on this earth was dead and gone. For all his faults, Rob had looked after her more than either of her parents had, and she had always hoped that perhaps one day he would clean himself up and be free of his debts so he could lead a normal life, but now he would never get the chance.

She got up from the couch and headed back to the bedroom to get ready.

Three weeks ago – Kiara

Marco spoke to her a week later, the first time they had a chance to talk properly since Rob had died.

The girls had returned to New York to work on more tracks in the studio. The label that had signed them had got them all apartments in a tall block in Manhattan, and Marco came to her apartment one evening.

Kiara was alone. Sierra and Megan were having dinner, Michelle was catching up with her family in New Jersey, and Alicia was on a date with a basketball star. When she told the girls she was going out they had all whooped in excitement and teased her endlessly. Kiara had helped her pick out her outfit that evening in Alicia's apartment, tossing dresses and shirts and pants on the bed, discarding combinations for being too girly, too slutty, too demure. Eventually Alicia had gone to her date, skin glowing, smelling of Ghost Deep Night.

Kiara had returned to her own apartment and ordered Chinese food. Her apartment felt cold and empty, and she had very few personal possessions to put in it. No trinkets from childhood, no gifts from family. She had piles of clothes and shoes and makeup from designers, plus purses and jewellery, but virtually nothing to cook with and nothing she truly loved. It wasn't her home. She slept with the lights on whenever she was there, which wasn't often.

She had just finished eating when Marco tapped on the door. He breezed in.

"Hey, want a drink?" she asked, as he settled onto her couch. The apartment had been furnished already when she moved in so nothing she had really reflected her tastes. The couch was a dark red, a deep soft leather that swallowed her like a mouth when she laid on it to watch TV.

"No thanks sweetheart." He tapped the couch next to him. "Let's talk."

At first, the other girls had made comments about Marco's closeness to Kiara. He certainly spent more time alone in conversation with her than the others. If only they knew, she thought, how complicated and murky her past was and how much she needed him to help her to keep things hidden. The other girls soon realised nothing romantic or sexual was happening between them. Marco was bisexual and had a boyfriend, plus Kiara had insisted she wasn't interested in dating at all.

She slid onto the couch next to him, waiting expectantly.

"Well, good news," he began. "You've been asked to do an exclusive TV interview with Beth Winters."

Two weeks ago – The Jacobs

"Kiara's interviewing with Beth Winters in a few weeks! We must watch it!"

Sarah's text buzzed into the phones of Janet, Victor and Shane late one afternoon. Shane had immediately texted back and they arranged to watch the interview at Sarah's house the evening it aired.

Janet was hopeful that perhaps this interview would help them to understand what Kiara had been through, knowing that Beth Winters was likely to ask probing questions as she did for all her guests. She just couldn't understand why Kiara still hadn't been in touch, and maybe they would finally get some answers.

One week ago – Kiara

"Are you nervous?" Alicia asked Kiara, as they sipped wine in Alicia's apartment with Sierra.

Kiara nodded.

"You're so lucky," Sierra said, a slight hint of envy in her voice. "Her ratings are so high, this is great exposure for you."

"I'd rather not do it," Kiara sighed, "Marco really twisted my arm with this one."

Sierra frowned and poured herself another glass of wine, studying Kiara over the rim. "Why? It's not like you have anything to hide is it?" she asked, a harder edge to her voice.

Kiara smiled weakly and shook her head. "No, of course not."

The interview

The studio was completely silent, the crew motionless. Kiara could see Marco over Beth's shoulder, nodding grimly from where he stood off camera, Alicia next to him with her hands pressed to her mouth. Kiara had never told the other girls that she had been raped either so this was a moment of revelation for all of them too, as well as the audience who would watch the interview when it aired.

"I was so afraid. I was seventeen and had never done anything with a guy before, and it was painful and terrifying and I couldn't fight him off," Kiara said quietly, her eyes shimmering with tears, her face pale. "It is without a doubt the worst thing that has ever happened to me, and I live with the memory of it every day."

The tears flowed down her face and Beth handed her a tissue.

***

The Jacobs listened in horrified silence.

"Oh my god, I feel sick," Sarah said in a low voice, burying her head against Victor's shoulder. Janet cried. "Why didn't she tell us?" she sobbed. Victor's jaw was clenched and anger simmered in his eyes.

Shane listened until the commercial break, then walked out to the patio without saying a word. He smashed his bottle of beer onto the stone and yelled into the sky, fists clenched in rage at what Kiara's father had allowed to happen, at what that man had done to her, and at the years that had been lost because of them.

***

"Kiara, I really am shocked and so sorry to hear about these terrible things that have happened to you." Beth leaned forward and her grey eyes were damp with tears, and Kiara couldn't tell if she was being sincere or not.

They hadn't lingered on the details of that night. Kiara genuinely didn't know the man who had been in the trailer that evening, and now that her father was dead she was sure that he would never be found out. As they carried on with the interview, she talked briefly about living in New York and how she had found work as a stripper to make ends meet. Fortunately, Beth's team didn't know about Rob and Marco agreed that it was best Kiara didn't speak about him, so she kept the details vague of her time in the city.

"I hated being a stripper," Kiara said, "but it paid the bills and meant I didn't have to live on the streets."

Beth nodded. "And then you found some bar work and it was there that your current manager Marco actually heard you singing for the first time?"

Kiara grinned, her skin tight from the tears. "I didn't know it was him who left the flyer for the auditions till after I got accepted into the group. It was like he was some kind of very hip, very tanned guardian angel," she laughed, and she could see Marco grinning from the side of the set.

She was glad that the bulk of the interview was nearly done now, the heat of the lights was starting to make her feel woozy and nauseated.

"Kiara, you're a true survivor, having gone through such a lot so young, and are a role model now to those who have been abused or who can't see a way to make their dreams a reality," Beth said.

"One thing I can't quite understand though, is why you haven't got back in touch with the family who helped you when you were younger. You said earlier how much you loved them and remembered their kindness. Why haven't you contacted them?" Beth asked.

Kiara sat silently for a moment. There were many times she had considered emailing Victor's company asking to be put in touch, or picking up the phone, or even writing a letter. Every time though, something had stopped her. It was only recently that she had been able to put a name to what it was.

"Shame," she said, finally. "I was ashamed. Of everything I had done and everything I had been through. I was too ashamed. I'm not the girl they knew back then, and I think maybe they wouldn't want to know the person I am today, with all this baggage." The tears were on her cheeks again, as much as she wished they weren't.

Beth nodded and paused while Kiara wiped her eyes. "Well Kiara, what would you say if you knew that they were waiting and hoping for you to get in touch with them? What would you do if you knew for sure that they were desperate to see you again?"

A crew member ran up to Beth and handed her a card. The front of the card was a close-up of a rose, deep red, the petals delicately unfurled. There was no caption.

"Dear Kiara," Beth began to read from inside the card. "We are so proud of you and your success. More than that, we are so glad to see you are safe and well." She paused, looking at Kiara, who stared at her unblinking and unreadable.

"We want you to know that we have missed you and thought of you every single day since you left. We love you and we hope we will see you again one day. Love, Janet, Victor, Shane and Sarah Jacobs."

Kiara took a breath. Beth handed her the card and she held it with shaking hands, scanning the writing. There a phone number scrawled along the bottom that Beth hadn't read out loud. Her heart slammed inside her chest. She was trying so hard not to burst into tears and had to bury her head in her hands and count to ten to compose herself. Beth watched her and waited till she raised her head again.

"The Jacobs, of Jacobs Sports Management fame, who were there for you all those years, are waiting for you to get in touch with them Kiara. Do you think you'll do that now you've seen that card?"

Kiara looked directly into the camera, able to say only one word. "Yes."

Beth smiled. "Well that's all we have time for tonight. Thank you so much Kiara for your honesty and bravery in talking about your difficult past and all you've been through to become the person you are today. Good night, everyone."

The signal was given and the cameras switched off. Beth leaned in to Kiara, who was sitting like stone, unmoving. "I hope that wasn't too hard for you. Your management were very good at prepping me for all of it beforehand so I hope I was able to help you along," Beth said to her in a low voice.

Kiara looked at her in confusion, before Beth patted her on the shoulder and walked off, several crew members congratulating her on a great interview. Kiara stood up shakily and walked off the set. Alicia ran up, and without saying anything pulled her into a full body hug, holding her tight.

"I had no idea," she whispered to Kiara. She pulled back and held Kiara at arm's length. "You okay?"

Kiara shook her head and looked down at the card, turning it over in her hands. There was a date in the inside corner. It had been sent eight months previously. Kiara could see Marco smiling with his arms folded, nodding and laughing with the crew. She walked away from Alicia and strode towards him, and his smile faded as he saw her expression. She raised her hand and slapped him across the face, a hard crack resounding through the air.

He grabbed his jaw as she walked away, taking Alicia by the hand, as the hum of the set came to a surprised halt around them.

**

The girls huddled together in Kiara's apartment.

"What is Marco going to do?" Michelle asked, her eyes wide.

Kiara shrugged. "Nothing. He deserved it and he knows it. He's letting it go."

"Are you?" Sierra asked, incredulously.

Kiara sighed. "I'm still mad about what he did, but at least I know now what he is capable of in the name of getting the right story."

"Are you going to call the number in the card Kiara?" Megan asked.

They all looked at her expectantly.

"The interview airs tomorrow night," she said, hesitantly. "So maybe I'll call a few days after that."

Alicia looked frustrated. "A few days?" she said, raising an eyebrow.

"Maybe they won't see it straight away. Maybe they won't watch it at all." Kiara shrugged.

Michelle grabbed the card and waved it in her face, "Hell-o, did you not read this? They are obviously desperate to see you again. Of course they will watch your interview."

Sierra nodded. "Definitely Kiara. You have to call them. They'll know you've gotten their card when they see the interview."

Kiara nodded. "We'll see."

**

"Who wrote that card?" said Victor, indignantly, raising his voice over the end titles of the show as the interview finished. He looked accusingly at Shane and Sarah. "We agreed, no contact until she was ready to get in touch with us."

Janet stood up from the couch and folded her arms. "Actually Victor, I sent that card."

They looked up at her, surprised. Janet had always been someone to keep the peace and didn't like to seek out disagreements. She was usually happy to go along with Victor's advice on most things.

"You heard her – she was ashamed, she didn't know if we would want to hear from her. She needed to be told that we were waiting for her, so I'm glad I sent that card and I don't regret it, although how Beth Winters got hold of it I'll never know."

"Did you put any contact details in the card mom?" Sarah asked.

Janet nodded. "A cell phone number."

"Yours?" asked Sarah.

Janet shook her head and smiled. "Shane's."

As she said it, Shane's cell phone began to beep in his pocket. Janet flinched in surprise.

"Oh my god Shane, answer it, answer it, answer it!" Sarah shrieked as he searched through his pockets with shaking hands.

"Hello, Shane Jacobs," he answered. Victor, Janet and Sarah stared at him as he listened, and then he turned to them and grinned.

"Hi Kiara, it's so good to hear your voice," he said, as Sarah jumped around the living room and Victor started laughing.

The reunion

"What do I wear?" Kiara asked Alicia, who was curled up on the bed.

"You know Kiara, you really should make this place more homely," Alicia said, gazing around.

"That's not what I asked! I don't need interior decorating advice right now Ali!" Kiara threw a purse at her. Alicia giggled and deflected the purse.

"Seriously, what do I wear?" Kiara pleaded, rifling through racks of clothes she didn't even know she had, sent to her for free.

"I don't know, Kiara. What does it matter? They'll be so thrilled to see you that you could turn up in full dominatrix gear and I don't think they would care." Alicia started laughing again.

"How about this?" Kiara said, pulling out a pale blue dress. Alicia nodded, "Looks good."

Kiara started pulling off her t-shirt and jeans to try it on. The girls had gotten so used to being naked in front of each other all the time as they raced to change clothes between performances that it really didn't bother Kiara to change in front of them anymore. She pulled the dress over her head and checked it in the mirror.

"Hey, how's things going with Sebastian?" she asked Alicia, as she turned around in front of the mirror.

Alicia smiled. "Sooo good."

Kiara jumped on the bed. "Are you in love?" she asked Alicia, smiling.

Alicia made a motion to show her lips were zipped. "I can't say," she said, "but I will tell you that he is great in bed."

Kiara laughed and covered her mouth in fake shock. She turned around and Alicia started to braid her hair, gently folding in her curls and leaving a few strays at the front.

"When are you going to start dating?" she asked Kiara as she focused on the braid. Kiara gave a short laugh. "Never. I have no interest in dating."

She faced Alicia. "Never say never," Alicia said, waving her finger at her, then looked her over and smiled. "You look beautiful. Are you ready?" Alicia asked her.

"Absolutely."

***

It had taken a few weeks for Kiara to find a time when she was free to meet the Jacobs. Marco had asked if the reunion could be filmed. She had glared at him so angrily that he laughed and held up his hands in mock surrender. They had an uneasy truce since the interview. He had apologised for keeping the card from her, for blindsiding her on camera like that, and had pleaded for forgiveness. She gave it – despite her anger, she was still absurdly fond of him, although she trusted him less than before.

They had arranged to meet in the penthouse suite of a hotel in New York. Kiara's label often used them as they could be trusted to keep any photographers out, which couldn't be guaranteed anywhere else, even at the house in Connecticut.

She travelled to the hotel in a sleek car with blacked out windows, the seats cool against her legs. The Jacobs would already be there waiting for her. She had decided to phone them as soon as the interview aired, on the insistence of the other girls, who had sat her down, put a phone in her hand, dialled the number and left the room.

It was Shane who answered the phone, but she could hear Sarah in the background demanding he put it on speakerphone. They had spoken only briefly, awkwardly, agreeing that they would arrange a time to meet through the group's assistant. Janet had come onto the phone before they ended the call, speaking softly, her voice shaded with tears – "We can't wait to see you again."

Right now, she was feeling a mix of nervous excitement and dread. She was scared about how much they had moved on and how much she had changed, and worried if things would be stilted and strange between them.

The car pulled up outside and she jumped out quickly, striding into the hotel and nodding to the receptionist as she entered the elevator, her heels tapping on the marble floor. The elevator began to rise and so did her nerves in her throat. She tried to breathe deeply and she wished she had drunk something to take the edge off before she came. The elevator slid open with a soft hush and she stepped out onto plush carpeting in front of the penthouse door.

The Jacobs were sitting down when she came in, Sarah, Victor and Janet on the couch and Shane on one of the chairs beside them. They looked up quickly as she came in and gently shut the door behind her. As she started walking over to them, her heels dragging on the thick carpeting, Janet stood up and walked over to her and, without a word, wrapped her arms round her and held her closely, pulling her in tight. Kiara buried her face in her shoulder and breathed in vanilla and sandalwood and Janet said in a shaking voice, "I'm so happy to see you."

Janet stepped back and then Sarah was already there waiting to hug her too, half-crying and half-laughing and telling her she looked amazing. Victor was next as she turned around and he grabbed her in a tight hug saying, "It's so good to have you back," and then Shane was wrapping his arms around her and holding her so close she could barely breathe. She was laughing as he released her and they sat down, Kiara on a chair facing them, smiling so hard her cheeks were aching, and it wasn't awkward or stilted, it was perfect.

They had so much to talk about. They focused on talking about how things were now, the group and their success, how they had seen her video on YouTube nearly eleven months ago, asking about where Kiara lived now and what the other girls were like, catching up about Sarah's marriage to Tim, the company and how it had grown and how Kiara had seen them on TV and in the newspapers too. Shane showed her photos of Joshua and she cooed breathlessly over them and asked how Melanie was and only then was there a pause and he told her sadly that things hadn't worked out. But Sarah had steamed right back into questions about the group and what it was like being so famous, and that they had seen her in the sexiest women in the world list and Kiara laughed, embarrassed.

To them, she was the same kind and funny girl they had known, but now so confident, radiant and beautiful. Gone were the frayed jeans and the ill-fitting shoes. She didn't have much makeup on but her eyes glowed like a summer sky and a few red curls gently brushed her face.

Janet had a small paper bag at her feet and she handed it over to Kiara. "These were a few little things I managed to save for you," she said.

Kiara delved into the bag. "My notebooks!" she said, waving them around. "All my lyrics are here," she said, flicking through the pages, laughing at the childish hand and immature rhymes. She came to the page with the love hearts, Shane's name etched carefully into each one, and quickly slammed the book shut, blushing and hanging her head with a smile. She looked sideways at Sarah, who had seen the page and had covered her mouth with her hand, laughing.

"Oh my god, that's embarrassing," Kiara whispered to her, and they started giggling uncontrollably. Janet knew what they were laughing about, but Victor and Shane couldn't see the page and looked bemused.

"Thank you for saving these Janet," Kiara turned to her. "I thought my dad got rid of all my stuff from the trailer."

"Why would you think that?" Victor asked her.

Kiara nibbled on her lower lip and took a short breath. "I went there."

"I knew it, I knew you had been back," Shane said, sitting straight up, "It was you, wasn't it? Who burned the trailer?"

Kiara looked at him in surprise. "Yeah, how did you know?"

"I just knew," he said, and looked at his family triumphantly, feeling vindicated.

"I know I shouldn't have done it, but…" Kiara trailed off and looked at her knees, not wanting to bring dark and difficult topics into the happy conversation.

Janet put an arm around her and then for the first time there was a silence, there were lots of questions still to be asked, but no one wanted to break the joyful bubble in which they found themselves. Shane was the first to speak. He had so much to ask her but he knew now wasn't the right time, and all the frustration and anger and guilt he had felt had dissipated the moment she walked in the door and he was just happy to see her.

"Kiara, anytime you want to talk, to any of us, you can if you want to. Anytime, okay?" he leaned forward and his dark eyes looked into hers, and the memory of kissing him leapt into her thoughts, no more than a flicker of a memory, and she smiled back at him.

163

"Thank you."

Six months reunited

Kiara lay back in the car and watched the pale skies slide past as they wound their way towards the Jacobs' house from the airport. She had landed from Paris a few hours before, jet lagged and exhausted, and desperate to get to the Jacobs and spend Christmas with them for the first time in so many years. She had been in touch with the Jacobs by phone and text, regularly pinging messages back and forth as she travelled around doing performances and recordings. She had wanted to see more of them, but the label had scheduled so much activity that the group was rarely in one city for more than a few days at a time.

This year each of the girls had demanded a proper break of at least a week to go and visit family and friends. They had worked hard over the past year with barely a rest, and it was time to relax. They had said goodbye in Paris and all flown to various places and homes across the US.

At first, Kiara hadn't been sure what she would do to fill a week and she had hesitantly phoned Janet who instantly told her she should spend the entire week with them. Sarah and Tim would be there for a few days, Shane too, Joshua for a day as well. For the first time in many years, Kiara was looking forward to Christmas.

She had no time to buy or wrap any presents and had picked up armloads of things at the airport instead, makeup, perfumes, cologne, French wines, and chocolates, handing over her credit card without flinching at the cost, signing an autograph for the store assistant, and hoping the Jacobs would be happy with the selection.

Kiara had closed her eyes for a moment in the car, woozy from lack of sleep, and then was woken up as they pulled into the drive at the Jacobs' house. Sarah was opening the front door and Victor and Shane were bounding out to help her with her bags, stunned at how much baggage she had, and Tim was walking out swiftly to greet her for the first time.

She wrapped her arms round Sarah and gave her a kiss on the cheek, patting her on the tummy to feel her baby bump, which was still small, only being four months along. They dragged her and her bags inside the house, dumping them in the hall, and Sarah grabbed her by the hand and pulled her into the kitchen for coffee and cake. The whole house smelled of cinnamon and pine, the warm air wrapping around her in a welcome contrast to the bitter cold outside.

She was trying to have a conversation with Tim, with frequent interruptions from everyone asking her about the tour, and she started to lose focus and answer the wrong person with the wrong answer, and they started laughing as she told them she didn't even know what time it was and perhaps she better have a shower and nap.

Janet showed her to the guest room and Shane and Victor helped to cart her bags up there. She couldn't quite believe she was here again, eight years after she had left, now twenty-five, wealthy, famous, and loved. She felt a deep sense of joy as she lay back against the pillows and breathed in the sweet smell of the clean sheets.

***

It was late afternoon when she woke up, the sky dimming and cheerful voices floating up to her from downstairs. She showered and changed into jeans and a plain black sweater, leaving her hair loose, and headed downstairs. She walked to the kitchen, where Janet was busy preparing dinner.

"How are you feeling?" she asked, as Kiara walked in.

"I feel great!" she said, perkily. "Need any help?"

"It's all pretty much done," said Janet, wiping her hands on a towel. "Coffee?"

Kiara nodded and took the coffee cup gratefully, hoping it would help to chase away the blurry edges of her tiredness.

"Sarah is having a lie down too, she feels pretty tired out with the pregnancy, but the guys are in the living room if you want to hang out with them," Janet said, sipping her coffee.

"Or, I could hang out with you?" Kiara asked, grinning.

Janet smiled and sat at the table, patting the chair next to her. They had a good hour to catch up, the first time they had talked alone. They talked about how things had been in the time Kiara had been away, the weddings, the deaths, the successes, the sorrows. Kiara cried to hear that Mary had passed away, and that Ted was now in a home for the elderly, where dementia had robbed him of memory and muscle control. She was delighted to hear that Moira was dating and on a cruise in the Mediterranean. She asked about Tim's parents, down in Omaha, and how Janet and Victor got on with them, and they briefly talked about Shane and Melanie, but Janet said it was better that Shane updated her on that.

Kiara told Janet about the girls, about Alicia's spark and strength, Michelle's quiet kindness, Megan's icy ambition behind which she hid a goofy sense of humour, Sierra's beauty and elegance, and about Marco and how he drove them all insane but he had managed them well even though they didn't always see eye to eye.

Sarah came down to help set up for dinner and she and Kiara prepared the table, lit the candles, and set the Christmas tree lights flashing. The table was crowded and noisy, food piled high and wine poured generously, and they all ate and drank too much and collapsed lazily in the living room afterwards, tipsy and hot, Kiara begging to see Sarah's wedding photos and then collapsing into laughter as they reminisced about movie nights and pool parties. Tim was left out of much of the conversation but sat happily stroking his wife's leg, laughing along, before Sarah felt too tired and they went to bed, and then Janet and Victor left Kiara and Shane to carry on talking late into the night.

Shane poured them both whiskey and Kiara winced as she gulped it down too fast and spluttered, Shane laughing and whacking her on the back, and pouring her another glass when she held hers up for a refill. He told her all about Joshua and how he was growing up so quickly.

"And Melanie?" she asked, tentatively, "What happened Shane?"

Shane grimaced. "The truth is all so…" he paused for a moment, "mundane. I worked too many hours, was gone too much, and she was alone with the baby. I guess she got fed up." He frowned, swirling the whiskey in his glass. "I suppose I thought we would have a break, then I would get the chance to try again, try to make a go of things, but before I knew it I was being sent divorce papers, and then she was seeing someone else. It all went so wrong, so quickly." He downed his glass and poured another.

Kiara patted his arm. "I'm so sorry Shane, I really am."

He turned his head to smile at her, dark eyes glinting in the dim lamplight. "And you?" he asked.

"And me what?" she smiled back.

"Dating anyone? I bet you have loads of guys chasing you now, number nine," he laughed, referring to her place on the world's sexiest women list.

She laughed with him but shook her head. "No way, Shane. I'm not dating anyone." Her smiled faded a little. "So much has happened that I'm not sure I want to be in any relationship." She

166

looked at him sadly, and he put his arm around her and gave her a hug, just like he used to when she was struggling at school and he had no other way to help her.

"I think a lot more happened to you than what you said on the TV," he said, gently.

Kiara pulled back from him and nodded. "What, you think I'd tell all my deep dark secrets to Beth Winters?" she said, grinning.

Shane shook his head. "I hope not."

He leaned back on the couch and folded his hands behind his head, looking at her. "Want to tell me?"

Kiara raised an eyebrow. "I'm not sure you could handle it Shane," she smiled but her eyes were serious.

"Try me."

Kiara had drunk enough to consider telling Shane the parts of the story she had missed out for Beth, about Rob and Dan and the drugs, and the less sanitised version of what it was really like in the strip club. She curled up against him and told him in a low voice the parts she had missed or the things she had skimmed over.

"Wooooow," he breathed out, when she had finished. They were silent for a few moments, her head on his chest, his heartbeat starting to make her feel sleepy.

"Hey, have you ever spoken to anyone about, well, everything?" he asked her, murmuring into the top of her head, his lips close to her hair.

"Marco knows everything," she said.

"No, Kiara," Shane sat up so she turned to face him, "I meant have you gotten any help for what you've been through? Like, did Marco suggest someone you could talk to about it all, to try to work through all this stuff that you've experienced?"

She frowned at him. "Like a shrink? I'm not crazy, you know."

He shrugged. "You don't have to be crazy to see a therapist. You've really been through some shit and it might help to talk to someone."

She pressed her lips together. "I don't need to see anyone Shane. Honestly, I'm fine. Okay?"

He looked at her for a moment, her blue eyes defiant, and he nodded. "Good to hear."

She got up to leave, but as she turned to walk out of the room, he called out after her. "I thought it was my fault you left."

She swung back round, eyes wide with surprise. He looked at her from the couch.

"Why would you think that?" she said, steadying herself on the doorframe, the alcohol making the ground sway gently beneath her.

"Because I pushed you away that night," he replied, his eyes searching her face for her reaction.

"Oh," she said. She walked up to him and bent down to hug him. She spoke into his ear. "It was *not* your fault. You made life more bearable than I can say."

She kissed him on the cheek, straightened up and walked out of the room.

***

Kiara put her hands in her pockets, breathing in the cold morning air. Her head pounded from the night before and her feet felt numb in her thin sneakers.

She looked up at the trees and closed her eyes, feeling drops of icy slush fall fat and wet onto her hair and cheeks. There was nothing left of the trailer, her childhood home, only earth and leaves covered with an icy smattering of snow.

She heard footsteps crunching behind her and swung round to see Victor approaching.

"Morning kiddo," he said, walking up to her. "I thought you'd be out here."

She smiled at him and linked her arm through his, leaning her head on his shoulder.

"Tired?" he asked her.

"Hungover," she said, grimacing, and they both laughed, the sound gently chiming out in the cold air through the trees.

They stood there in companionable silence, shifting their feet from the frozen ground. Kiara's feet were soaked through and she shivered.

"Have you been to the grave?" Victor asked her.

She shook her head.

"I'll take you there if you want to go." He said, his pale blue eyes squinting against the steel grey skies. He looked so much older than she remembered, his eyes more lined, the cold wind blowing strands of hair over his forehead.

"I don't want to go. Is that bad?" she turned to him and asked.

Victor smiled. "Not if you don't want to go."

They turned and starting walking back to the house together.

"You know, it took me years to go to my father's grave," he said, as they walked. She nodded in silence, their feet crunching over mounds of ice, the white crystals muddied from the earth underneath.

"I was so angry at him for so long. I was glad when I went eventually, but it took me a long time to get there," he continued.

"Maybe one day I'll go," she said, quietly.

He put his arm around her and they trudged back across the garden to the house, where Janet and Tim were preparing coffee.

***

Kiara apologised again and again that the gifts weren't wrapped as she handed them out later that afternoon, but no one cared. There was a chaos of presents, ribbons and wrapping strewn everywhere. There was a celebratory feeling in the air, with Sarah pregnant and Kiara back again.

Shane was subdued, thinking of Melanie and Joshua, but he was soon laughing and joking with Tim and enjoying a drink with Victor, trying to put his son out of his mind until tomorrow when he would be seeing him. He knew Melanie wasn't far away, visiting Alma and Kent, and the thought of their presence nearby made him ache with sadness, but he tried to focus on being present with his family.

Janet brought down a huge bag of gifts and set it before Kiara.

"Are all these for me?" Kiara said, staring at the bag, wide-eyed. "I really don't need anything," she said, hesitantly.

"Kiara, there's seven years of birthday and Christmas gifts in there," Janet said.

"We always set them aside for you, hoping one day you'd be back to open them," Sarah added.

Kiara bowed her head, tears pricking at her eyes, and took out the gifts, lining them up according to the years marked on the labels. She started with her eighteenth birthday present. Janet had bought it before she had run away – a beautiful gold necklace with a 'K' and a single teardrop diamond. Kiara turned to Shane to put the necklace on her, and she lifted her hair out of the way as he clasped it round her neck, wiping tears from her cheeks. They all cheered and started to laugh as Tim started a very out of tune rendition of Happy Birthday.

Every Christmas gift she opened met with a cheer of "Merry Christmas!" and every birthday gift prompted another terrible round of singing, each worse than the previous, until she slumped on the floor, weak from laughter, holding her sides.

Janet stood up, Sarah joining her. "We have one final gift for you Kiara," Janet announced.

"Stand up," Sarah held out her hand to Kiara and pulled her off the floor, turned her around and wrapped a scarf around her eyes.

Kiara giggled and allowed herself to be propelled along by Shane, his hands on her arms, pushing her along from behind. She felt them cross the hallway floor and go into the dining room where they stopped her and pulled off the scarf. She was standing in front of the piano, where someone had draped a large red bow on it.

Mouth open, she turned to Janet. "You're giving me the piano?" she said, shocked, knowing how much the piano meant to Janet and to the whole family.

"It was your mom's, how can I possibly accept this?" she said, running her hands over its familiar smooth contours.

"Well, now it's yours," Janet said, smiling. "We wanted to keep it in the family, after all."

She looked at them and blinked more tears away, and with great ceremony sat at the keys and began to play and sing for them, Janet leaning her head against the wood, watching her proudly.

**

Kiara heard a soft knock on the door. It was gone midnight and she assumed everyone was asleep, so she was surprised to find Sarah standing outside her bedroom.

"Hey what's up?" she asked.

"I can't sleep and saw your light on," Sarah said.

Kiara beckoned her in and shut the door. Sarah sat on the bed, Kiara beside her.

"How are you feeling?" Kiara asked.

"A little nauseous, but fine," Sarah murmured, one hand stroking her stomach. "What's that?" she said, nodding towards the nightstand, where Kiara had a small bottle of pills and a bottle of vodka.

Kiara winced inwardly and wished she had remembered to put them away. She was normally so careful to keep the pills and alcohol hidden, and even when she was on tour she made sure the other girls didn't see them. She tried to sound nonchalant. "Just some sleeping pills. Sometimes I have trouble sleeping when I'm on tour."

"But you're not on tour now," Sarah said, looking concerned, squinting at the label on the bottle.

Kiara quickly reached across and swept the pills and bottles into the drawer. "I just forgot to put them away, that's all," she said hurriedly, hoping Sarah would change the subject.

Marco had suggested that she try the pills when he found out about her reliance on alcohol to sleep. She knew she wasn't supposed to mix them with alcohol, but the combination seemed to work so well with a little vodka chaser, enough to put her out without nightmares and not so much that she felt too ill to get going the next morning.

She had hoped that she wouldn't need them when she was at the Jacobs' house but the first night she had lain awake, visions flitting in and out of the dark, the shadows appearing to grow and loom threateningly, even in this room that smelled like summer florals and that she knew was safe in. She lay there thinking about Rob and about her father, and her head started to pound and her stomach churn. She had dry-heaved in the bathroom till she had given in and downed a few mouthfuls of vodka and taken a pill, feeling a welcome cloudiness chase away the nausea and the anxious churning.

"Tim is really lovely," Kiara said to Sarah, changing the subject.

Sarah smiled. "He's wonderful, I'm so lucky to have him."

They chatted for a while about how they met. Sarah's friend Amber was a patient of Tim's and thought they would be a good match, so she had set them up on a date together.

"It's a shame about Shane and Melanie," Sarah said, looking at Kiara from the corner of her eyes.

Kiara nodded. "He's really cut up about it. So awful."

Sarah looked at her, grinning, and poked her in the foot. "But he *is* single now though…"

Kiara glanced at her and raised her eyebrows. "So?"

"Well, you've always liked him," Sarah trailed off.

Kiara shook her head, two red circles blooming on her cheeks. "No, that page in my notebook was just me being silly, kid stuff."

Sarah sat up and gave her a shove. "C'mon Kiara, you adored him. We all knew, even without seeing your notebook," she said, matter-of-factly.

Kiara's blush deepened and spread down her neck. "Nooooo, it wasn't like that," she protested, while Sarah grinned at her.

"Well, all I'm saying is he's single now and so are you." Sarah lay back on the bed, relaxing with her hands behind her head, propped up on a pillow.

Kiara shook her head. "I'm really not looking to date anyone," she said.

"Why not?" Sarah replied.

Kiara thought for a moment. "Too much baggage."

"Any guy would be lucky to have you," Sarah said, rolling over and standing up from the bed. "Sorry sweetie, I've got to get to sleep now, all of a sudden I feel completely exhausted and I feel like I might fall asleep right here!"

Kiara nodded and wished her goodnight, then opened the drawer and fished out the pills.

***

The following morning Shane was up early waiting for Melanie to drop Joshua off for the day, when his phoned buzzed. *"Running late, be there by 9.30."*

He frowned and sipped his coffee, tapping his hands on the table impatiently. Sarah walked in and poured herself a glass of water, sitting down at the table with him.

"Nauseous?" he asked her.

"A little, but it's really not so bad anymore. Is Melanie on her way?" she asked.

"Soon," he said, and studied his phone, flicking through Melanie's Facebook feed, full of Christmas photos of Joshua.

"Shane," Sarah said, hesitantly.

"Yup," he said, not looking up from his phone.

"Can I talk to you about Kiara?" she said. He looked up. "Sure."

She told him about the pills and the vodka bottles. They had both noticed that she drunk quite a bit in the evenings, that her lights were on late, that she frequently had headaches in the morning, but Shane had thought perhaps it was just because it was the holidays and she was enjoying herself. Pills and vodka on the nightstand seemed like a bad sign.

"I did ask her if she had spoken to anyone, you know, about the rape and all the other stuff she went through," said Shane.

"She told you everything?" Sarah asked.

Shane shrugged. "Pretty much. But she hasn't spoken to anyone about it, apart from her douchebag manager." He frowned. "You'd think the label would want to make sure she got some support rather than getting her to air that shit on camera for ratings."

They sat there quietly, the kitchen clock marking off the minutes, till the front door rang.

"It's Melanie. Let's talk about this later, okay?" Shane said, standing up and walking to the door.

"Hi Shane," Melanie handed Joshua over, who squirmed and grabbed her hair with his fists. She managed to loosen his grip and passed him to Shane. He chattered excitedly in Shane's arms, wriggling energetically.

"Merry Christmas," he said, as they stood there awkwardly, a cold breeze snaking into the house.

"You want to come in for a coffee?" he asked her, hoping that she might relent and come inside.

She shook her head, glancing at the car behind her. "I have to get going. I'll pick him up later, okay?"

He nodded. Melanie's gaze was suddenly averted, her green eyes looking past Shane into the house. Kiara walked down the stairs, still in her pyjamas, yawning and stretching, cat-like and sleepy. She walked behind Shane and caught a glimpse of Melanie at the open door and waved before heading to the kitchen.

"So, she's back?" she said to Shane.

He grinned and nodded. "She came straight here from Paris. It's good to have her back again."

Melanie smiled. "I'm happy for you guys that she's back," and she meant it, remembering Victor and Janet's distress for those years when Kiara had been lost to them.

Melanie waved goodbye to Joshua and headed for the car, hopping in the passenger seat. Shane didn't try to see who was in the driver's side. He turned and shut the door, carrying Joshua into the living room to meet Kiara, who was now sipping coffee and laying on the couch. She spent hours laying on the floor playing with him, making funny faces to make him laugh, zooming sticky plastic toy cars around the floor. She was reminded of Isaac and felt a pang of sadness at not having seen her friends for so long. She pinged Betty a message to wish them *Feliz Navidad* with a string of kisses.

A short while before lunch she realised she was still in her pyjamas and stood up to go and change, leaving Joshua with Sarah and Tim and heading up to her room. She stopped abruptly in the doorway as she found Shane sitting on the bed, reading the label on her pills.

"What are you doing?" she demanded, hands on hips, a red flush sweeping over her cheeks.

Shane looked up and shook the bottle at her, pointing to the small pile of empty liquor bottles he had pulled out of the nightstand drawer.

"Are you taking this stuff every night?" he asked.

She clenched her fists at her side, feeling a hot anger rise in her stomach. "That's none of your business, Shane."

He raised his eyebrows. "Hey, I just want to make sure you're okay, and this," he swung his hand over the bottles, "this is not okay."

She marched up to him and grabbed the pills and stuffed everything back into the drawer, the glass clinking angrily as she laid bottle after bottle back inside.

"Please don't go through my things," she snapped at him.

He stepped back, his eyes drawn and lips pressed together, annoyed.

"We care about you, unlike that manager of yours that you're always talking about. Does he know about this?" He jabbed a finger at the nightstand.

Kiara folded her arms, annoyance making her heart beat faster, her pulse scudding in her throat. "Yes, he does actually."

She turned her back to Shane and began straightening the bedclothes, pulling them violently. "You should be downstairs with Joshua. He's the one you need to take care of, not me."

Shane stood behind her, resolute and unmoving. She swung round and put her hands on his shoulders and pushed him backwards out of the room.

"Get the hell out!" she shrieked.

Janet passed by at the top of the stairs, pausing in surprise. Shane looked at her and shook his head, shocked. He had never seen Kiara angry before, she had always tried so hard to be meek and quiet and pliable.

"This isn't you. The Kiara I know would *never* push people out of a room," he said to her firmly, leaning against the doorway.

"That girl is gone," Kiara told him flatly, her mouth pressed into a thin line. "I know how to take care of myself Shane, you don't need to worry about me."

He raised his eyebrows. "Take care of yourself? That's what you call it? Drinking yourself to sleep, just like your dad used to do?" The words came out before he thought about them, they fell out into the air and though he felt his mom's gentle hand on his shoulder and her voice telling him to leave Kiara be, he said it anyway.

Kiara slammed the door in his face and the slam echoed around the house as she threw herself angrily on the bed, furious at his interfering, his words running over and over in her mind.

She stayed curled up on the bed for a while, her heart thudding so angrily she could feel the frustration reverberating through her entire body. She closed her eyes and balled her hands into fists over them, trying to breathe. After a little while she stopped trembling and, as she thought of how hurt Shane had looked when she pushed him out of the room, a wave of guilt passed through her, swiping off the hard edges off her anger.

She knew that he was right. The fact that she still needed the pills and the alcohol to sleep at night wasn't normal. She was no longer in Hunts Point, no longer in the trailer, there was no one there to hurt her, and yet as she lay in bed each night her thoughts were always stuck in those places. As soon as it got dark and quiet, even on tour, she could feel the memories encroaching upon her.

Up on stage amidst the noise, the lights, the music, the dancing, everything else went away, just like it had done when she sat downstairs playing the piano as a child, dreaming of another life. When she was with the girls or with the Jacobs these past few days, a sense of acceptance and happiness enveloped her. But on her own at night every room became her childhood bedroom in the trailer, or Rob's room in Hunts Point, every sound an intruder, every breeze the breath of someone lying in wait.

She didn't know how to make it better, but she had trusted Rob when he said alcohol would quiet the demons, and she had trusted Marco when he said the pills would give her some peace. She had trusted them because, unlike Shane, Rob and Marco had their own sufferings they were trying to blot out – Rob the memories of the children's homes and surviving with Dan after running away, and Marco, growing up bisexual in a family he never dared to tell, and being kicked out when he fell in love with a friend who betrayed his secret. She was damaged like they had been, and she trusted their advice on how to get by.

Still, she knew the Jacobs would be worried, and even if they didn't understand, she had to try to make them see that everything would be okay, that she could fend for herself now, and that she wasn't a 'problem' to be taken care of anymore.

She got up and showered, standing under the blasting hot water till it turned her skin rose-pink, then got dressed and headed downstairs. Sarah and Tim were out visiting one of Sarah's old friends, Janet was talking with Victor in the living room. The smell of Janet's homemade mulled wine hung heavy in the air, a smell of warmth and home and hope. Kiara remembered breathing it in when

175

she was younger and being allowed a sip when she had turned fourteen.

She found Shane in the kitchen. Joshua was having a nap, tired out from all the activity. She walked up to him and wrapped her arms around his neck, pressing him close.

"I'm sorry," she whispered in his ear.

He hugged her tightly and they stayed like that for a moment before Victor strolled in to top up his wine. "Woah! Sorry for interrupting," he said, holding up his hands.

Kiara broke off from Shane and laughed. "Not to worry Victor, I was just apologising for being a crazy bitch."

Shane laughed too and the awkwardness was broken, cups were filled with mulled wine and normal conversations resumed. Shane didn't try to talk to her about the pills again, but every night when she climbed the stairs to her bedroom he hugged her harder than before and told her she could always talk to him if she needed, and he watched her go to her bedroom and worried about what haunted her and the things she felt she couldn't share.

***

There were tears when it was time to depart. Kiara was to head straight to the airport to fly to Amsterdam for more promotions. As her car pulled up in the driveway, she kissed the Jacobs goodbye, promising Sarah that she would come to her baby shower in the spring if she could and was determined to invite them round to her apartment in New York one day.

As the car pulled away, she felt a terrible sense of déjà vu, the memory of leaving and fleeing and realising that she wouldn't see them again for an unknown amount of time. Even though this time she was going to a job she loved and she would see them again soon, the feeling of dread lingered on her like a cold finger stabbing her in the stomach, until she arrived in Amsterdam and checked into her hotel, where the paparazzi and Marco were already waiting for her.

Nine months reunited

As hard as she tried, it was difficult to find the time to meet up with the Jacobs.

The group released an album and the singles did well. They toured, rehearsed, recorded, and performed. They had few days off, scattered around cities she didn't know and never saw much of apart from the hotel and the airport and whatever stage they were performing on. They did early morning radio shows and whole days of interviews to promote the album and Kiara had regular questions fired at her from interviewers about her reunion with the Jacobs.

Kiara's status as lead vocalist was never in question by the label or the press, but Megan in particular and Sierra sometimes complained when a new track was tailored to Kiara's range and their parts spliced around hers. Marco always shushed them and soothed them, rolling his eyes at their complaints behind their backs.

When they were in New York, they always went back to the club where they started, where Frank was still manager, gathering with him in his office to say hello and performing nights there unannounced, to the delight and surprise of the crowds.

There had been a lot of press attention in the nine months since the Beth Winter's interview. Some of Kiara's old classmates had surfaced, giving meaningless quotes about how they were friends and always thought she was a great singer. One guy, whose name she didn't recognise, gallingly suggested he had shared a kiss with her when they were sixteen, under the headline "Kiara's first kiss?" Frieda, their new press manager now Anna had left, had rung Kiara to let her know the story would be coming out the next day. Kiara had issued a comment to say he was lying, and the story had gone no further. Shane had texted her the headline with a laughing emoji and she had smiled – the fleeting kiss they had shared that night remained their secret.

There was constant speculation about the girls and their love lives. Sierra and Alicia were dating – Sierra was enjoying a fierce infatuation with a handsome backing dancer and Alicia was now seeing a music producer she met at a party. Photos of the couples appeared in glossy magazines, while inaccurate stories often surfaced about the other members of the group being romantically linked to people both famous and ordinary.

Kiara managed to have Sarah around her apartment one evening in late March. Kiara was back from Europe and had an evening that didn't involve parties or performances. She ordered pizza and sipped red wine while Sarah stuck to mineral water, now seven months pregnant. Shane couldn't make it as he was organising a friend's bachelor party, but Kiara was happy to spend time with Sarah alone and she would see Shane for his birthday in a few weeks anyway. They spent a lazy evening eating and talking, Sarah offering tips on how to decorate, Kiara delightedly showing her the piano Victor had arranged to be delivered and laughing as she recounted the difficulty they had getting it up to the apartment.

"So, are any of those stories true?" Sarah asked.

"No! They're all a load of garbage," Kiara said, pulling another slice of pizza from the box.

Sarah looked at her. "I don't know how you stay so slim," she said enviously, rubbing a hand self-consciously over her swollen belly.

"I spend most nights dancing, most days rehearsing. Burns a whole lotta calories," said Kiara, draining the wine from her glass.

"What about the first kiss story? I recognised that guy from school," Sarah said.

"Did you? I didn't. I have no idea who he is!" Kiara exclaimed, giggling. "He was definitely not my first kiss," she added, shaking her head and smiling.

Sarah rarely asked Kiara about dating, and Kiara never told her much either, but Sarah's curiosity was sparked. "Who was it then?" she asked.

Kiara put down her wine glass and raised an eyebrow. "Seriously Sarah, I was one of the most unpopular girls in school. Boys weren't interested. And then I left, and I was just focusing on staying alive. So, kissing really hasn't been top of my priorities, you know?"

Sarah frowned. "Are you telling me you've never been kissed?"

"No, I've been kissed, of course I have," Kiara could feel her cheeks starting to redden and began to fiddle with her napkin, shredding tiny pieces and placing them on the table.

"Have you ever slept with anyone?" Sarah asked, not wanting to stop digging, still at heart the same gossipy girl she had always been.

Kiara sat in silence for a moment before replying. "Apart from the rape, I've not had sex, no."

Sarah felt terrible for prying. She had assumed Kiara would have been with men now that she was famous, wealthy, drop-dead gorgeous, and travelling all over the world. She forgot that what started Kiara on that journey was a horrible violation.

"I'm sorry, I shouldn't have asked," Sarah said, leaning over and squeezing Kiara's arm.

"Hey no, it's okay, really. I'm used to people wanting to know about my private life," she said. She glanced over at Sarah. "I'm enjoying just being me, not having to worry about what some guy wants. Except for Marco," she said, laughing.

"Yeah Marco, what's the deal with him?" Sarah asked.

"How do you mean?"

"You talk about him a lot." Sarah raised her eyebrows at Kiara.

"Oh no, Marco's got a boyfriend, there's nothing romantic between us at all," Kiara made a face at the thought of it, making Sarah laugh.

"Do you ever think about, you know, getting married and stuff?"

Kiara shook her head slowly. "Not really, no. I'm just focused on the here and now, one day at a time," she said, and smiled brightly.

Sarah nodded and Kiara flicked through the TV channels to find a movie they wanted to watch. Sarah rubbed a hand on her stomach, feeling her baby stir inside her gently, and couldn't help but feel that Kiara, for all her fame and fortune, was missing out on a lot.

Ten months reunited

"Are you ready yet?" Megan shrieked at Michelle.

Kiara, Alicia, Sierra and Megan were all waiting in Michelle's apartment. Michelle was always the late one, constantly losing her shoes or scrabbling around in her purses to locate her keys.

They were all going to a party thrown by their record label – a huge event with lots of famous names attending. Kiara wasn't bothered about going to the party but was happy to spend an evening with the other girls. She had chosen a short gold sequinned dress and golden heels with delicate straps winding their way up her ankles. Michelle hopped out of her bathroom, squeezing on a shoe, and grabbed her jacket, and in a mist of perfume they made their way to the car that was waiting for them.

The party was taking place at an exclusive club. The air was throbbing with music and strobe lights, there was a packed dance floor and music videos were being streamed onto the walls and over thick red velvet drapes. The girls were immediately whisked around the room to greet various people, shaking sweaty hands, leaning in to hear names and immediately forgetting them, smiling, nodding, looking forward to the part of the evening when they could just get on the dance floor and close their eyes and move to the music, without caring who saw or heard.

Marco was saying something in Kiara's ear, beckoning someone over to greet the group. The man turned to Alicia first, so his back was towards Kiara, then he swung around and took her hand with a cold, heavy grasp. Her eyes met his, dark blue like the ocean, and he grinned at her. "Marianna, I mean Kiara, how lovely to meet you," and Andrew Daniels put her hand to his mouth and pressed his lips against her skin.

Kiara stared at him in horror, her eyes wide, mouth open. Marco nudged her in the ribs, sharply. "Kiara, Andrew Daniels is an executive with the company, having just been head-hunted from Ventura records." She nodded and stammered hello, then excused herself to run to the bathroom.

Stumbling through the crowds, her arms outstretched in front of her, she made it to the cubicle before retching and vomiting. She knelt on the cool tiles and the black and white mosaic danced before her eyes. She put a hand on the shiny black cubicle door to steady herself, and heard Alicia hissing, "Kiara, are you okay?" her feet tapping along anxiously in front of each cubicle.

"I'm fine, just had too much to drink," she called out. She knew Alicia wouldn't buy it as she had hardly drunk anything yet, but she could hear other women chattering and she didn't know what else to say. She could see Alicia's feet, dark and smooth with bright pink nails, her silver shoes gleaming under the door. "Do you need anything?" Alicia asked, hesitantly.

"No, I'll be fine in a minute," she said, and saw Alicia's feet turn and leave.

She pulled herself up shakily, willing herself to breathe, her chest tight like a drum and her breathing irregular. She counted to ten and breathed out as slowly and quietly as she could. Her mind was spinning over and over. What was she going to do? She knew it would be frowned upon to run off like that, or to leave early, so she had to see out this party, then decide what to do about Andrew Daniels.

She stood up, grabbing toilet paper and dabbing at her underarms, where a cold sweat had seeped through her deodorant. She opened the door and washed her hands, rinsing her mouth out, reapplied her lip gloss and smoothed her hair, which she had straightened for once. It reached halfway down her back in thick red waves, still not entirely straight despite her best efforts.

She marched back into the club and searched for the girls. She grabbed some champagne off a waiter and downed it quickly, wincing as it burned her throat after the vomiting, feeling it stick across her teeth. She ran her tongue over her teeth and swallowed hard, trying to stay calm and walk steadily. A hand grabbed her arm and she turned around, thinking it was Marco. It was Andrew.

"Hey, don't run off again, please," he said, smiling at her, his hand tightening on her arm. "It's so nice to see you."

There was something in his smile that she found intensely threatening, but he put an arm round her waist and manoeuvred her firmly through the crowd to one of the booths on the side, secluded from the dance floor and sheltered by swooping drapes like theatre curtains. Marco saw her and gave her the thumbs up, thinking that she was schmoozing the new executive. She gave him a wide-eyed stare and mouthed "help", but he laughed, assuming she was joking.

Andrew put his hand on the small of her back and pushed her gently into the booth, sliding in beside her to block her in. Her legs stuck to the white leather.

"I bet you didn't expect to see me here, did you?" Andrew laughed.

She shook her head. "It's a surprise," she said, the words sticking in her throat. She coughed and Andrew reached out to grab a glass of champagne from the table. She sipped it, eyeing him nervously.

"A nice one, I hope," he chuckled. "I was surprised too, to see you performing, my little friend Marianna who always delivered my special packages for me."

Kiara flinched. "Tell me, does the label know about your secret past? It certainly wasn't mentioned in that TV interview you did," he said, leaning in confidentially.

"They know," she said, trying to sound confident, tilting her chin up and looking at him straight in the eyes. "You can't tell them anything I haven't already told them," she added.

"Maybe not," he said thoughtfully, "although I know lots of journalists who would love to have a tip-off to help them start digging up dirt on our lovely Femme Fatale lead singer." He ran a finger down her arm. "The label would never know it was me, and you wouldn't be able to prove it."

Kiara's hands started to sweat, her stomach tensing. The way he grinned at her made her feel threatened, trapped like a shark with his prey.

"What do you want?" she asked him, desperately looking over his shoulder to see if there was anyone she could wave to, but there was only a faceless crowd of moving shapes in the dark.

"I just want to be friends Kiara," he leaned in and started running his hand up her thigh, and pushed his lips against hers, forcing her head back, his tongue in her mouth. He leaned his weight on her and she managed to grab his hand on her thigh and stop it from going any higher, but his other hand squeezed her breasts so hard that she gasped in pain. His hand on her leg moved to grab hers in one quick movement, wrapping his fingers round her wrist and pulling her hand towards his crotch, placing her hand on his pants where she could feel that he was hard.

She bit down on his lip as hard as she could and his head jerked back in pain, anger flashing in his eyes, and she kneed him in the crotch as she slid over his lap and fled, sobbing, fighting through the crowds, and called the driver so he could get her back to the apartment immediately.

***

She was still curled up in the foetal position the following morning, fully dressed with last night's makeup streaked down her face, when Marco came in, using his spare key.

"What the fuck Kiara?" he stood in her bedroom doorway, hands on hips, eyeing the empty vodka bottles on the floor. She didn't move, although she was awake. She felt like she was made of stone, entirely numb, and freezing cold.

Marco marched over and grabbed her arm, forcing her to sit up. The sudden movement made the world tilt and she ran for the bathroom to vomit. She retched painfully for ten minutes, clinging to the edge of the bowl, spit running out of her mouth and down her chin. She knew she looked a mess and Marco was never inclined to listen to someone in a state. She washed her face with a warm washcloth, cleaned her teeth and combed her hair, but it didn't help much. Her face was pale with flakes of mascara still underneath her eyes, which were red from the vomiting. She knew she smelled of stale perfume and sweat.

She walked into the kitchen, where Marco was sitting at the table, looking furious, his dark eyes drawn and jaw clenched. "You wanna tell me what's going on?" he demanded, rapping his knuckles on the table. Kiara breathed deeply. Marco only did that when he was really pissed off.

"Andrew Daniels sexually assaulted me," she said, quietly and quickly, not wanting to let the words out of her head, lest she never get them back and was unable to speak of it at all.

"That's funny, he says you assaulted him. And he's got the injuries to prove it," Marco said, tautly.

She looked at him in shock. "He forced himself on me!" she said, indignantly.

"He's got a nasty cut lip where you bit him, plus nail marks on his hands. He says you led him on then turned on him," Marco's

182

rapping intensified in speed and volume. "We all saw you walk with him to the booth Kiara, he had his arm round you, it looked like you were both pretty cosy in there, and you looked comfortable to me, to everyone who saw you both."

Tears came to her eyes. "Marco, no, you don't understand, it wasn't like that. He knows me from before, I used to deliver his drugs, he was threatening me..." Marco interrupted her before she could finish. "He knows about the drugs?"

She nodded miserably.

"Fuck, and you go and piss him off? Well done, sweetheart." Marco's voice turned sharply sarcastic. He ran his hand through his hair and sighed.

"I'm sorry, but he grabbed me and I didn't want him to," Kiara stated to cry, tears splashing onto the kitchen table.

Marco stared coldly at her. "I'm sick of constantly bailing you out and cleaning up after your dramas."

She stared at him through a shiny haze of tears.

"I will make sure he doesn't press charges or reveal your dirty little secrets Kiara, and you will apologise to him and keep him sweet, do you understand?"

"But, he..." she stammered, but Marco had already walked out of the apartment.

Eleven months reunited

Marco made sure that Andrew Daniels neither pressed charges nor told anyone about Kiara's past. He gave her Andrew's number and she apologised over the phone, putting on a sweet voice, laughing hollowly, purring various flatteries and excuses until he was mollified. Marco had nodded at her, pleased, and she had felt a sense of shame and revulsion rise in her that she hadn't felt since the strip club. She thought things were supposed to be better now, that she had a say, that she had control over what was done and said to her, but it was all a pretence.

It became harder to perform without drinking first, harder to sleep without more pills, harder to party without crying for hours afterwards, fearful of being alone with men, of their hands and eyes on her, of Marco's cold anger and the threat of his protection being removed.

She managed to pull herself together to visit Sarah and her baby, Eleanor, a few weeks after the birth. Sarah's house had been a mess of baby presents and clothes, Janet running around making coffee for visitors, Shane popping by to visit his niece, Tim completely exhausted and ecstatic at the same time. She had smiled and asked questions, cooed over the baby, all the time desperate for a drink and feeling that she was just going through the motions, an observer rather than a participant. She left, subdued, exhausted and aching for normality, for someone to look at her the way Tim looked at Sarah and not with disdain or lust.

Twelve months reunited

Femme Fatale star Kiara's disaster on stage

Fans were shocked by Femme Fatale's show in London's O2 arena last night, when lead singer Kiara appeared worse for wear, stumbling over the dance moves and slurring the lyrics. Fans said she looked drunk or even like she was on drugs. Her management have said that the star hasn't been well and they are making sure she gets better before her next performance.

Thirteen months reunited

"What the hell is wrong with you?" screamed Megan, as Kiara opened the door to the dance studio and stumbled inside, two hours late for rehearsals.

Sierra, Michelle and Alicia stood stone-faced and silent as she walked towards them, clutching a bottle of water, pale-faced and sweaty.

"Um, sorry I overslept," she muttered, putting a hand to her forehead. The room was hot, her vision blurry, and she sat on the wooden floor with her head between her legs.

Sierra glanced at Marco angrily. "Are you going to say something? She's ruined nearly every performance this past week, and last month was a disaster too. We're only able to cover it up so much and people are noticing."

Kiara looked up and stared at them as they talked, but her vision was unfocused and her face expressionless and vacant. She was so tired. She woke up feeling so sick and in pain every morning that taking a shower made her nauseated, and only by drinking alcohol could she make the pain subside long enough to get dressed and make it down to rehearsal, aware that she could smell the vodka still emanating from every pore and so could everyone else that she worked with. She knew it was unprofessional and she hated letting the group down, but she had lost the energy to pretend that everything was okay.

Alicia walked over to Marco. "She needs help," she said, folding her arms.

"She needs a fucking head doctor," snapped Megan.

Marco walked to Kiara and stood in front of her, grabbing her arms and hauling her to her feet, heavy and uncoordinated. "Go back to bed," he said, in disgust.

Fourteen months reunited

Femme Fatale – a four piece?

Kiara Anderson, lead singer of hit group Femme Fatale, has been notably missing in the group's latest round of album promotions. Her management has issued a statement to say she has been unwell and is taking some time off to recover, while the group continues to promote their second album. Group member Sierra said: "We've been working so hard recently and it's really caught up with Kiara. We can't wait for her to get back on her feet but it's so important she has time to recover."

***

"Kiara, what's going on? Are you ok? Shane xxx."

"Hey sweetie, reading some stuff about you, hope you're ok. Please call, Janet x."

Kiara's phoned buzzed against the nightstand, again. She squinted at the screen, 2pm. She turned the phone off, rolling back over in the gloom of her hotel room, and fell back to sleep.

***

Kiara sat facing Sierra, Michelle, Megan, and Alicia. Marco and several of the label's executives, plus their PR manager Frieda, gathered in the room. They were at a suite in LA, where the group was finalising their second album.

Alicia and Sierra were trying to hold back tears, unsuccessfully, swabbing at their faces with bunches of damp Kleenex, while Michelle looked at the floor and Megan stared angrily at Kiara.

Marco was speaking and Kiara understood the words, but it was as though she hadn't heard them. She stared at him in a blank stupor and nodded.

"Kiara, we are flying you back to New York. The group have decided it's time for you to leave."

Part Four
Healing

Three days after the group

Kiara was dragged from her sleep by a violent thudding invading the edges of her dream then forcing its way into her consciousness. She opened her eyes. She didn't know what time it was, but her drapes were drawn so the room was dark and murky.

She raised herself up on her elbow and listened to the noise till the fog in her brain cleared and she realised someone was banging on the door to her apartment. She grabbed her robe and wrapped it around her then shuffled to the door. She ached all over, as though she had been fighting throughout the night, and her head felt dull and painful.

She opened the door to find Shane, Victor and Janet outside. She stepped aside to let them in and they filed inside wordlessly and sat on her couch, making room amidst the clothes, shoes and old magazines strewn over it.

"You look terrible," Janet said, after a moment of quiet, her face etched with concern.

Kiara nodded. "I feel terrible." She sat on a chair, feeling heavy and exhausted, and rested her pounding head on her arm.

"We've been really worried about you," Shane said, gently. When Kiara didn't reply, he added – "there's been loads of news articles about you being ill and leaving the group."

Kiara felt a sob rising in her throat and choked it back. "They kicked me out," she said, speaking into her arm. She was devastated when it happened, but she wasn't surprised. She just couldn't carry on anymore, couldn't keep pretending to hold it together. She thought she was doing okay but after what happened with Andrew something had snapped inside her and she couldn't keep up the façade. She no longer wanted to be in the spotlight, she didn't want to pout and smile and dance when inside she felt like she was dying.

Her arm felt wet and she realised tears had run from her eyes. She wiped them with a shaky hand.

"Are you eating anything?" Janet asked. Kiara shook her head, she couldn't remember the last time she ate. She had come straight back to the apartment from LA and stayed in bed for the past two, maybe three days, she couldn't remember exactly.

"I can fix you something now if you like?" Janet offered hopefully, but Kiara declined. Her stomach was cowering inside her, feeling like it had been pummelled and dipped in acid.

"Can you tell us what happened?" Victor asked, leaning forward and patting her arm.

Kiara sat for a moment wondering if she had the energy or the words to tell them, but she felt as though she should explain why she was such as mess. She told them about the night with Andrew in the club, and how Marco had reacted, and how she began to unravel after that, how the pills and the alcohol were no longer just a crutch to get through the night but to get through the day too. She said it all quietly and matter-of-factly, looking at the floor, while Shane's face darkened and Janet pressed her fingers to her lips. Kiara began to cry when she told them about the group's decision to ask her to leave LA, and that she didn't have the energy to fight for it and she had just wanted to come back here and sleep.

Janet stood up and wrapped her arms around her, even though Kiara was sure she must smell awful, as she hadn't showered in days, only stepping into the bathroom to vomit or dry-heave hopelessly over the basin.

"I'm going to run you a bath okay? Then while you're in the tub I'm going to pack some of your clothes."

Kiara nodded and didn't bother to ask what for or where they would go. The apartment was rented by the label so she knew she would have to leave soon enough anyway.

Shane went to the kitchen and began cleaning up, clanging plates and glasses angrily, making her wince. He hadn't said a word and she wasn't sure what he was thinking. She knew he had warned her about the pills and the booze and thought he was mad at her for not listening to him and taking his advice. Victor poured her a glass of water and handed her some Advil, which she took gratefully, trying not to flinch each time Shane clattered something in the kitchen.

Janet took her by the hand and led her to the bathroom, helping her into the tub. She lay there, hot and limp, and let Janet wash her hair, gently stroking her curls and rinsing away the suds. Kiara remembered how embarrassed she had been when Janet took her bra shopping and right now she was too worn down to feel embarrassed about letting her bathe her. She looked up at Janet and she wasn't sure if the moisture on her face was bathwater or tears, and she thought about how her own mother should have been there. She grabbed Janet's hand and kissed it, pressing it to her cheek, and Janet smiled back at her.

She helped her out of the tub and wrapped a large towel around her, and while Kiara sat on the bed Janet opened the drapes and started methodically packing a suitcase. Kiara watched her quietly, and Shane popped his head round the door to give her a coffee. She sipped it slowly, her throat raw from days of alcohol and throwing up, her heart pounding in her chest, but the Advil had taken off some of the worst edges of the headache. She thanked him and smiled up at him and he stared at her sadly as she sat wan and thin in her towel.

Janet laid out some clothes on the bed and left her to get dressed, slowly and painfully, the world tilting one way and then the next every time she moved her head, the effort exhausting her. When she came back out of the bedroom, Shane, Victor and Janet were ready to go, the kitchen tidy, her suitcase waiting by the door. Victor took her arm, Shane lifted her case, and she followed them out.

As they arrived in the parking lot, Victor and Janet hugged her goodbye and headed off to their car, where a young woman was waiting.

"Who's that?" she asked.

Shane grinned. "Your decoy."

Kiara looked confused. The young woman pulled on a baseball cap and jumped in the back seat. Victor and Janet drove out of the parking lot, Kiara watching them go, while Shane loaded her case into the trunk of a black car. "Did you get a new car?" she asked, not recognising this one.

"Nope. It's a rental," he said, slamming the trunk shut and climbing in the driver's side.

"Why?"

"Photographers have been camped outside your building for days," he said, starting the engine with a soft rumble. "Hopefully mom and dad's car with your decoy in will distract them and let us slip away."

Kiara leant back into the seat, cool air drifting over her face from the vent. "You guys are geniuses," she said, feeling intensely grateful for all they had planned to help her, even before they had set foot in her apartment, even though she hadn't answered her phone for days.

After five minutes Shane pulled smoothly out of the parking lot and drove swiftly through and out of the city as Kiara stared out of the window in silence.

"Are you mad at me?" she asked.

"I'm not angry at you," Shane said, though there was tension in his voice.

"You seem angry."

"I'm angry about the way you've been treated," he said.

"Oh," she said, and didn't know what to say, so they lapsed into silence.

It was only after forty-five minutes that she remembered to ask where they were going. Shane laughed. "I was wondering when you were going to ask that. We're going to the beach house."

Despite feeling so ill, Kiara sat up and looked at him, her face brightening. "Really? Oh, that's good news."

She had been desperate to go to the beach house for years, and now she was finally going there. Shane smiled, gripping the wheel. "Well, you can stay there for as long as you like. Tim's been up there recently and stocked up the food, got the bedrooms ready. Sarah has him well-trained."

"Will Sarah be there?" Kiara asked.

Shane shook his head. "Not with the baby, it's a bit difficult for her to be there."

He glanced at Kiara and back at the road. "I'll be staying with you though."

"What about work?"

"That's the benefit of my dad also being my boss," Shane laughed.

Victor, Janet, Sarah and Shane had discussed what to do and had formulated a plan to get Kiara out of the city where they hoped they could talk to her, keep her out of the press, and away from her management. They didn't know how bad things were, but they knew that she needed their help, so Tim had been dispatched to ready the beach house, and Victor and Janet got one of their friend's daughters to come in case they needed a decoy.

Janet had immediately offered to stay in the beach house with Kiara, but Victor had interjected, and said that Shane should do it. Since the divorce Shane had been working longer hours than before, sleeping badly, and needed a break, plus he thought it would be better for Shane to stay with Kiara and make sure she was safe from any prying eyes, whereas Janet would hardly be able to tackle any rogue photographers.

Shane and Kiara were silent for the rest of the journey. Kiara drifted to sleep, waking up when they arrived.

"Welcome to the beach house," Shane said, extending his hand to her to help her down from the passenger side.

***

Janet and Victor joined them that evening, confident that the photographers had left them. They sat down to chicken and mashed potatoes, Kiara eating tiny mouthfuls and leaving most of it. After dinner, they curled up on the two large couches, delightfully squishy, with mugs of hot chocolate. Victor cleared his throat and Kiara knew that a serious discussion was about to take place. She gulped her hot chocolate and burnt her tongue, wincing at the rawness.

"Kiara, I've instructed our lawyers to talk to your label," Victor began.

Kiara hadn't expected this. "Why?"

"Because they may be in breach of contract and they certainly have negated their duty of care towards you when you made serious allegations against one of their producers," Victor replied.

Kiara looked panicked. "I don't want to take that any further Victor, please, I want to forget that whole incident."

Victor shook his head. "I'm sorry sweetheart but this needs to be raised in the discussions about how the label have treated you. It doesn't mean getting the police involved, if you don't want to take things that way."

She nodded, lacking the energy to protest.

Victor continued. "We would very much like for you to stay here, in the beach house, but it's entirely your choice. Shane will stay here with you as long as you want to be here."

She looked at Shane and reached across to squeeze his arm, mouthing 'thank you' at him.

"We would like you to get some help Kiara," Janet said, leaning forward, looking into Kiara's eyes. "Is that something you might consider?"

Kiara stared back, blankly. "What type of help?"

Janet glanced at Victor and Shane. "Well, we think that perhaps it might be good for you to talk through some of the things that have happened to you."

"We can get someone to come here, someone you can talk to in complete confidence," she continued.

Kiara nodded. "Okay."

"We'd also like you to talk to a doctor about the pills and the alcohol, to see what they suggest to help you," Victor added.

Kiara agreed to everything they suggested and excused herself to go up to one of the bedrooms and lie down, not paying attention to where she was, just desperate to sleep, and she crashed out fully clothed in the first bedroom she came to, throat dry and head thumping.

Four days after the group

It was early when she woke, a pale blue dawn outside with fingers of orange clawing through the flat clouds and a mist of warm rain smattering against the glass. She sat up in bed, still feeling tired, aching and nauseated.

Someone had taken her shoes off and tucked her under a blanket, putting her suitcase at the end of the bed. She threw off the blanket and grabbed the case, unzipping it and grabbing a wash bag Janet had packed for her, with a jumble of lotions inside. There was a towel hanging over the small chair in the corner of the room and Kiara took it and padded down the hallway, unsure which of the doors led to the bathroom. The house was old, the wooden floor warped and groaning under her feet as she shuffled softly in her socks. She listened at each door she came to, not wanting to barge in and disturb Shane by mistake. She could hear someone's deep and even breathing in one room and assumed that was him. Testing the other doors, she found another bedroom, and then the bathroom.

She showered, the warm water slapping painfully against her aching skin, the heat and dampness making her feel nauseous, and wrapped herself in the blue towel, relishing its softness. As she opened the door to the bathroom, she saw Shane leaning against the doorway to his room, and she jumped in surprise.

"I'm so sorry, did I wake you up?" she said, pulling the towel tighter around her.

He smiled and shook his head. His dark hair was ruffled from sleep, his voice gravelly. "Nope. You're up early."

"What time is it?" she asked.

"6.15am," he said, running a hand through his hair, stretching his arms out in a yawn afterwards.

"I guess I went to sleep pretty early," she said.

She walked to her room as Shane passed her in the hallway, heading to the bathroom. He turned as she went to close the door to get dressed. "I'll go and make some coffee if you like?"

She nodded, smiled at him, and got dressed. By the time she had dressed he was downstairs, still in his crumpled t-shirt and boxers. He handed her a cup of coffee, and she breathed it in gratefully, still woozy. She pushed a stray curl out of her eyes and smiled up at him.

"Bacon?" he asked. It had been a long time since she had eaten breakfast, usually she felt too ill in the mornings, but she nodded, not wanting to turn down his kindness.

"Bacon sounds great."

It felt strange to be waking up in a house with just him and her. They'd always been surrounded by people before, and she was suddenly very aware of how it was just going to be the two of them for the majority of the time. She watched him cooking and wondered if this was what marriage was like, if this was what he used to do with Melanie. He turned and saw her staring and she felt embarrassed and carried her coffee to the large windows in the living room.

The house nestled straight onto the beach, on the curve of an inlet, their own tiny private strip of sand directly outside the veranda. Across the inlet there were other houses in the distance, their outlines of grey and white reflecting in the dark water. Verdant green grass wrapped around the land to the side of the house, the back overhung by deep green trees and shrubs, coated in a fine dew. It was calm, shady, and utterly peaceful. The morning air was cool and damp and she opened the door to the veranda, wandering out, the steam rising from her coffee and wafting in the light breeze. The only sounds were the water gently slapping against the shoreline and the birds cawing into the air. Shane followed her out.

"It's beautiful, isn't it?" he asked her.

She nodded, closing her eyes and taking a deep breath of pure air.

"So many good childhood memories playing in that water," he said, scanning the inlet. "We were always sad that you couldn't come with us."

"Me too," she said, remembering how her father had vehemently opposed her going, giving her a sharp slap round the head when she had kept asking. It was a topic she didn't persist with.

Shane crossed his arms in front of him and she could see the goose bumps rippling up his skin. Although it was a summer day the misty rain made it feel cooler and the sun hadn't heated the air yet. "You're cold," she said.

"Yup, going back in now," he admitted defeat and went back in, the smell of breakfast drifting to her warmly as he opened the door and returned inside.

She followed him back in and they shared bacon and eggs, fresh orange juice, and toast with butter sliding down hotly in golden streams. Tim had done a good job with the groceries.

Kiara lifted her orange juice – "to the best breakfast I have ever had," and they clinked glasses and spent breakfast talking about Shane's memories of long summers at the beach house, when Kiara had been left behind, desperate for their return, and she tried to ignore her stomach flinching with every bite.

***

Sarah came to visit that afternoon, leaving the baby with Tim, and they spent the afternoon curled up on chairs on the veranda, sipping iced tea and eating the brownies Sarah had made. Shane left them alone to talk, and Kiara filled Sarah in on what had happened with the group, Sarah's eyes growing wide with indignation.

When Sarah left a few hours later Kiara found Shane in his room with his laptop open, his phone pressed to his ear. He beckoned her in and she sat on the edge of his bed, waiting for him to finish. He hung up and shut his laptop. "That was the lawyers. They've got a meeting with the label in a few days. Do you want me to fill you in on the details?" he asked.

She thought for a moment then shook her head. "No, I'd rather not be kept in the loop. I'm happy to just be here not having to think about any of it right now," she said.

He nodded. "Okay, no problem. We will tell you only what you have to know."

"Thanks Shane, really, for all this," she waved her hand around, "for staying here, taking time out of your life for me, for all the hassle it's caused." She looked at the floor. "I'm very grateful."

He reached over and squeezed her shoulder. "It's no problem, really. I needed the time off too, you know."

She nodded. "Working hard lately?"

He grinned. "Always. I deserve a break."

"If you can call looking after a pill-popping ex-girl group singer a break," she laughed.

He laughed with her and they headed downstairs to fix dinner together. They lounged on the deep soft couches afterwards, munching popcorn and watching a movie, although they chatted throughout and neither of them paid attention to the TV.

As the evening turned into a dark blue night, Kiara started to feel uneasy. She had felt nauseated for most of the day, forcing food down and trying to ignore the shaking in her hands, but as night fell her skin began to prickle, her throat tightened and she felt terribly sick, pain running up and down her legs. She started shifting about, trying to get more comfortable.

"You okay?" Shane said, noticing her fidgeting.

"Um yeah, I just don't feel too good," she muttered.

She got up to grab a glass of water and the room spun like a carousel. She sunk to her knees, hands on the couch, and Shane pulled her up but she started to heave and ran with her hands over her mouth, just making it to the downstairs bathroom, heaving and retching till nothing remained except painful spasms. She rested her head on the basin and ran the faucet, rinsing her mouth out under the stream, desperately trying to stop her stomach heaving.

She lurched out of the bathroom, pale and sweating. "I'm going to bed," she said to Shane, throwing herself towards the stairs to give herself the momentum to get up, but she sunk again onto her knees on the third step and hung her head to rest on the wood. She felt Shane behind her, lifting her up and carrying her to her room. She lay limply on the bed and he covered her with a blanket. She was stiff and shivering yet sweating.

"Can I get you anything?" he asked, brushing away a damp curl from her forehead.

She shook her head and he told her she could call him for anything, anytime in the night, but she barely heard him. As his footsteps walked away she knew she would need to vomit again, but she wasn't able to get to the bathroom this time and retched into the trash can in her room, again and again, throughout the whole night.

***

The doctor frowned at her over his glasses, his milky grey eyes squinting underneath wiry eyebrows. He made notes as she talked about what she usually drank and when, how much, how many pills, how she felt now. He was a specialist in treating addicts, and the JSM company often called on his expertise when one of their clients was struggling and wanted to get better without having to go to rehab and endure the adverse publicity.

197

"You're going to feel terrible for a good few days yet, but afterwards when your body adjusts you'll start to feel better," the doctor said, gravely. "I'm going to prescribe something to help you for the first few days but you must stop taking it after that, and I'll be checking on your progress every day this week and gradually reducing the dose, okay?"

She nodded.

"I'm also concerned that you are underweight. You need to eat a good diet and bulk up a little," he carried on. "How does that sound to you?" he said, glancing at her.

"I can do that," she said, though her voice faltered a little. She wasn't sure she could. When she couldn't take anything to help her sleep at night she would lie awake for hours, ears buzzing, only to fall in and out of nightmares, and wake feeling afraid and exhausted.

The doctor nodded. "I'll be back tomorrow to see how you're getting along, although you can always call my number, anytime."

She took his card and he left the bedroom. He creaked down the stairs and she heard the low murmur of his voice, talking with Janet, who had popped over while Shane was out visiting Joshua for the day. Shane had been torn about whether or not to go, and she could see the anxiety on his face when he found her limp and hoarse in the morning, but she urged him to go and see his son, knowing how much it meant to him to have those precious visits.

She heard the door shut and the doctor leave. Janet bustled around downstairs, Kiara heard cupboard doors opening and cutlery clinking, and she closed her eyes and tried to picture the water lapping gently outside, imagining the fresh clean air running over her.

She heard Janet come upstairs, walking softly on the warped floors and pushing open the bedroom door a small way to check on her. Kiara opened her eyes.

"I'm not asleep," she said, and waved Janet over.

She came and sat on the edge of the bed and Kiara propped herself up on her elbows, shoving a pillow behind her neck.

"How are you feeling?" Janet asked her.

Kiara made a face. "Rough."

Janet smiled grimly. "Shane said you were very sick all night."

Kiara sighed. Poor Shane, having to stay here with her. "It was pretty bad. The doctor says that I'll feel better in a few days as my body adjusts."

Janet nodded and looked at the floor briefly before raising her head.

"Kiara," she began hesitantly, pressing her lips together and smearing her dusky pink lipstick slightly. "We've arranged for a therapist to come here tomorrow so you can start to work through some of the things that are troubling you."

Kiara nodded and Janet carried on quickly. "If you don't like him or want to stop or feel uncomfortable at any time you can say so."

"Sure, I understand," Kiara said, her stomach washing around inside her, feeling full and empty at the same time. The thought of talking to a complete stranger about the things that kept her up at night was terrifying, but Kiara would try because the Jacobs had asked her to, and she felt she owed it to them.

"Thank you for being willing to try," Janet leaned across and took her hand. Janet's skin was soft and papery, Kiara's cold and moist. "Things will get better, you know."

Kiara exhaled slowly. "I hope so."

***

"You're living with her?" Derek said, incredulously, raising his beer to his lips and taking a long swig.

"Yup," said Shane.

"Hang on a minute, I have to get this right," Derek said, shaking his head. "This is *the* Kiara Anderson we're talking about?"

Shane nodded.

"And just you two alone in a house, together, all the time?"

Shane shrugged. "Pretty much, yeah."

Derek exhaled, blowing out his cheeks. "Wow. That's a lot of temptation," he said.

Shane looked surprised. "What do you mean?"

Derek's eyebrows shot up towards his forehead. "Are you kidding me? Are we talking about the same woman here? She's so hot. How you're keeping your hands off her I have no idea."

He glanced at Shane. "Unless you're not keeping your hands off?" He grinned and nodded suggestively.

Shane laughed. "I don't see her like that," he said, drinking from the bottle. "I've known her a long time, and she needs a friend right now. That's all it is."

"Just friends, huh?" Derek said, thoughtfully. "Maybe you could introduce me and I could be her friend too," he said, grinning at Shane.

"And what about CeeCee?" Shane said.

"Ah yeah, forgot about the wife," Derek said, and they laughed.

After the divorce, many of Shane's friends had drifted away, their wives were friends with Melanie, and the husbands followed suit. It had become awkward to meet up with them knowing they had spent the previous evening dining with Melanie and Kyle. But Derek had stayed in touch and Shane tried to meet up with him when they could both spare the time. Shane had spent a good few hours with Joshua before Melanie needed to take him to a party, and he had time to spare for a beer with Derek before heading back to the beach house.

Seeing Melanie always made his heart lurch, no matter how much he wanted to be free from her spell. Each time he hoped that either he wouldn't feel that familiar pull of affection, or that she might open the door and wrap her arms around him again, declaring all to be a mistake. He ached for his former life, waking up beside her, lazy Sunday morning sex, walks to the park, date nights, the taste of her kisses, being entwined with her at night, her legs entangled with his.

Shane's phone buzzed. He checked the message and drained the last of his beer. "Gotta get back," he said, standing up, clapping Derek on the shoulder.

"Feel free to invite me over, anytime," Derek called out to him, as Shane headed back to his car.

Six days after the group

"So, what do we talk about?" Kiara asked Graham, as they sat in the living room. Graham had sandy hair streaked with grey, and wore thick framed glasses, the dark brown of the frames gently gleaming in the lamplight beside his chair, where he sat with his ankles neatly together and his hands folded in his lap, relaxed and tidy.

"Well, we can talk about anything you want to Kiara," he said, his voice deep and soft. His eyes were a warm hazel and had a hint of a smile in them even when his face was serious.

They sat in silence for a few moments, Kiara picking at a stray thread from her sleeve. She wrapped it round her finger, squeezing it tight, watching the blood rush to the skin and throb slightly before she released it.

"Why don't we start with just how you're feeling today?" Graham said, breaking the silence.

Kiara nodded, relieved, but still the session seemed to stretch out, flat and unfulfilled. There were so many silences when Kiara would listen to the rain thrumming on the roof and watch it course down the windows, the clock in the living room ticking out the empty moments.

"You know, I used to sit for hours and watch the rain run down the window in my bedroom in the trailer," she said.

Graham nodded. "What was the trailer like? Can you describe it to me?"

She started to tell him about the trailer, but she could barely finish her sentence when her throat closed up and she started to shake, the hot tea in her cup slopping over to her fingers and dripping onto her jeans. Talking about the trailer and the way it looked and felt and smelled just made her remember what had happened to her there and the way it had looked when she set it alight to burn.

"Kiara, we can stop if you want to," Graham said, gently, leaning forwards, the first movement he had made in the session so far, apart from unfolding and folding his fingers every now and again.

She nodded. The session lasted an hour but she felt it like it was much longer and was relieved when he left.

Shane heard the door go and Graham's car crunch on the gravel. He came downstairs, having busied himself with some emails on his laptop while Kiara had her session. He found her curled up in front of the window, arms wrapped round her legs and her head resting on her knees, staring out of the window. She was still aching all over, her hands setting off into violent trembles without warning. The doctor had told her this would happen and she wished she could curl up and sleep until it felt better, but sleep had evaded her the past two nights.

"Hey, how did it go?" he asked. She looked up and smiled at him. "Not bad," she said.

He leaned back against the window frame, the paint starting to peel off in small cream flakes, and she unfurled her legs and lay them over his lap. They watched the heavy summer storm unfurl over the inlet and rest over the house, the rain increasing in violence and the thunder looming overhead.

"How are things with the label?" she asked, tentatively.

He looked at her. "Well, they've released you from your contract, and have paid you a sum for ending it and for the way they handled your allegations against Daniel Andrews."

"Wow," she said, surprised.

He nodded. "Our lawyers really went to town on them for what Marco did after you reported that assault to him. They threatened to go public, so it wasn't hard to persuade them to come to an agreement."

He continued. "They released a statement to the press to say that you were suffering from exhaustion and are taking time away from the group. When the time is right, they'll announce that you have left as a mutual decision," he continued.

She nodded, silently tracing the rain down the window.

"That's great Shane, thank you," she said, feeling again a swell of gratitude for her friends who took care of her and expected nothing in return.

"We're sending people to pack up your things in the apartment and to bring them here, if that's okay with you?"

"Yes, that's fine."

"Good to hear," he shoved her legs off him and stretched his hand out to hers, pulling her up. "Come and help me fix dinner. I'm not your slave, Anderson," he said, laughing, and she followed him to the kitchen, even though the thought of dinner made her stomach lurch to her throat.

Two months after the group

Summer changed to fall and the skies turned a paler shade of blue, the sun glinting off the water as the leaves turned to gold on the trees.

Each day had its own peaceful routine. An early morning walk by the water, breakfast on the veranda, her appointment with Graham, lunch, and quiet afternoons reading, playing the piano that had been sent from the apartment, and learning to play the guitar that Shane bought her, patiently strumming chord after chord, sucking her sore fingertips which were red with string marks afterwards. The doctor came regularly and was pleased with her progress. The insomnia continued but the aching subsided, the trembling lessened, and she was able to eat without feeling terrible afterwards.

Sarah brought baby Eleanor to visit and Kiara kissed her chubby soft cheeks and stroked her hair, pronouncing her to be the most beautiful baby in the world while Sarah beamed with delight. Victor came and she walked with him arm in arm along the waterfront and he would tell her about his new signings and which teams were playing well that year.

Kiara learnt to play Wonderwall by Oasis, one of Shane's favourites, and performed it at a family dinner in the Jacobs' house. And then for the first time in a long time she picked up a pencil and started scratching out her own lyrics on a yellow legal pad, scribbling and crossing out, strumming, Shane laughing at her as she walked around murmuring half-formed lyrics.

She played whatever she wrote for him, on the piano or on the guitar, and he always applauded and said it was great, and even though she asked if he had any criticism for her he never did.

Shane visited Joshua whenever he could and when Melanie allowed it, and he worked on projects his father sent through. Kiara avoided using a computer in case she was too tempted to look up the headlines about herself, watch the disastrous videos of drunken performances she knew would be on YouTube, or read the speculation that her career was over. Sometimes she got a text from Alicia, saying she was missed, or messages from Betty and Veronica, whose other brother never made his way to them, though they refused to give up hope.

Marco had contacted her once too. *"I'm sorry how things went down. I hope you're ok,"* was all he said in his text.

"Thank you," was her reply, short but not meant to be blunt. She bore him no anger. He hadn't been kind to her, but he had helped her on many occasions and she wasn't one to burn bridges, just trailers, she thought to herself, smiling in spite of the awfulness of it all.

Shane was with her every evening except when he was out seeing Joshua or with friends. They watched endless compilations of the greatest boxing matches or basketball's best-ever players, wrestling matches, and old films, working their way through eighties and nineties classics. She felt his presence in the house at night, knowing he was there, keeping her safe, though she slept lightly and woke startled by any sound.

Her sleep was no longer the deep amnesia of one brought on by pills and booze, but light and fitful, still grappling away nightmares, sometimes lying awake for hours. One night she must have been screaming in her sleep because she felt Shane shaking her, and she had taken a few moments to come out of it, not knowing if she was in the real world or in a dream, and Shane had held her in bed till she drifted off to sleep again. She barely remembered it the next day till he had sheepishly mentioned it and asked if she had minded, and she had shaken her head, of course she hadn't.

Since then if he heard her screaming, he would come to her room and wake her and slide into her bed and press her close and tell her she was safe until she was calm again. She began to crave his warmth beside her in bed, the solidity of his chest where she could listen to his heartbeat soothing her to sleep, the smell of him, the feel of his body pressing against hers as he held her and told her everything would be okay.

Shane had hesitated to intrude on her in the night, but couldn't bear to listen to her nightmares anymore and was glad to be able to comfort his friend. It had been hard adjusting to an empty bed and the truth was that he liked to be with Kiara in the night, his arms around her, breathing in the scent of lavender and honey on her skin. Although nothing sexual happened in their night-time encounters he had felt tempted to kiss her one night when she had tilted her face up towards his, but he turned away, knowing that it wasn't appropriate or right to take advantage of her in that way, and Melanie's bright green eyes flashed into his mind as though she were watching him.

One morning Janet had found them in Kiara's bed together, Kiara still curled up and asleep, and he had stumbled out embarrassed to explain why he was there in her room. She had listened coolly and nodded, but he wasn't sure she understood that nothing had occurred between them.

Kiara continued her sessions with Graham. Some went better than others, but she was able to talk to him and found his presence calming. They talked about her father, about her mother, about her anger towards her parents for letting her down, and her feelings of fear that she wasn't good enough to be loved by either of them. They talked about school and the other kids and how they had made her feel worthless and insignificant. She told him about what it had been like in Hunts Point, the constant fear and discomfort, the reliance on Rob, the things she had seen people do, the things she had done as well, and the strip club and how she had felt soiled by all of it. She sobbed as she told Graham about Rob's death and how she had left him there in Hunts Point and how she was afraid that he had suffered and died alone, and that she couldn't bear the thought of it.

Eventually, she was able to talk about the rape too. She had hidden it as deep as she could inside herself, trampled it down as far as it would go in her subconscious, hoping it wouldn't surface again. To have to dig it up and force the memories back to the surface was like exhuming a long-dead corpse and having to study its rotten features with a magnifying glass.

Eventually though, it began to feel like cleaning out a basement and opening the windows to let rays of light in, one by one. It was hard and it was awful, but it was the first time she was actually confronting things that had happened rather than running away from them or trying to force them out of her mind. All the anger and shame and fear had to be wrung out of her, so she talked and cried while Graham listened, and she started to feel things inside her healing, ever so slowly.

Three months after the group

After a while, Kiara felt that it was time to visit her father's grave and decided to track down her mother's and Rob's at the same time. Kiara wanted some closure and felt that seeing the place where each had ended up would help.

She asked Shane to go with her and he readily agreed. Her father's grave was easy to find – in a corner of the local cemetery, marked by a simple grey stone with his name, date of birth and date of death. It was only later that Kiara found out that the Jacobs had paid for the burial and the headstone. Shane had left her alone, wondering among the headstones, a cold November rain misting over them, and Kiara hadn't cried or raged but had felt a sense of calm that her father was gone and there was nothing more that could be said or done.

She started a search for her mother's grave, but she wasn't sure where her mother ended up or even if she had died under another name, so after a while she gave up, frustrated and unsure if she would ever find out where her mother was buried.

It was Rob's grave that was the most shocking to her. With no traceable family and no money, Rob had been given a city burial on Hart Island in New York. Kiara had no idea what the place was until she looked it up online, horrified to read of the fate of those buried there – coffins stacked up together and lowered into their final resting place by prison inmates. Visits were not allowed, though there were campaigns to open the island to those who wanted to pay their respects.

She wept to think of Rob abandoned and alone out there, lying in the dank earth surrounded by people he never knew in life but who became his neighbours in death, on that murky green strip of land surrounded by cold dark waters. She had cried for days, a terrible restless feeling of guilt upon her she couldn't shake off. She felt that she would carry that guilt with her all her life and hoped that the island would one day be opened to visitors so she could see

Rob's final resting place for herself, and at least make sure that he was not forgotten.

***

Fall passed its peak and the leaves fell with the arrival of cold winter winds blowing across the inlet, the waters darkened and the mornings turned cold.

Victor was sitting out on the veranda with Kiara one afternoon, curled up under rugs, the horizon bright and far before them over the water, the pale blue sky glazed with thin white clouds.

"I've got something to ask you, but you can say no if you want to," he said.

She waited expectantly.

"It's the annual charity ball for JSM next month and I'd really like you to perform, if you'd be okay with that?" he said.

"I'd love to," she said, without hesitating. She felt ready to go back on stage, but under her own terms, just her and the piano, maybe even singing her own songs eventually.

Victor grinned, blue eyes dancing. "That's great! You can sing whatever you want."

She clapped her hands in excitement, already running over the songs in her head that she might perform. She had kept quite a few of her beautiful clothes so she wasn't worried about what to wear. The most important thing wasn't the clothing or the makeup or the dancing, this time, it was going to be about her voice.

Four months after the group

Shane laughed at how excited she was on the day of the ball, as she fluttered round the beach house anxiously, checking the time every ten minutes. She painted her nails, did her makeup, and chose a teal strapless dress that clung to her tightly down to the waist, then floated down to the floor. She left her hair down, curls streaming down her back. She had put on weight, her skin was peachy and glowing, her eyes bright, her body no longer dehydrated and toxic with alcohol.

She and Shane were travelling together from the beach house, and she glided down the stairs where he was waiting in his tux and there was a moment when he had a glimpse of the Kiara that everyone else in the world seemed to see, but she fell down the last step and stumbled into him and they both laughed and the moment passed.

She was happy to take his arm when they arrived at the ball, and they smiled for the photographers, blinded by cameras flashing, and she clung to Shane's arm to steady her on her heels. They looked at each other and Shane mouthed at her *"this is crazy"* and she laughed, used to being in the middle of a throng of photographers like this.

When they got inside she headed off to prepare for her performance. She had spoken to the instrumentalists the week before, with a rehearsal two days ago, so she felt confident everything would go smoothly. But she was nervous about standing up there on her own, singing some of her own songs, wondering what people would think of her.

She needn't have worried, and the nerves dissipated as soon as she was on stage. The performance was how she had hoped being a singer would be, her and her voice only, singing songs she loved or had written. Afterwards people were swirling around her with congratulations, handshakes, and celebratory smiles.

Sarah greeted her excitedly, exclaiming over her dress. Moira had also made it to the event with her new partner, Lawrence. She was wearing a chic black shift dress, her silver hair gleaming and trademark necklaces draped over her chest. She greeted Kiara with a warm hug.

"It's so good to see you darling, you look much better than you did when you were in that awful group," said Moira, never one to hold back.

Kiara laughed, knowing she was right. "That's good to hear."

Kiara felt a tap on her shoulder and swung round, shrieking in delight to see Alicia standing there, shimmering in a purple bodycon dress with huge silver earrings swishing from her earlobes. They hugged tightly.

"What are you doing here?" Kiara asked.

Alicia grinned. "My ex, the basketball player, invited me. We're still friends," she said, leaning in confidentially, "sometimes with benefits," and winked at Kiara, who feigned shock.

"I loved your set. Did you write some of those songs?" Alicia asked.

Kiara nodded, beaming.

"It suits you," Alicia said.

"What does?"

"Looking happy for once," Alicia said, and squeezed her hand. Kiara squeezed back. She had genuinely missed Alicia the most out of all the girls and was delighted that she was there tonight.

"How are things with the group?" Kiara asked hesitantly, not wanting to bring an awkward edge to the conversation, but upon seeing Alicia she was desperately curious.

Alicia bit her lip. "Umm okay I guess." She looked around to see who might be in earshot, and murmured to her, "It won't last much longer."

Kiara raised an eyebrow and nodded her head for Alicia to continue.

"Megan is desperate to go solo, and Michelle is fed up with it all," she said, in a low voice.

"And you?" Kiara asked.

Alicia grinned, her bright white teeth gleaming against the deep red of her lip gloss. "I'm sure I'll do alright," she said, and Kiara believed that she would.

"What about you? You've been totally off the radar," Alicia said.

Kiara nodded, smiling. "I've been staying with Shane, getting better, doing some work on myself," she said.

"Wait, living with a guy? Oh my god, tell me everything!" Alicia squealed, and Kiara hushed her as a few heads nearby turned in surprise.

"No, not like that. Just staying with him at the family beach house, you know, while I get better," Kiara explained.

"Ah," Alicia said, but looked incredulous.

"Really! I swear. There's nothing between us," Kiara said.

"So, where is this Shane?" Alicia asked. "I've seen him on TV, but it would be great to meet him properly."

Kiara nodded and scanned the room, searching for him. She spotted him chatting to David Knox, a boxer JSM had just signed, and waved frantically to get his attention. David saw her waving and laughed, nudging Shane to turn around. She beckoned him over and he shuffled through the crowd, greeting people on the way.

"Hey," he said, finally reaching them.

"Shane, this is Alicia, Alicia, Shane," Kiara said.

"It's great to meet you, I've heard lots about you," Shane said, greeting Alicia with a kiss on the cheek.

"Likewise!" Alicia said.

"All good things I hope," Shane said, glancing at Kiara and grinning.

"Oh totally," said Alicia, giving Kiara a look.

Shane was distracted by someone who dived into their conversation and he turned his back momentarily.

"Wow," Alicia mouthed at Kiara, then whispered in her ear, "the way he looks at you, you can't tell me you're just friends."

Kiara shook her head and whispered back, "You're wrong. Just friends."

The group that was playing after Kiara's set started to play a version of Fields of Gold and couples drifted to the dance floor. Alicia leaned over and tapped Shane.

"Are you gonna ask my girl to dance? Can't leave the lady of the moment standing here on her own, you know," she said, boldly.

Shane laughed. "Of course," he said, and held out his hand to Kiara, who was cringing from Alicia's heavy-handed intervention.

They walked to the edge of the dance floor and Shane wrapped an arm around her waist, one hand folding over hers. He seemed oblivious to the eyes that followed them, but she felt their gazes resting on them as they swayed to the song, and her face warmed under the scrutiny.

Shane was laughing about something someone had said to him that night and was relating it to her, but he tailed off for a moment and paused.

"What's up?" she asked.

He shook his head. "Nothing. Just..." he hesitated. "I just realised I'm dancing with the most beautiful woman in the room." His eyes met hers and he tightened his arm around her, and she was suddenly very aware of his hand holding hers. She couldn't quite meet his gaze anymore and dropped her eyes.

"I didn't mean to embarrass you," he said, quickly, and she looked up and shook her head.

"Do you see what I see?" Moira said, leaning in to Janet as they watched the couples and Moira spotted Shane and Kiara dancing on the other side of the room.

"What's that?" said Janet.

"Love is in the air," Moira intoned, nodding her head at Shane.

Sarah was next to Moira and she clapped her hands excitedly. "They are definitely falling in love, it's so obvious," she said, delightedly.

"Hmm I'm not so sure," said Janet.

"Can't you see it?" asked Moira.

Janet shook her head and observed them dancing. She could see the fondness between them growing, but as it did her unease also grew. She was worried that Kiara was still vulnerable, Shane was still hung up on Melanie, and it could lead to them making a terrible mistake or someone getting hurt. She didn't share Sarah's easy enthusiasm about it.

"Sarah, promise me you won't meddle okay?" she said, suddenly.

Sarah looked surprised and held up her hands. "As if I would!"

Janet looked at her knowingly and Sarah smiled. "Okay fine," she acquiesced.

***

The following day Shane opened his laptop and checked the news. There he was, holding hands with Kiara when they arrived at the ball, she turning her head back to him and smiling at each other, under the headline, *New love for Femme Fatale star?*

Other news used the selfie Alicia had put on her Twitter account, captioned *"Great to catch up with Kiara at the #JSMball tonight,"* sparking off speculation that Kiara was going to re-join the group.

A YouTube video of Kiara performing at the ball already had hundreds of thousands of views, leading to other speculation in the gossip pages that she was preparing to launch a solo career.

Shane laughed and shut his laptop.

Four months after the group

The Jacobs and Kiara spent Christmas together in the Connecticut house, the home filled with the scent of mulled wine and cinnamon. Melanie dropped Joshua off for a day, and Sarah announced that she was pregnant again, even though Eleanor was only seven months old, and it was totally unexpected and unplanned, but she and Tim were delighted.

Unlike last year Kiara didn't drink, and spent the evenings sipping cocoa with marshmallows, curled up in front of the fire in the living room, thankful for how peaceful everything seemed.

Five months after the group

It didn't take long for labels to get in touch with Kiara about potential solo options after the video from the ball went online.

Contact from a label based in Miami interested her the most. They had a track record of working with artists and letting them have creative input, and Kiara knew that she wasn't willing to bend to anyone's direction except her own. She had made up her mind that she wanted to do things her way and if that meant singing in nightclubs to audiences of twenty people, then so be it. She talked to the label on the phone and they asked her to spend a few days meeting with them and discussing her ideas in mid-January.

She was excitedly packing for the trip when Shane came to her room. He was going to spend a few days in the city catching up on some work and visiting Joshua while she was away, and she planned to visit Betty and Veronica while she was in Florida which would extend her trip by another day or two, but she couldn't wait to see them.

As he watched her packing, a feeling of apprehension he couldn't explain came over him. She was excited and eager, but he had a dark feeling in the pit of his stomach. He didn't want her to go. They hadn't been apart for more than a day for almost six months, and he realised with a jolt that he dreaded being away from her. He wrapped his arms around her and held her for a moment. She was surprised and wriggled free, laughing.

"Hey, I have to finish!" she said, playfully throwing a sock at him.

He sat on the bed and watched. She blushed as she packed her underwear and it sparked off a fury of thoughts in his mind about what she would look like in it and he had to turn his head away when he realised he was staring at her in a way that was much more than friends would do. She finished and zipped up her case, not noticing his sudden discomfort.

"I'll miss you," he said, taking her hands.

She didn't show it but the thought of being apart from him made her tremble inwardly. He had been her rock and her protector these past few months and she relied on him more than she cared to admit. She knew she would miss his physical presence and the peace she felt when she was with him. She had thought more than once in the past few weeks about what Alicia had said to her at the ball, and about the way they had danced together, but Shane hadn't said anything to her over Christmas and she assumed he would if he wanted to take things further, so perhaps he didn't and she was just reading into things that weren't there.

She smiled and kissed him on the cheek. "I'll miss you too," she said, using her thumb to wipe the lip gloss off his face, and prepared to leave for her flight.

***

"I have to talk to you." Kiara's phoned beeped as the message from Sarah came through, and Kiara felt a jolt of nerves in her chest as she saw the message.

"Is anything wrong?!" she replied.

"No. Just when you have time, call me," Sarah responded.

Kiara felt a little relieved and phoned Sarah later that evening when she had returned to the hotel and was waiting for her room service to arrive.

"Hey what's up? Is everything okay?" Kiara asked as Sarah picked up the phone.

"Everything's fine. How's things going down there?" Sarah asked. Kiara felt a slight twinge of annoyance, if Sarah just wanted to catch up she wished she hadn't requested it so dramatically. She told Sarah about the meetings with the label and producers, and how they had some great ideas and conversations about the flavour of a potential solo album.

Sarah listened patiently.

"So, I wanted to talk to you about something…" Sarah trailed off, "but I'm not supposed to meddle."

Kiara smiled and sighed. "Sarah, you obviously want to tell me some gossip."

Sarah laughed. "You know me too well."

"Well, what is it? I swear I won't tell anyone," Kiara promised.

"Shane came to visit yesterday for dinner," Sarah started. Kiara felt a flicker of fear that Sarah was going to tell her some gossip about Shane and a new love interest, just like when Sarah had announced Shane's relationship with Melanie at the dinner table that one evening so many years ago. Kiara took a breath.

"He is crazy about you," Sarah said.

Kiara thought she didn't hear properly, and her heart scudded in her chest like a stone skipping across water. "What?"

"He's totally crazy about you," Sarah repeated, a triumphant gleam in her voice.

Kiara was silent for a moment. "What did he say?" she asked, eventually.

"Well, he didn't say that exactly, but I was asking about you and he just went on and on about how much he misses you and how much fun it's been at the beach house and how proud he is of you, and how amazing you looked at the ball and stuff like that."

Kiara exhaled, a breath she didn't even realise she had been holding in.

"Sarah, that's nothing, I mean, that's just normal," Kiara said, stammering a little, both disappointed and relieved at the same time.

"No really, the way he said it, honestly Kiara, I would be seriously surprised if he doesn't try to tell you how he feels when you get back," Sarah insisted.

"Okay, well, we will see," Kiara said, not wanting to think about all the questions and confusions and hopes that arose from what Sarah was saying.

"Don't you feel something for him too?" Sarah asked, sounding deflated that her news didn't elicit a more excited response.

"I don't know," Kiara said, but in truth she knew that she felt something deeper than friendship for Shane. She tended to quash those feelings when they arose, when she watched him cooking breakfast, or coming out of the bathroom, towel round his waist, hair dripping, or when he slid into her bed at night to comfort her. She didn't want to hope for such things, Shane having always been out of her reach until now.

"You don't know? C'mon Kiara, anyone who sees you two together can see the spark between you," Sarah said, incredulously.

"I guess we will see when I get back, won't we?" Kiara said, then changed the subject and they talked about how Eleanor was getting on and how Sarah's new pregnancy was progressing.

After they hung up, Kiara ate her room service and lay on the bed, feeling overwhelmed by possibilities.

***

Shane had been twitchy and awkward with her on the way home from the airport. He had greeted her enthusiastically enough but seemed nervous and distracted as they drove back to the beach house. She chatted on the way back about how the meetings with the label had gone and how delighted she had been to see Betty and Veronica and Isaac again. Suyapa had returned to Honduras last year, missing her home and the rest of the family, especially after the death of their brother in Mexico, unconfirmed but taken as a given.

Shane had nodded tersely, smiling occasionally with short answers. Something was on his mind, but she didn't ask him what it was. She thought about the conversation she had with Sarah and his behaviour didn't fit at all. She felt nervous as they approached the house, wondering if he was going to tell her something that could potentially change the course of both their lives.

She had thought about it over the past few days, what she would do if he did tell her that he had feelings for her, imagining being with him, and the idea of it made her smile and bite her lip with pleasure, and as her time to return approached she started to hope that Sarah was right.

They pulled up and unloaded her bags, and she went to shower and change. When she came downstairs he had already made her a coffee and invited her out to the veranda. She knew he was preparing to tell her something and her whole body felt infused with nervous anticipation, tingling and trembling as she sat outside with him, the air cold and crisp compared to the clingy Florida humidity.

"Kiara, I need to tell you something," he began, clearing his throat.

She nodded and smiled, "Sure. What's up?"

He took a deep breath and looked her in the eye. "Melanie and I are giving things another try."

Her heart sank, cold and heavy, into her stomach, and she looked into the blackness of her coffee and wished she could dive into its darkness and hide.

**

Shane had been completely shocked when Melanie had invited him around, sat him down and told her she wanted to give their marriage another try. He had only just begun to imagine what life with someone else could be like, with someone in particular, when Melanie had dropped this surprise on him.

He felt partly furious with her for her timing, her presumption that he would even want to, and partly pleased that she had tried someone else on for size and found that she still wanted him, even after their divorce was long finalised. There was a sense of vindication, that she had been wrong all along, and a sense of sadness and disappointment as he thought of Kiara and how close they had become and the potential and the possibility of being with her.

But in the end, there was no choice for him, not when he looked at Joshua and knew that he owed it to his son to give his marriage another try and for Joshua to grow up with two united parents, as he himself had been blessed to experience. So, he had agreed, and he and Melanie had been busy working out the details. He would move back into the house, on the condition that he could make sure Kiara would be okay and sorted first.

Melanie had agreed and had dared to ask him if the rumours were true, if he and Kiara were or had been a couple. He had shaken his head, angrily, thinking of Melanie and Kyle and the months they had been together, and she hadn't asked any further.

Melanie believed him and was relieved. She had seen the pictures in the magazines, read the rumours online, and an unexpected jealousy had leapt into her heart. Since her and Kyle had made things official, the heat of the affair had worn off and become mundane, and the mundanity of her life with Kyle just simply wasn't as nice as the life she had with Shane.

She missed Shane's trusting nature and his easy kindness. Perhaps because of the way their relationship began Kyle was a lot less trusting than Shane and his paranoia was irritating. Kyle was bringing in plenty of money but life with Shane had always been so easy, especially when it came to his family, who adored Joshua, whereas Kyle's mother was a cold and distant austere woman who disapproved of their relationship.

Melanie had been used to being the only woman Shane saw, he had idolised her for years, and when she saw that same look being directed at someone else, especially knowing where Kiara had come from, she knew she had to turn his gaze back to her again.

Kyle had been livid, making threats to reveal the duration of their affair to Shane, then begging her to reconsider, but her mind was made up. Shane was coming back to her, where he always belonged.

***

Shane had told the news to Janet, Victor, Sarah and Tim in person, meeting them at the house in Connecticut, the day before Kiara came home.

Janet and Victor nodded mutely, Janet forcing a smile, and sounding pleased about being able to see Joshua more. Victor patted his son on the back and knew in his heart that Shane and Melanie were in for a tough ride, to try to salvage their marriage from the furnace of divorce and distrust, but he supported Shane's choice. Sarah had sputtered, amazed, and had been the only one to ask, *"But what about Kiara?"* and Shane's eyes had darkened as he had snapped back *"This is my chance to be a dad to Joshua again, and I am sure Kiara will understand that,"* and Sarah had lapsed into stunned silence at how angry he seemed.

Sarah phoned Kiara the night she returned, knowing that Shane had broken the news to her.

"Kiara, how are you?"

Kiara shut the door to her bedroom and sat on the bed, surrounded by the debris of her suitcase. "Well, um, I'm fine."

"Really?"

Kiara sighed. "Yes."

"Did Shane tell you…" Kiara cut Sarah off mid-sentence. "Yes, he did and I'm very happy for him," she said, firmly, hoping that if she kept repeating those words then maybe they would turn into real feelings.

Sarah was silent. "I'm sorry, Kiara," she said, after a pause.

Kiara shrugged, though Sarah couldn't see her. "Don't be. I'll be just fine."

Six months after the group

Kiara didn't want to be a burden and encouraged Shane to leave and move back in with Melanie as soon as he could, helping him to pack, making jokes, smiling brightly till her jaw ached, but really wanting to rip the clothes from his suitcase and beg him to stay with her.

Despite her disappointment, she wasn't angry. She knew that Shane needed to be with Joshua, to be a proper father, and he had loved Melanie for so many years, the pieces just fit together in a way she and him never did. He had never told anyone that he had feelings for her, and certainly hadn't told her that himself, so she couldn't hold him to words he had never spoken and feelings he had never admitted and may not even have.

She was ready to start another chapter in life. She had her final session with Graham and thanked him for everything he had done for her. She packed up her things and arranged to move to Florida to work on her solo album, where she could spend days in balmy sunshine and see her friends. When it came to the piano, she and Shane had stood in front of it, and he had offered to arrange for it to be transported to Florida.

She leaned on it and stroked the keys. "Maybe we should leave it here," she said, and smiled at him, and she wished with everything she had that he would change his mind and choose her, but he just nodded and continued loading the suitcases into the car.

Ten months after the group

Shane's office intercom beeped. "Mr Jacobs, there's a man here to speak with you." Margaret's voice came through, tinny and insistent.

Shane frowned and checked his diary. "I haven't got any appointments scheduled," he buzzed back.

"He says it's urgent. Kyle Williams?" she said.

Shane scowled as he realised it was the man Melanie had been seeing after the divorce. Unsure what to do, his finger hovered over the buzzer. Eventually he pressed it down. "Send him in," he said.

Kyle strode into Shane's office. Dressed in an expensive suit, with expertly styled blond hair, he looked poised and confident, and a little aggressive. Shane stood up and pointed at the chair in front of his desk.

"Do you want to sit down?"

Kyle nodded tersely and sat in the chair. They didn't bother with small talk or greetings. Kyle's visit had the air of a serious matter and Shane was in no mood to keep him there for longer than he had to be. He was affronted at the gall of the man for turning up to his office.

"Have you received the notifications from my lawyer?" Kyle began, leaning forward and folding his hands together on Shane's desk.

Shane folded his arms over his chest. "No."

"They have sent three letters in the past four months to your house and had no response," Kyle said.

"Well, I haven't received them, so that would be why," Shane said.

Kyle looked taken aback and Shane was pleased to have wrong-footed him.

"Ah," Kyle said.

"Whatever your lawyers have to say in a letter, you can say to me now and speed things along a little," Shane said, curtly.

Kyle looked uncertain. "I didn't want to bring this to your attention in this way," he said.

Shane smiled tensely. "I guess you'll have to, seeing as I didn't get these mysterious missing letters."

Kyle sighed and, unfolding his hands, reached into his leather case, bringing out a sheaf of papers, which he rifled through. Shane tapped his fingers on his desk impatiently, and Kyle frowned. Selecting a piece of paper, he placed it on the desk and slid it in front of Shane. He looked down and the colour left his face.

Throat tight, he said to Kyle, "This can't be true."

Kyle nodded. "I'm afraid it is. Go ahead and repeat the test if you like. The result will be the same."

Shane looked at the paper in front of him and felt a deep sickness spread through his chest and stomach. Kyle stood up. "I will ask my lawyers to redirect their letters to your office to ensure they don't go missing again." He left Shane with his head in his hands, hunched over the desk, reading the words over and over again.

Child: Jacobs, Joshua
Alleged father: Williams, Kyle
Probability of paternity: 99.99%

***

Shane threw the coffee cup onto the kitchen floor, where it smashed violently, fragments and slivers of porcelain spattering out from the impact. Melanie paled and flinched.

"You need to tell me the truth. Now," Shane said, his fists clenched, one resting on top of the kitchen counter where the paternity test lay.

Melanie had never seen Shane so angry. When he had come home early and said nothing, thrusting the paper at her, her heart had pounded so hard her face had gone numb. She stared at his red eyes and knew she had to tell him.

"I didn't know he was Joshua's father," she said.

"Bullshit," Shane said, furiously, his face flushed, sweat breaking out on his forehead.

"I'm telling the truth. I only found out four months ago when he sent through the test results," she looked at the floor, studying the fragments, thinking how they reflected the life they had built together.

"The test results that were addressed to me?" he asked, accusingly.

"When I saw the envelope from his lawyer's firm I knew it couldn't be good. So yeah, I hid them from you," she said, defiantly.

"What did you think was going to happen? That I wouldn't find out eventually?" he yelled.

"I wasn't thinking straight! I told you, I thought you were Joshua's dad. I was in shock!" she shrieked and turned on her heel and walked to the couch, sitting down heavily.

Shane followed her and stood in front of the couch, his arms folded.

"So, you were with him even when we were married," he said, not asking but stating.

She nodded.

"And he is Joshua's father."

Again, she nodded, tears running down her cheeks, and she felt overwhelmed by regret.

All the fight left him, and Shane sat down in a chair and raised his hands to his face, ran them agitatedly through his hair, and cried.

***

Kiara stared out at the smoggy London sky, punctured in places by tall steel buildings lighting up the evening. She had always liked London, it had the energy of New York but with all its unique history ingrained into the city, everywhere you turned there was the past meeting the present. The first time she came here with Femme Fatale she had no time to explore, and the second time the girls had been out a few times to clubs but they hadn't seen the real sights. This time, promoting her new solo work around Europe, she made sure there was time in the schedule to have a few days to walk around, her hair tucked under a baseball cap, anonymous amongst the crowds, riding the red buses slowly grinding their way through the city traffic under the smoky rain.

She got Sarah's message when she got back to the hotel room and made herself an instant coffee, wincing at the gritty bitterness and chucking in several packets of sugar, while listening to Sarah's voicemail. She checked her watch. 7pm in London, 2pm in New York. Sarah might be out to lunch with her mommy friends, but Kiara would give her a try. Sarah picked up on the first ring, knowing it would be Kiara as no one else called her from an international number.

"Kiara, thanks for calling me back," Sarah said, breathlessly.

"Everything okay?" Kiara asked, warily. Sarah's voicemail had put her on edge, the tone in Sarah's voice had been dull and tense in the message, and not like her usual cheery self.

"No," Sarah said, and proceeded, in between choking sobs that left her gasping, to tell Kiara what had happened with Shane and Melanie. Kiara listened in silence, tears running down her face, hand over her mouth.

"Oh my god," she said, when Sarah had related the update.

"I know," said Sarah, miserably. "It's just," she paused, "devastating," she said, the word bursting through a sob.

"Joshua isn't his son, he's not my nephew, mom is absolutely distraught, Shane is a wreck," Sarah said. "That *bitch*," she cried, angrily.

"Where is she now? Do you think they can work it out?" Kiara asked.

"God no! Shane is furious. I've never seen him so mad. And Melanie's gone to Milan to stay with Jade for a while. I have no idea what she's going to do, but I guess that other guy is Joshua's dad so he will be involved, it's his right I suppose."

Kiara let out a long sigh and took a gulp of coffee, burning her tongue.

"What is Shane doing?" she asked, worried for her friend.

"He's renting again, working all hours. Trying to forget I guess, but he needs a break," Sarah replied.

They chatted for a while about how Sarah's pregnancy was going and how Eleanor was, before hanging up. Kiara let out a shaky sigh. She couldn't even imagine what Shane was going through. She punched in his office number, which she knew off by heart. She thought he was most likely to be there, and he picked up.

"Shane Jacobs," he answered, brusquely.

"Hey Shane," she said.

"Oh hey," his voice softened. "London calling," he joked, in a terrible English accent.

"I spoke to Sarah," she said, softly.

"Hmmm," he said.

"I'm so sorry," she whispered.

He exhaled on the other end, his breath making the line crackle. "It's a mess," he said, finally.

"How are you doing?" she asked.

"Well, I've now lost my wife and my son, so pretty bad," he said. He was trying to keep his voice light, but she could hear the strain and his voice cracked over the word 'son'.

"If you ever need someone to talk to," she said, "you know how to get hold of me."

"Thanks," he said. "How are things going for you over the pond?" he asked, changing the subject.

"Good. I'll be moving around Europe for a bit for a good few weeks, then I'd like to come back here to do some performances in London, maybe a month or two." Kiara was enjoying playing lots of independent venues, performing her songs to small but appreciative audiences, a far cry from the heady glamour of her Femme Fatale days.

"I'm glad it's going well. How are you doing?" he said, and she knew what he was really asking.

"I'm fine Shane, really. I'm on my own a lot which is so different from being with the girls, but apart from that I'm enjoying myself," she replied.

The loneliness was more acute than she thought it would be, but it wasn't the girls she missed. It was Shane's presence she felt the lack of the most, especially at night when she couldn't sleep and lay awake watching BBC world news, the same stories again and again, till she could drift off. Her management made sure the minibars were always empty in any hotel she checked into, and she relied on plenty of coffee to get her through the days after particularly bad nights. The nightmares were less frequent and Graham had taught her lots of techniques for dealing with the old fears whenever they surfaced, which was less often than before.

London had lots of beautiful old churches and she liked to sit in them when they were empty and quiet, breathing in the musty air from the creaking wooden pews and thinking of new lyrics in her head. She was alone but she had a peace about it. She felt stronger than she had done before and for the first time in her life she felt a sense of pride in who she was and what she was capable of.

"Well, maybe I'll come out for a vacation in London and visit you," Shane said, wearily. "I could use a break from all this."

She smiled. "You're always welcome, Shane."

As they hung up she frowned at how he had tried to hide how badly he was hurting. She ordered room service and curled up on the bed for another long night, the dark hours stretching before her, empty and quiet.

Twelve months after the group

Kiara ended up being in London for much longer than she had planned. The promotional tour went extremely well and she arranged to work on some new material in some studios just outside of London. The label rented her a small apartment and she kept a quiet life, although she still did magazine and TV interviews, and attended the occasional awards ceremony or movie premier.

She received an unexpected phone call from Marco while she was in London. He was there working with another singer and wanted to know if she would like to meet for a coffee. She agreed readily. He came around to her apartment, looking as tanned as ever, though slightly more worn around the eyes.

He hugged her. "Good to see you," he said, sitting down on the couch. "I love your new album. You put it together so quickly but it's fantastic, it's like it poured out of you fully formed," he said.

She smiled at the rare compliment. "Thanks Marco," she said, sliding onto the couch beside him, tucking one leg under her and handing him a coffee. "It just came together so well, and I guess it made sense to get it out fairly quickly, while people still remember who I am," she grinned.

He eyed her. "You're looking well. A bit fatter, but better," he grinned and she knew he was joking.

They caught up about the group, about his new protégé, and about her new label. It wasn't long before he had to leave but as he walked out of the door, he turned around and grabbed her in a hug and squeezed her tight.

"I really am sorry for everything," he whispered in her ear.

She nodded, not quite believing it was Marco saying this to her. He held her at arm's length and looked her in the eyes. "I'm proud of you. You're a survivor. Like me," he said, flashing his white teeth at her and leaving before she could reply.

***

"I'm coming to London," Shane's text had arrived at 4am, shocking her awake with a jolt. She calculated that it was 11pm in New York and thought that maybe he was drunk.

"Serious?" she texted back.

"Yup. Put me up or hotel?" he replied.

"Stay with me," she texted, laughing that he would even think of staying in a hotel.

He texted her the details of his flight, in a week's time, and she lay back and smiled all night even though she couldn't sleep.

***

She was at the studios when his flight arrived so she arranged for a car to pick him up and take him to her apartment where she would meet him afterwards. When she got back, he was flat out asleep in the spare room so she left him for a few hours before she woke him up for dinner.

222

"I cooked!" she announced proudly, as he stared at her bleary-eyed and smiling in between yawns.

"You didn't?" he asked, incredulously.

She gestured to the kitchen where two pizzas sat steaming from the oven, and he laughed. They ate with their fingers in front of the TV, talking about her life in London, about the best places to visit, and about the family. Later in the evening, he updated her about Melanie and Joshua. Kyle had proposed to Melanie, and she had said yes. Kiara nodded along silently.

"That must be so hard," she said, rubbing his arm sympathetically.

"You have no idea," he said, looking at her. "It's like, a death," he said, struggling to find the right words for how losing Joshua felt, "but that person is still alive, just they have been taken away from you forever."

"And Melanie?" she said.

He shrugged. "I was getting over her before we got back together, I really was. I'm not sure I'll get over losing Joshua though."

They stayed up late talking it through. He had decided to take a vacation after working hours and hours to distract himself, and she was the first person he thought of.

"It's your turn to put me back together now," he said, grinning. "You owe me, Anderson," and she laughed.

She took a week off and they spent the days exploring London. It was the height of summer and the air was hot and moist and the Thames sparkled in the sun like a coiled road of diamonds through the city. They stood in awe on the Millennium bridge, looking out over the boats passing beneath and staring up at the dome of St Paul's Cathedral, grey and gleaming against the blue sky. Shane was keen to see Windsor Castle so they took a day trip there, walking around the castle grounds, marvelling how it looked looming proudly over the town. They had dinners in Chinatown and in riverside pubs, laughing at each other's pronunciations of British words and both agreeing that 'fish and chips' were fantastic.

One day they took a boat trip down the Thames, sitting on the outside even though there was drizzle in the air, and Shane put his arm round her and pulled her close to him. She curled her hand in his and rested on his shoulder, tempted to close her eyes but not wanting to miss a single sight along the river.

They climbed up to the observatory in Greenwich, the green unfolding before them leading to the expanse of the city spread along the horizon, and she sighed and declared it to be the most beautiful city she had ever been to. Shane had smiled at her and held her hand on the steep path down the hill and hadn't let go of her hand the rest of the walk back to the boat.

***

That evening, Shane turned to her on the couch.

"I have something important to tell you," he said, earnestly and seriously. She turned off the TV and gave him her full attention, and he fetched an envelope from his suitcase.

Unfolding the paper inside, he looked at her carefully, and said: "Do you remember the researcher we asked to look into finding your mom's grave?"

Confused, she nodded. She had given up the search and left the task to a researcher. She had assumed they hadn't found anything, and this wasn't quite the conversation she was expecting.

"Well," he continued, smoothing out the folds on the paper, "they found her and where she was buried. She died ten years ago, in Wisconsin."

Kiara frowned. "No, that's not right. She died when I was eight, so that would have been in 1993."

Shane shook his head. "I'm so sorry Kiara, your dad lied to you."

Aghast, Kiara's mouth opened and shut and she had no words. She felt a burning anger rise in her against her father, whom she had taken so long to make peace with after his death, yet here he was, still hurting her long after he had died. And then she felt anger at her mother, who had died when she was eighteen, not eight, and had so many more years in which she could have contacted her again and chose not to.

Shane saw her face flush and took her hand. "I know this is a shock," he said, gently.

She looked at him and nodded, the tension in her mouth crumbling into shaking sobs. Shane held her tightly and spoke into her hair. "I'm sorry Kiara, but there's something else."

"Oh god, what now?" she groaned, and in spite of it all, she and Shane laughed, Kiara blurrily wiping away tears.

"Go on, hit me with it Jacobs," she said.

"The researcher contacted her husband, and it turns out that she had tried to come back for you, when you were three, but your

dad…" Shane hesitated. She leaned forward, nodding at him to continue. "Your dad told her you were dead."

Horrified, she lifted her hands to her mouth, more tears splashing down onto her fingers.

"That bastard!" she shrieked and thumped her fist down on the couch.

Sobbing, she covered her face with her hands. "I don't get it, he *hated* me. Why didn't he just let her take me?"

Shane shook his head. "I guess it was to hurt her, to spite her, for what she did," he paused. "Sometimes children get used as emotional weapons," he said, sadly, thinking of how Melanie had used his desire to be a father to entice him back to her when he knew that his heart had gone another way.

"The thing is, Kiara, it turns out that your mom, well, she had another child," he said, softly.

She looked up, surprised. "What?"

He nodded. "She had a boy, born in 1990. Five years younger than you."

She stared at him wide-eyed. "Is he alive?"

"Yes."

Shane passed her the paper, which contained the name, date of birth, location and occupation of her half-brother, and then Shane took out a photo and passed it to her. Blue eyes stared brightly back at her, a confident grin, and a shock of dark red hair. Matthew Murphy, her half-brother.

"I have a brother," she said, stunned.

"Does he know?" she asked Shane, quickly. Shane shook his head.

"The researcher didn't tell your mom's widow anything. He thought you died like your father said and I guess he either hasn't seen you on TV or doesn't think you're the same person as the baby your mom left behind."

"Oh my god, all this time I thought I didn't have any family left," she said, and she couldn't continue because she was overwhelmed with tears again. Shane held her for hours while she cried on his shoulder, and he continued to hold her the entire night long when he slid into her bed for the first time in a long time.

***

The following day, they went to London and paused by Tower Bridge, leaning on the railings over the river, watching the boatloads of tourists drifting by.

"Are you going to get in touch with him?" Shane asked her.

She drew a breath of the air, damp from the river. "Yes, but when I'm back in the States. I expect it'll be a bit of a shock." She smiled. "I can't believe I actually have a brother out there," she said, shaking her head.

Shane smiled. "Life certainly has its twists and turns, doesn't it?"

"It's all so, unexpected," she said. Looking at the tower glowing over them, she added, "There's so much water under the bridge that I could drown in it."

"I know what you mean," he said. He looked at her and smiled. "Seems like just yesterday we were in Connecticut and you were bounding through the back gate."

She looked at him and felt a pang of sadness at the simplicity and certainty that time had gradually stolen from them.

"Can I ask you a question, Shane?" she said, cautiously. She was nervous and her hand trembled slightly, but she needed to know.

He turned to face her. "Go on."

"Did you arrange this trip specifically to bring me that news?" she asked.

He nodded and her heart dipped. She didn't say anything further and they stood as the crowds passed them by, taking selfies in front of the bridge, a muddle of languages and faces in the middle of which they stood in their own thoughts.

"There was another reason though," he said, suddenly.

"More news about my crazy family?" she said, raising an eyebrow, and grinning.

He laughed and shook his head.

"Then what?" she asked, trying to sound casual, but her heart had started to beat fast hopeful thuds.

He took a step closer to her. "I wanted to see you, to be near you again," he said in a low voice, suddenly desperately nervous about telling her how he really felt and how much he wanted to be with her. He had been trying to find the right moment for the past few days, irritated by his own hesitation, but now she had given him the prompt he needed.

She studied his face and he reached out a hand to brush away a stray curl that was blowing across her forehead in the breeze.

"What do you think about that?" he said.

"About what?" she said, widening her eyes, not wanting to be mistaken about what he might say again, hardly daring to hope that he might tell her the words she longed to hear.

The bustle of the crowds around them seemed to fade away as he paused and gently pressed a hand to her cheek. "I'm in love with you, Kiara," he said, searching her eyes and hoping she felt the same. The radiant smile she gave him in return told him he wasn't mistaken.

He pulled her close to him and leaned in to kiss her. She tilted her head back and closed her eyes, relishing the warmth of his mouth on hers, the smell of his cologne, the feel of his hands on her lower back, gently pulling her to him. As he kissed her, she was as happy as she had been the night when she was seventeen and everything had been perfect for that one moment, except now it was more than a fleeting moment and he wasn't pushing her away this time. She ran her fingers through his hair and pulled him closer, her heart quickening and her skin tingling with joy at knowing he wanted her, after all the years of friendship and unfulfilled longing.

When they finished the kiss he drew back and smiled at her and took her hand. No words were needed to say what they both already knew, what they had known for a while, each in their own hearts. They turned and walked back along the river, their arms entwined, each ready to start a new chapter, this time together.